Shadow Patterns

Bob & Ann, I hope you enjoy my book as much as I did enjoy writing it!

Marcia Prather Adams

Marcia Prather Adams

Guild Press of Indiana
Camel, IN 46032

DEDICATION

To my four children—Jeff, John, Beth, Bill and their families.

March, 1983 . . .

Chapter One

Janelle Jamison locked the door of her apartment, walked across the thick-piled white carpet to the elevator and touched the down button. Looking in the glass of the elevator door as it slowly opened, she smoothed some loose strands of blond hair into her French chignon and straightened the light blue, ribbon knit jacket of her St. John suit. She paused, considering the reflection. Large grey eyes looked back at her with sadness.

The elevator door slid closed, and soon she entered the chrome and glass lobby of the apartment complex. High heeled Bruno sandals tapped out a staccato beat as she walked across the expanse of marble floor to the double doors, greeted the doorman, and walked out of the air conditioned lobby into the warmth of the Dallas spring. The March air was scented with smells of fresh-cut grass and flowering hyacinths. Mockingbirds chirped their songs and lush azalea blossoms burst with brilliant russet, pink and scarlet. She hardly noticed. Even the monotonous drone of early morning traffic, the pulsating energy of the city which was her usual wake-up call, did not penetrate her numbness. It had been eleven months today. The brittle pain of it all, particularly that first, revelatory moment, was still intense. It should have receded to the edge of her consciousness as pain usually did over time, but it hadn't.

I'm leaving you, Jan. I can't keep wanting to be with someone else. She replayed the scene at least twice a day. Maybe it was the rock-hard set of Jerry's jaw that had made it so difficult to bear. The trapped look. The honesty that had reached out to give her a knockout punch. He was desperate to get away from her.

She stopped by her car at the curb and squeezed her eyes shut for a moment to stop the memories that replayed like a jumbled-up tape. Then, absently, she unlocked the door, slid into the driver's seat and sat there motionless, gripping the steering wheel with long nails that dug into the soft leather covering. The scene played on.

Janelle, I mean it. I love someone else, have for some time. He'd turned from her stunned look. Shoulders hunched, hands thrust deep into his pockets, he moved his head slowly from side to side as if he himself doubted his own words.

Mandy and I've been seeing each other for over a year. Just fun, no strings. He'd grasped the fireplace mantel for support as he'd stared into the fire. After a long pause, he'd sucked in a deep breath and hesitantly whispered, *She needs me. You don't.*

Janelle felt a lump rise in her throat at the memory of what came next. There had been blatant pride in Jerry's eyes as he had looked straight at her and said. *She's pregnant, Jan.* It was that shameless pride that hurt.

Janelle slapped the wheel and threw her head back against the seat. Startled back to reality, she glanced out the window to see if anyone was watching, then shakily started the car.

There was something sadly mocking in all this. Jerry had made it plain from the first time they'd made love that he didn't want a child. She thought about their conversation, always the same refrain. *Clutter up your life with kids? No, you're the only one I want to come home to.* Not to have a child had been an adjustment for her, but after all, the doctor had told her she would have difficulty ever conceiving, and she'd been content with their life. So, had Mandy tricked him? No, he seemed genuinely pleased that he was to be a father. They must have considered the consequences of their affair, at least Mandy must have. Janelle's mind raced and she grimaced at the ugly implication of her thinking, but didn't even try to control the bitterness she felt for the woman who had taken Jerry away from her. It hurt too much, to only blame herself for the pain—Jerry hadn't wanted a child with her, but had with Mandy.

She'd tried to ignore the seamy Texas tabloids, the transmitters of gossip, that had invaded their privacy by printing stories, conjectures, and half-truths, about the breakup of a couple that had had its share of pictures on the social pages:

PEOPLE WATCHING——
Janelle Jamison Taylor, one of the loveliest leading ladies of charity causes and a top executive of the largest insurance company in Texas, and her

husband, Jerry D. Taylor, Prince Charming of philanthropy and consort of the queen of finance, have for four years been described as the ideal couple with beauty, brains, and wealth. Their ideal marriage image has been shattered with the news of impending divorce.

The Three J Educational Television Production Company, underwritten by the Jamison Group, was founded by the Taylors two years ago. Three J's production, HIDE AND SEEK, is an educational program aired on closed circuit TV in the junior and senior high schools of the city.

BUSINESS BRIEFS AND WHISPERS——

In a public announcement Jerry D. Taylor resigned as public relations director and advertising manager for the Jamison Insurance Group. "Unforeseen circumstances make my resignation necessary," he said. "I will continue to co-produce the Three J Educational Television Production Company until a replacement can be found."

The question insiders are asking is, "When is one of the unforeseen circumstances to be announced?"

For eleven months, she'd had a feeling of animated suspension, as if she was up above looking down on all the hullabaloo. Even the earlier divorce decree itself had seemed unreal. But yesterday, when the property settlement had been finalized, and four years of marriage had been finally wiped out, she'd felt the divorce deeply.

In sun-streaked brilliance, traffic moved toward downtown Dallas along Turtle Creek Boulevard. A motor started up as the groundskeeper began the daily ritual of trimming the lush foliage that surrounded the condominium complex, and a postal van drove by the side street where she sat.

"Come on, Janelle, get going! You've got two accounts overdue, an insurance claim to cover in Houston, a new TV script to review, and here you sit." Her scolding helped a little and she relaxed. "As Daddy used to say, 'It's OK to feel sorry for yourself as long as you don't expect the other guy to join in.'" Wearily she smiled, eased her BMW into gear, and headed toward the intersection of Holland and Turtle Creek Boulevard as she considered all of the deadlines she had to meet for the day.

Seeing an opening in the ribbon of cars, she punched hard on the accelerator and rolled the steering wheel in a tight turn to enter the right lane of traffic. Speed adjusted to the fast pace set by the car in front of her, she relaxed just as the glare of bright sunshine off the top of a car shot into her eyes. She flinched; her car veered a fraction to the left. A searing whine pierced the air like an electric saw cutting through a solid piece of oak, as metal ripped through metal. Instinctively, Janelle swung the front wheels and swerved from the injured car, then straightened her car just inches from the curb at the same time her convertible wobbled back and forth into the southbound traffic.

She needed to stop—get out of traffic. But how could you take care of an accident in morning rush hour? Nerves skipped and pulsed at the base of her skull; pain shot up her neck, causing black spots that distorted her vision. She shook her head and breathed deeply to help relieve the tension. She braked for a red light behind a black sedan and cautiously looked around to see if the injured car was in sight. There it was, to the left of her car. No mistake! A midnight-blue Maserati wore a gash like a jagged wound of ripped metal in the gleaming finish of the right hand door. Janelle rolled down her window. She opened her mouth to speak, then hesitated as she saw the window of the blue car slide halfway down.

Before she could utter a word, a deep voice bellowed from the leather interior of the Maserati. "What do you think your car is—an electric can opener?"

Janelle could not see the person through the tinted window, but anger was making his voice shake. Her voice quivered as she answered him. "Please, let's talk. Pull over there." She motioned to her right where a residential street opened off the boulevard. The light turned green; she signaled a right turn, and steered her car onto the quiet side-street. Glancing in the rearview mirror, she saw the sleek car follow her around the corner and stop behind hers.

She turned off the ignition, brushed damp hands against her skirt, and taking a deep breath, gripped the door handle. She needed to stay calm and talk to—whoever it was.

Just then, a door slammed and she glanced in the rearview mirror to see a very tall, broad shoulder man walking purposely toward her car. His exaggerated shadow hovered over her little car like that of a big bear ready to attack.

The man bounded to the right side of her enclosed sports car, yanked at the resisting door handle, then leaned over and scowled at Janelle through the closed window. "Who in the hell do you think you are to lurch out in traffic like that?" he roared through the glass. Steely blue eyes glared at her.

He was still shouting through the glass. What was he saying? She lowered the window " . . . careless attitude with no thought of others on the road but yourself." The shock of his angry tirade erased her guilt, turning it to defiance.

"I had an opening in traffic, so there was ample time for me to get in the right hand lane! Perhaps *you*," she snapped, "veered into me!" Her usually low voice come out a high screech.

She shocked herself at the outburst and felt her anger drain away as she noted the face had left the right window. She let out a sigh that ended in a squeak when his face suddenly appeared at the window beside her. Those steel blue eyes skewered hers in a locked stare.

He blinked, then said in a deadly calm voice, "You can't get away with that excuse for your reckless driving! Come look where my car is ripped and you will see wh . . . y," he ground out the word slowly, through clenched teeth. "It wasn't my fault!"

He stood to the left of her car, legs spread apart, arms folded over chest in a stance that seemed to challenge her to get out.

The nerve and conceit of the man! Janelle's head pounded with indignation. She slung open the door with such force that it slapped the tall stranger in the groin. With a grimace of pain, he staggered back before he could get his balance.

Good! A smug grin played on her face as she stamped her feet down on the pavement, flounced out of the car, and yanked her skirt over exposed thighs. Drawing herself up to her full five foot five inches, hands on hips, she prepared to face the man eye to eye. Instead, she found herself looking at two long arms folded over a broad chest. Defiantly, she looked up at six feet five inches of Texan—his frown of anger changed to what appeared to be an appreciative grin as he appraised her from head to toe. She thrust out her chin as if ready to physically defy his sensual appraisal.

The scene changed. The burly man looked surprised and shifted his gaze to the ground. He expelled an exasperated breath, raked a hand through his thick hair, and slowly said, without looking up, "Well, will you look at my car?"

Janelle spun on her heel and walked to his car where she proceeded to examine the extent of the damage.

She let her breath out slowly. It was pretty awful. A long jagged slash ran along the front fender and door of the low-slung sports car like an open zipper. She knew she should apologize. But did he think her irresponsible and incapable of driving? She would not be treated like a zany female. "Oh, that can be fixed fairly easily," she said airily.

"Ma'am, a branding iron out in open-range country couldn't have done a more searing job!"

"Still, it can be fixed."

He harshly grumbled, but a softness in his blue eyes made the words seem less stern. "You must be an expert on cars," his glance roamed casually over her, "Or, do you do body work? If so," he moved slowly toward her a teasing gleam in his eyes and a one-sided grin on his face more provocative than lascivious, "maybe we were destined to *bump* into each other and can negotiate a deal."

Her eyes widened as he came toward her with a slow, catlike grace, exuding animal magnetism, and stopped within inches of her face. She stepped back just a little.

It took a few moments to catch her breath; then, deliberately ignoring the implied offer, she said, defiantly. "I know a competent garage at the corner of Oaklawn and Maple. Take your car there and have an estimate made for my insurance company. Of course, there should be at least two other estimates made in addition to a police report which I'll rely on you to get."

Nervously, she searched, drew out a card from her purse, and extended it toward him, tensing her arm so the trembling of her hand would not show. "You need not bother to give me identification. I'm *sure* I will hear from you again!" Without a backward glance, heart thumping in time with her steps, Janelle turned and quickly walked to her car.

"I'll be damned!" He said it just loud enough for her to hear. "How can anyone so lovely looking have such gol-darn bad manners?"

Janelle did not look at him as she made a U-turn and again eased her car onto Turtle Creek Boulevard.

Chapter Two

Fifteen minutes later, Janelle rushed into the elevator of the Jamison Building and savagely punched the button to the 25th floor. Within ten seconds, she walked out of the elevator onto the pale grey carpeting of the hall and swept by her favorite Texas hill country painting without a glance. Bad manners indeed! The man had insulted her after trying to bully and seduce her. Well, she'd seen bad manners but never . . . . She'd pushed open the glass doors which displayed her name in gold letters and swished into the comfortably furnished waiting room. She passed her secretary, Jean, seated at the reception desk, and with a crisp greeting and absent wave, continued on into her private office, and slammed the door.

Just inside her office, she stopped for a moment and allowed the beauty of the carefully planned room to calm her. Grey walls and silver blue carpeting set a relaxed tone for soft shades of peach and green fabric-covered couches and chairs arranged in conversational groups to the left of the entrance. To the right in the large room stood a mahogany desk flanked by two high-backed leather chairs backed by a computer work center.

Janelle walked past the workcenter to gaze at the beauty of the cityscape framed in the large window. Below her was the Dallas Art Museum that from her lofty view resembled a giant white space ship with turrets and walkways. Just last week she'd walked into the gallery to see an exhibit of one of her favorites, Claude Monet.

Her mother and she had seen the artist's works at his home in Giverny, when they'd gone to France a few years before. She'd come back to Dallas inspired by the impressionist and, for her new office, had chosen pale spring shades, fresh, bright, and feathery like Monet's garden paintings, that subverted weight and boundaries in airy space. She thought it providential that Monet's masterpieces were enjoyed and accepted here in her solid, no nonsense Texas city, that some still thought of as a tough cowboy town.

The face of the rugged man with his weathered skin flashed in her mind. Smothered thoughts of the Maserati episode rekindled. She felt a slow burn of shame. Her face flushed. Her skin felt moist with what— *arousal?* She jerked off her jacket, jammed it in the nearby closet, and slammed the door with such force that it shook the mirror on the wall. "Attracted to him! I'd rather be mauled by a mangy cougar!"

No. She was kidding herself. She'd actually liked, loved his looks. He's probably a male model, she thought, grinning. Calmer now that she'd reviewed the episode, she really needed to apologize to Jean for being so abrupt when she came in to the office.

She rubbed tension from her neck as she looked through the file laid out on her desk. Dalton Petroleum Company. It was one of the biggest insurance deals she'd ever supervised, involving 500 employees, equipment, rig liability and sundry items. It had kept her insurance staff busy for over two months getting the policies coordinated and rates established. She thumbed through the report. There was a separate self-insured retention policy.

And of course, this wasn't the only place she was having to think deeply about the oil industry. On the fifth floor of the building, the educational TV program she supervised was at work on the very subject. She thought of the changes since Jerry had left the project. The stage had been changed to a more informal arrangement. Floor pillows and couches had replaced the desk and chairs. The relaxed setting allowed the kids to lounge in comfort as they wrangled over the pros and cons of the oil industry. In the first two segments of this series on the oil industry, the research team had explained the Emergency Petroleum Allocation Act which was to cultivate foreign oil supplies and had entangled the domestic oil industry in massive bureaucratic red tape. Robyn Grant, one of the seniors on the panel, had done excellent research on the oil diplomacy of the Carter and Ford administrations. She hoped the studio setup for the taping was OK. They'd never had the setting quite so relaxed.

Janelle knew that politics would be a part of the discussion, but that was what some of the television programs were for—to give young people of the city a chance to see the beneficial and the distasteful elements of special interest groups involved in governmental decisions.

Jerry and she'd formed the Three J Educational Television Production Company three years before to educate and entertain junior high and high-school students of Dallas. It was their baby—the only one they'd had as a team. Janelle had named the show HIDE AND SEEK. Jerry had obtained the approval of the Dallas Educational Commission to distribute the in-house videos to the schools. And the two of them, plus several others from the city and the Jamison group, approved each show's content.

That first show had been a weak forecast of things to come. But it was still passably informative and entertaining. The two of them and students chosen to help research the topic, "Friends and Favorites in the Schools" had come up with a memorable program on popular clothes, popular morals, and cliques. It had been a mad scramble, but they had met the deadline requirements of the school officials and the *Dallas Morning News* previewed and headlined: "Innovative HIDE AND SEEK is a searching educational experience for Dallas students."

Without Jerry, she'd had a double load of demands and concentration needed for the kids programs, but it certainly had helped her shake the grief that often threatened to choke her. Now, the kids needed an expert and it was her job to get one and she had no ideas.

The intercom light glowed. She punched it. "Janelle. Can you come into my office?"

Damn! It was Jeb. She was supposed to be in his office fifteen minutes ago! Quickly, she sorted through files and picked out papers, reminding herself that she needed to check with Jeb about the offshore rig indemnity clause for this DPCO oil package. She walked out and stopped to drop some folders on her secretary's desk. "These can be filed and the new list of students there on top can be duplicated and sent to the research group, Jean." Janelle touched the young woman's arm. "I'm sorry I was abrupt with you when I came in. I had to sort out things for Jeb, and felt rushed."

Jean glanced up questioningly then grinned, "No problem, Janelle, I can tell when you're inside your head. Helen's at the dentist. She said she'd be back by the time of the meeting. I have the kids' stuff she left for you here."

If everything had gone on the rocks for her, Helen at least, had something going. Janelle was nurturing a growing romance between Jeb and Helen, but it wasn't advancing as well as she would like. The two most wonderful people in her world needed to get together in a setting other than the office. At least, that was the goal this week.

She gave her secretary a teasing smile. "Think you have enough work to keep you busy?" Janelle knew Jean had the energy of two people and often complained if the stack of papers wasn't tall enough.

"Can't think of another thing to be done." Jean leaned back in the swivel chair and gestured to the papers. "I'll just sit back and drink some coffee until you come back, chief."

"I'll be in Jeb's office if you need me." Smiling, Janelle walked out the door and continued down the hall. With people like Jean working for her, competent and vital, she had no right to be gloomy. The bright morning and promised challenge of the DPCO project blotted out the past. To hell with loneliness and guilt.

Jeb, talking on the phone when she entered his office, smiled and held up one finger, signaling that he would be off in a minute.

Janelle noted the six wooden chairs lined up like soldiers in front of the uncluttered desk, the neat stacks of journals and insurance forms on the walnut credenza behind his desk. Even the earth tones of russet and beige with tints of midnight blue used in the plaid upholstery fabrics evoked a feeling of no nonsense.

She studied the Blackborn oil painting of mallard ducks. It was a subtle study in space in which the colorful birds seemed poised, ready to fly toward the window and the Dallas skyline. For an instant, the birds' flight reminded her of her marriage to Jerry. He was gone, the courts had acted, but she was in suspended animation. She walked to the portrait of her father which hung on the wall opposite Jeb's desk. Her father's presence was still as vibrant in the office as it had been for the years he'd occupied it. As Jeb's voice droned on in the background, her mind hyper-jumped to a painful time three years before in this office.

Her dad had called her into his office, and, dutifully, Janelle had come and stood waiting to commence business. Her father was sitting at his desk seemingly embarrassed or distracted. His face was flushed, his eyes would not meet hers, and he kept running his hands through his hair as if the motion would somehow relieve his tension.

"Jan, this is about Jeb. Like you, Jeb grew up in the company. He came to work for us when he was twenty-four years old. You know that—he'd worked in the oil fields as a rookie after high school to make enough money to go to business college." His thoughts seemed to drift away. "He'd answered an ad in the *Dallas Morning News* that brought him to my office."

"Well, Dad, he'd had no former experience in the insurance field."

"Yes, but he had an eagerness to learn and a penchant for hard work. I hired that boy and he took his turn processing claims."

"I know all about this. It's legendary." What was he getting at?

"Came up through the ranks. I've been there to teach and encourage Jeb, but it was his love for his work and devotion to excellence that made him the executive he is today." John J. splayed his hands out on his desk, heaved himself up from the chair, and studied the desktop for a moment, then looked at her.

"He's conservative, steady and thoughtful. He takes hold of a problem like a golden retriever with a bone and does not give up on the problem until he is sure if it is good, or not good, for our client as well as for our company."

"Dad, Jeb is as important to me as he is to you."

The big, red-faced man came around the mahogany desk to stand beside her, hesitantly touched her shoulder, then walked away, hands thrust in pockets, to face that very Mallard painting.

Janelle was silent.

"I want Jeb to be president of the company after me." He turned—obviously he'd seen the shock in her eyes, her mouth open ready to reply. "No," he held up his hand, "Let me finish." He stopped to look at her through lowered brows. "You know how proud I am of you, Janelle, proud that another Jamison has come into the company so competently."

With a shrug of her shoulders, Janelle turned from him to look out the window. He held out a hand to her, then dropped it as she turned away from him. "You are my only child and if I had many more they could not own my heart and my pride as you do." John J. was not a demonstratively affectionate man and Janelle knew the confession was hard for him.

"What do you want to tell me, Dad? Just get it out of your gut, as you might say." Janelle walked back to him, patted his arm, and stood quietly waiting for him to continue.

For a moment, he solemnly studied her with eyes as grey as her own and deep with love. "I don't want you to be president of Jamison, Janelle, because you are a woman, and by God, I want you to remain that way!" His fists had tightened and his voice had escalated until he was almost shouting.

Janelle noted her father's defensive stance; she was startled by his explosive words. Jeb should be the logical choice for president if and when her dad retired—Jeb was ten years younger than her dad, and thirty-two years older than she was. He'd deserve the promotion. But her father demeaned Jeb's ability with what he'd just said. And the implied suggestion that she would never ever get a chance at the presidency because she was a woman, *that* she couldn't get out of her own gut.

"What makes you judge and jury?" Janelle's voice had shaken with unexpected rage. She held back the urge to yell, or cry or both.

He sighed and turned from her, "Janelle, I've lived a long time in this business, and I believe I know human nature fairly well. You're like me, Jani." It was his special name. "You've got drive and guts but it's misplaced here. You should be devoting your time to your home and Jerry, have some kids, get that . . . " he looked at her with a pleadingly shy grin, " . . . energy of yours directed to woman's work."

Woman's work? She'd known he was Old Texas in his views of women, but this—she exploded in true Jamison fashion. "I . . . came . . . to . . . work . . . for . . . you . . . in . . . the . . . summers," she took a deep breath. "I could have spent my days shopping at Neiman-Marcus and going skiing in Colorado. Apparently *these* are feminine activities approved of by outdated Texas thinking."

Her tone became more strident, "I went to business school and took courses on insurance business procedures, public relations, and government regulations instead of going the sorority route of my friends that you and mother saw as normal. I wanted to be prepared to come and work for the Jamison Insurance Company." She added resignedly, "You know all that."

With a deep sigh, she continued. "I've never asked favors and don't expect them, Dad. I thought—dreamed—I'd be president someday, but not *before* Jeb. But *damn* it!" She hesitated, and slowed her words. "If and when my turn comes to be the president of the Jamison Group, I hope like *hell* the dubious credentials of being a woman do not keep me from being considered!" Janelle had not raised her voice during the tirade, but noticed her father's face had drained of color. Apparently, he hadn't liked her use of expletives. She'd learned from him how to get a point across.

He stood looking at her with a piercingly cold look. Janelle felt a shiver of fear, but took a deep breath and lifted her chin. "And one more thing, I appreciate a woman in the home. My own mother has been a perfect example of what you're talking about. I love and respect Mother. She has an inner spirituality which she shares constantly."

Janelle had gone to the desk and picked up a photograph of her mother. "But she isn't me, Dad.

"You've worked with me. I trusted you to understand that." She'd turned to her dad. A glint of tears was in her father's eyes. He'd silently nodded his head as if he understood.

Jeb was hanging up the phone. As she turned to join him, it rang again. Jeb answered, then held his hand over the receiver. "Sorry Jan. "I'd better take this call too. Sit down, I'll be with you in a minute or— want to get together later?"

"I'll wait." Janelle moved to sit on the couch facing the portrait. Jeb was back on the phone.

In the portrait, the artist had caught the self-confidence of her father. The eyes showed his deep understanding and love of people. John J. had shown through his love for his wife, Nell, and his only daughter that he'd have ridden rough-shod over anyone who dared try to harm them. Janelle knew this. But often, as she was growing up, she felt left out. It was as if her parents' love for each other, deep and all absorbing, filled up all the space in their home. Perhaps she'd married Jerry so she could find her own special brand of love. But she and Jerry had never melded interests, hadn't shared many confidences. Why hadn't she shared with her husband her deep desire to have children?

It had come up in that meeting so long ago with her dad. All that talk about staying home, taking care of children. "Dad, Jerry and I don't want children. At least he doesn't and I've agreed. Jerry enjoys his work, our life together." Her voice quivered from the effort to talk this frankly with her father, especially since she'd always been the perfect daughter. "Dad, I need my career."

John J. expelled a deep breath and said in reply, "I've seen women who have gotten to the top of the executive ladder and when they got there, have seen them forget how to let a man pull out a chair for them. Or, are afraid that men intend to pull the chair out from under them." He continued, "Women executives seem to confront rather than negotiate. They're hard, Jani." His eyes were honest.

"God made man and woman, Jani. Two people together to build a family. That's the way it should be. You and your mother made me see the important part of a home—well, I guess you could say, before you were born, I lived insurance."

He was pacing back and forth like a caged animal. "I used to stay down here until eleven at night, go home, fall in bed, come back down here at seven AM. Your mother put up with me, God love her, But until *you* came," he emphasized, "my first priority was the business, and your mother. She shared every part of what I did. She made our success possible."

Janelle remembered thinking that it was true. Her mother gave the love, provided unconditional support. Her father set up the rules for the married relationship. Given that he considered women subordinates who were to wait to take orders, not give orders, his thesis was logical. Janelle knew by heart what she had said to her father after that.

"Dad, I have a home now, with Jerry. You have a home with Mother, yet come to the office each day for fulfillment. Don't you think I can do the same? I have a home I share with Jerry, and I love him, but I also have a job which I love. Am I so different from you?"

John J. shook his head slowly. And that had been that. Deeply disappointed, she had to face his decision as a fact to be accepted not a proposal to be debated. In a few days, she'd rebounded with her idea for a television program for students. He'd told her, "I'll give you thirty minutes to explain this hare-brained idea of yours." She smiled to herself remembering her eager presentation.

"Most schools are over-populated and over programmed with the supposed essentials for the education of the young people. It is impossible to hone in on finer details of some subjects—there aren't enough hours in the day, nor the educators to do the extra work. Educational TV has a real place here.

"There are networks ready to pick up a series relating to education. The administration in Washington has made it clear that education will be a top priority in the issuance of public funds both at the national and at the state levels.

"And there are some subjects that don't get studied in school. Who's talking about cliques that exclude kids and ruin their high school experience, about local industries that dominate the area with their power, about sexually transmitted diseases?"

"Wait a minute."

She ignored the interruption. "TV has become the teacher of our society. I want this *teacher,*" she emphasized the word, "to put some researched facts in front of students so they can make realistic choices in such things as their education, their future voting, their everyday lives. We'll call it HIDE AND SEEK for that's what it will be: taking things out of hiding so eager minds can seek answers."

He didn't want things taken out of hiding; still he'd listened. Maybe he thought he ought to offer her *something.* Later, Jeb had overcome her dad's resistance by pointing out that Janelle's program could be an advertising vehicle for the insurance company, and the design of the television topics would be good background material for insurance coverage changes. Her dad could sell it to the Jamison Board as his own project. Of course, John J. had liked that part.

It had been three years since she presented the plan to her dad. Now her dad was dead. Her mother too. Both had been killed that very year when their car was hit by a drunken driver as they drove from Padre to Dallas.

The day of their serious talk, had he been telling her to get out of business before it became her god? Little did she know that day how short a time she'd have with him, that Jerry and she would be divorced two years later. How she missed her parents. Janelle's throat ached with unspoken words. His eyes in the portrait seemed to stare into her soul, affectionate, yet challenging. Was there a rebuke in those eyes?

"Jan. Sorry to have kept you waiting," Jeb said. "That was the president of Dalton Petroleum Corporation. He wants to meet tomorrow.

I've read your progress report on DPCO and think we're ready to finalize the insurance plan for their company."

"We only delivered the completed package to California last week!" she said, surprised.

"Well, the big boss is in the city right now and wants to rehash some of the plan personally with us and make the final decision," Jeb shrugged. "I see no way that his company can refuse us!" He slapped his hand on the desk, and came around to face Janelle. "This multi-million dollar package is due to your fine work. Your father would be proud of you." He leaned down and kissed her on the cheek, an unaccustomed gesture for him.

Janelle studied Jeb's rugged good looks: grey hair, a face creased with definitive smile-lines around the eyes and mouth. He had a gentle manner that inspired trust. Her dad's faith had been justified. And Janelle understood why Helen was attracted to the man. "Helen took time out from the HIDE AND SEEK programing to help with the proposal. She's great on fine details," she said.

An idea hit her as she walked to the door. "Hey, maybe you can get the president of DPCO Oil to appear on the TV show the kids are working on this week! From what you've told me, he's charismatic and knowledgeable. What do you think?"

"Excellent idea. I'll ask him."

The hall was empty as she headed for the elevator.

It had taken Helen a long time to adjust to the fact that she could care for someone who was her superior in the business. That Jeb could see her as a woman, not a cog in the business wheel. Maybe it was her quiet sincerity that attracted him. She remembered her mother saying that Jeb's former wife, Sonya, had been a sweet woman who'd been involved in Dallas society. That she'd loved the glittering rounds of the Dallas social life while Jeb had wanted a home and quiet evenings. They'd been divorced after five years. That was fourteen years ago. Janelle knew he'd had women in his life since then, but his work seemed to be his real passion. And now, there was Helen. At least Janelle hoped that was the direction this office friendship was heading.

Janelle exited the elevator on the fifth floor and headed for the television studio. The idea of the important but unknown Mr. Dalton being interviewed by the students was exciting. Jeb had briefly worked for the man's father Ted Dalton. From a distance, he'd watched Ted Dalton's son grow up. The boy had come up through the ranks of the oil business and, much like his father, had a reputation for being well liked as an honest business man in the oil trade. Unlike his father, Jeb seemed to think the young man to be a free-thinking and an independent individual who liked flashy cars and beautiful women. Jeb had said the thirty-four-year old was a fast-track spender.

Jeb, having been brought up in the old school which emphasized Baptist morals, home values, and quiet living without the pretentious use of hard-earned money, seemed to categorize Mr. Dalton as a puzzler.

Jeb had added that he hadn't personally seen the man for several years, as he did not come to Dallas, rather sent his two business associates to the city. Dalton spent his time on the California coast, in Europe and the Near East, and on rare occasions visited the east Texas oil country. Still, he'd be a real addition to the program if they could land him.

Chapter Three

Janelle stopped just inside the studio door and listened to the com
ments of the students. "Hey Robyn!" Pete Rowenda, a street-
smart, Hispanic junior was entering the HIDE AND SEEK studio.
"We've got enough info on the oil business, but haven't gotten the go-
ahead to tape. What gives?"

Robyn Greer, a tall, lean eighteen-year-old with a thatch of curly
black hair, an angular face dominated by a large nose, and deep-set,
dark brown eyes was working with a group of teenagers who were busy
sorting papers on a low table. Robyn nodded his greeting to Janelle
and spoke to the group. "We have the first three segments taped and
are ready for the fourth and last tape with a celebrity interview. It's
possible for us to have the whole package ready for the schools by next
week," Robyn grinned. "We'll have to rush it, and definitely get these
research files on the last month's programs taken to the storage closet
and some of this oil industry research filed away."

Stacks of papers on the floor were ready for cardboard files which
were lined up along the wall. Floor pillows, Pepsi and Mountain Dew
cans, purses, notebooks, and backpacks were strewn over the floor on
one side of the studio, providing homey contrast to the gleaming television cameras, Kluge lamps, and large cam-lights spaced along the
opposite side of the room

"I suppose it'll get done," one girl said.

"Yeah." Another student moaned. "The group researching oil went
overboard with their notes and transcripts. This is just a part of it!"

Janelle enjoyed the lively group. These kids, the ones who presented
the researched information to the viewing audience on the HIDE AND
SEEK television programs, were mirror images of the viewing adoles-
cents. They were an exciting bunch that generated enthusiasm in their
peers; they could be trusted.

"Well," Julie Leoni sighed, "I had begun to think we were never going to finish this oil program!"

Julie, an eighteen-year-old Italian beauty with long black hair and brown eyes, was a favorite of the viewers. Janelle knew the girl received lots of mail from students and had chaired a program on some of their questions: Should a Protestant date a Catholic; How could a fourteen year old escape intimidation by older boys; How could you keep your best friend from stealing your boyfriend. Julie had given the viewing audience a tour of the kitchen of her father's Italian restaurant in Dallas and had explained the health laws, and the recycling programs of the city's food establishments. That program had received an excellence award for environmental education from the state.

"I'm really tired of it." Janelle watched a frustrated Julie grab a stack of papers and thrust them out to Pete and wondered why the girl seemed so upset.

"Aw, you just want to get on to the next program." The group all knew what the next topic was—in fact it was the most provocative and politically dangerous subject they'd ever done. The disease AIDS. Pete took the papers from her. "It's the hottest topic in town."

Apparently, Pete and Julie and the virus research team had completed their scientific segment of the AIDS series and were ready to tape the updated question and answer segments, which were to be led by Robyn.

"You two and the HIV virus research team did a super job on the scientific video. When you think the disease hadn't been fully diagnosed in America until four years ago, people need to be informed about the seriousness of the virus. Me included," Robyn admitted.

Pete walked over to Robyn. "Julie, the virus team and I are ready to move on the updated Q & A section. Are you ready to lead the discussion?" Janelle could feel a kind of tension in the room, probably an undercurrent of fear. The information they were getting was about HIV, and people were dying of the virus.

"Right on Pete," Colleen Blair said in a strong voice. "I know a guy who is HIV positive right now. He'd had a transfusion for a football injury and the blood was contaminated. This virus sure scares me. I can't stop thinking about it!"

Colleen was a walking, talking encyclopedia who'd been chosen as leader of the young women's program-planning because she was good at asking hard questions of the student research teams. Students seemed to trust the laid-back, bluejeaned, pigtailed, no-make-up Colleen. Janelle surmised Colleen was a successful mentor because she appeared unthreatening to those who wanted nothing to do with intellectuals.

"Yeah. No one seems interested in doing research on their own. They're waiting for our panel to tell them what to do," Pete Rowenda agreed. "My dad and sister have told me some pretty scary things about people who are HIV positive. I've told Julie some of the effects of the virus that they've seen first hand in the hospital where he's a staff doctor and she's a nurse. It's powerful bad, folks."

A slight frown clouded Robyn's face. "I don't know Pete," he said. "This material you and Julie have done is too sketchy.

"Sure it's sketchy. We've reams of material, but the censors haven't approved even half of it! Too many details, they said!" Julie looked at Robyn disgustedly. "If it hadn't been for Ms J and Jerry intervening, I bet the censor group would have refused to approve *all* the scary stuff on this freaky thing."

The censors, adults of the Dallas community, chosen for their expertise in public policy, had the power to veto taped material even though the adult scientific committee might approve it. Janelle recalled the bitter arguments between the science and censor committees as to what of the AIDS material should be shown to the schools. Over a year ago, Jerry'd been the one to obtain the first go-around of approval for taping the AIDS programs. Janelle hoped she'd be as effective with the two adult governing bodies when she presented the kids up-close question and answer segment.

"I think we have to sit on this one for awhile." Robyn dug his hands into his back pockets and shrugged his shoulders, his head bowed, as if to avoid looking at Julie and Pete. Robyn was always enthusiastic and eager to pursue ideas students sent to the group. Was AIDS scaring him? Or did he have a personal stake in some way?

Another panel member, Donna Meeker, spoke up, "Well, I know you've got college on your mind, but really, Robyn!" She walked over to Robyn and looked at him. "We have got to get going on this stuff. Nobody knows where it's all going. I sure as hell wish I'd been more savvy." Her voice died with a whisper.

No one present doubted that she was one who should be aware of the facts about AIDS. A voluptuously built redhead, a very popular girl with the late night roamers, she was the leader of the self-destructive fast-set who lived for the moment. Many of the viewers understood her. She relieved their own consciences.

Janelle, who'd been quietly observing and listening, moved coats and bags to sit on the couch. Robyn smiled his relief. "Hey, Ms. J! Have anything for us on our oil guest?"

Janelle nodded. "We'll know something after the meeting with Dalton Petroleum Company tomorrow. The president of the company sounds like a natural. Jeb knows the man personally and hopes to convince him to stay over in Dallas for another day to be interviewed."

The young faces she studied were so beautifully, unreservedly eager. Janelle felt a tug of longing for a child of her own. It wasn't rational. Her doctor had told her it would be almost impossible for her to conceive. Jerry's and her decision to remain childless had not seemed so extreme because of that. Now, she'd always wonder what would have happened if they'd tried. Aloud, she asked, "How's the rest of the oil program coming?"

Each of the students took turns reporting the research, taping final phase plans for the oil program. As Janelle listened in quiet pride, she recalled bringing each and everyone of these students into the program. The first day she'd gone out to recruit students for the documentary television programs, she'd met Robyn Greer at North Dallas High School. He'd been standing by the school entrance with three boys when Janelle started into the school building. "Hey! What do we have here?" one boy asked the others.

"A good lookin' babe who must be lost," another one snickered.

"Too old to be a babe, but maybe an old doll, hmmm?" the third boy added.

Robyn moved between Janelle and the boys. "Hey, guys. Don't you know a lady when you see one? Let her in." He shoved one of his friends aside and opened the door for Janelle.

The school assembly listened to Janelle's presentation on bringing a televised contemporary study program to the schools. Afterward, several came up to sign the roster. Robyn was one of them.

And who was he? "He's the leader of a punk group," the principal told her. "They're not bad kids as far as I know; they lack direction. Robyn lives with his mom and works at a car repair shop on weekends." The man shook his head. "Makes Bs, but seems to have no direction or interests other than just hanging out."

Then there was the day Donna Meeker had signed up with HIDE & SEEK. Janelle had gone to Hillcrest High School, set up her recruiting desk outside the cafeteria, and Donna appeared with other curious and enthusiastic students. She'd noticed Donna, who stood out with her mass of corn-braid hair, low cut, v-necked blouse and skintight jeans. The girl with the mascara eyes had hung back, leaning against a boy, looking much like a curious kitten afraid to eat, but interested in what was in the bowl. Her lowered eyes intently watched the other kids come up to the desk; then she finally shoved off the wall and came over to the table. "Could help on Saturdays!" Donna exclaimed. "I've got to have something to do on Saturdays during football season. The coach says I'm a distraction to the boys." The girl shrugged, hands on hips, head tilted to the side and looked defiantly at Janelle for a moment, then looked down at the floor.

First impressions are not always fair. Instinct suggesting the young woman might need direction like the Greer boy, paid off when she'd asked the girl to commit to at least two Saturdays a month for program duties. "Why not? Keep me out of trouble." Janelle recalled that the haunted look left the pretty girl's eyes for a moment.

Today in the studio, Janelle knew she had been right about Donna. This girl was willing to go for the difficult interviews—seek out buried answers. She now wore a size larger sweater, and the swish of the hips was less suggestive. And Robyn was the leader most respected by all the kids. It seemed the independent, bad-kid-types had turned out to be excellent leaders. Perhaps all they had needed was a signpost on the road and direction of how to get somewhere else but a dead end.

Janelle considered Julie Leoni. She was the daughter of Oscar and Gina Leoni, friends of Janelle's parents. This young woman, one of the most respected leaders, was living proof of what family love can do for a child. Julie was asking something—"Ms J, you heard us talking about the AIDS program. There seems to be some sort of delay. What's happening?"

Robyn looked over to Janelle with a questioning stare. "I'm checking to see how we can complete this program, but right now . . ."

Janelle hurriedly interrupted him. "It seems as if it's taking months longer than we anticipated. We've had to restructure and modify the AIDS material after Jerry left—the Dallas Educational Commission has asked us to send our current material to them, and it's hard to say what is current when every day new facts are being learned about the virus." She wiped tired eyes with her hand.

"We'll see to it Ms. J, don't you worry," Robyn, always attuned to others, said. "Since we can't proceed today, I suggest that we file the rest of this stuff and head out the door." Robyn looked questioningly at Janelle.

"Good idea! We'll be in touch with you about the oil baron's appearance on the show after tomorrow's oil meeting." Janelle smiled at each of the group. "And, Robyn, I believe Helen's scheduled the new filming of the AIDS program for the first of next month. She'll call you. The censor group has approved all the updates, but we'd better be very sure they go for the final material that we'll cover."

"Yeah. Hope they'll buy it," Robyn mused. The others looked at each other. The import of dealing with such a sensitive subject with a board made up of "Old Texas" people was registering.

Back in her office, after finishing up the file for the DPCO meeting, Janelle stretched her arms above her head and breathed in a sigh of relief. The HIDE AND SEEK television program Jerry and she had nurtured was growing all the time. His directing and public relations talents and her organizational skills had launched the program off the drawing board and into the schools, but the local student enthusiasm had made it a success.

Of course, the scheduling was a real bear. It had to be juggled to work around the participating students' classes and the camera crew's availability. Jean kept the phone wires hot penciling in the scheduling calender and notifying the two adult committees when the students' material was ready for critical viewing. Helen helped with production and kept a performance sheet on each student helping with the programs. The constant editing and re-editing, seeing the show to deadline had built strong relationships among adults and high school kids who usually didn't speak the same language.

Janelle and Jerry had been in charge of the overall planning, working with the research panel. Jerry chaired censor committee meetings, grumbling, "It's like the Hollywood Hays Office of the 1930s for Christ's sake." But her dad, Jeb, and the rest of the original planning group were firm in their wish to have censors. And her conservative insurance executive father, always looking down the path for risk, insisted they should hear any gripes of outrage before the videos were released.

Janelle picked up the day's folders and took them out to her secretary. "Jean, will you file these and update? Everything seems to be on schedule for this month's program on the oil industry. The first three AIDS tapes have been approved and printed. Helen needs to push the group to finish up the last one so we can have it all canned and ready to distribute."

Placing the AIDS folder on top of the others, Janelle continued, "I'll be in for the taping tomorrow. I don't know what time to tell the crew to be ready for Mr. DPCO Oil until Jeb has talked to him." Janelle dropped remaining papers on the already cluttered desk.

"Sure thing, chief," Jean answered smilingly—it was *CHIEF* only when Janelle seemed uptight.

Janelle walked toward the door, then returned. "Where's Helen? Has the dentist drilled to China?"

"She was in but her mouth hurt, so she left early."

That was unusual. Helen raised the blinds in the morning and was still at her desk when the maintenance crew came in to pick up the waste baskets. "I'll call her when I get home to see how she is," Janelle said. Jean nodded.

Janelle's thoughts jumped to the next day's meeting. "I forgot to tell Helen about the meeting with DPCO tomorrow. Please leave her a note. And Jean, when you go out for lunch, I'd sure like a grilled cheese sandwich and hot tea brought back to the office." She closed the door and prepared to work on the oil prospectus for the rest of the day.

Traffic was not too bad on the drive to the grocery on Oakland north and west of her apartment. After picking up milk, a beef pot pie, and coffee ice cream, she continued her cautious drive home on Turtle Creek. Azaleas brightened the green edges of the creek and glorious flowering dogwood and crab apple filled slopping lawns of stately mansions with color. She never tired of the drive with its wrought iron and stone gateways.

Slowing down as she passed the house where she'd lived her childhood, she noted new plantings by the driveway entrance and wondered if there were new owners. The house had been sold to an older couple at the death of her parents.

Huge, soft maple trees had been lushly green that day in June when she and Jerry were married. The large Tudor house had been surrounded by flowering crepe myrtle and tall, stately red oak, its stone veranda defined by rose topiaries and smilax. Tents with furling flags had spread out over a lawn where the royalty of Dallas, dressed in brilliant colors and black tuxedos, enjoyed the gala wedding reception of Janelle Jane Jamison and Jerome Theodore Taylor III. It was like a setting for the Cirque de Soleil, the French Circus, with she and Jerry the main attraction drifting through laughter and music, as they visited with over 500 guests. They'd lingered, though excited and eager to get away to Padre Island, her family's get-away-spot, for the first night of their honeymoon, then to fly abroad the next week and drive to a small French hotel, Le Mas D'Artigny. The intimate spot was set above St. Paul, an ancient fortified French village, and Saint Paul's monastery in the mountains above the Côte d' Azur. Legend had it that the Apostle Paul had traveled close by on the road winding up through the Loo River Canyon. And what joy to leave the extravaganza that had been their wedding. Much less joy to leave the marriage.

As she drove past the site of the morning fiasco, the Maserati man flashed in her mind. Righteous indignation burned again. Of everyone she could have hit why did it have to be that arrogant—she searched for adjectives—"attractive and sexually appealing" forced their way into her mind. She held her temper in check and cautiously followed the car in front of her. One accident a day was more than enough.

Janelle parked her car at the entrance of her apartment building, left her ignition key with Timothy, then dashed to the elevator. The light blinked the floors on the way to the penthouse. She was feeling ashamed. Clearly that man had both angered and attracted her. Was she so lonely that her heart jumped out at every handsome stranger?

Having closed the ornately carved apartment door, she grabbed the mail the cleaning lady had left on the chest-high brass and chrome hunt table in the entrance hall, hurried on to deposit the groceries in the kitchen, and returned to the shadowed living room. With a flip of a switch, soft lights pushed the darkness aside as she headed for the fireside couch and slowly sank into the softness of down-filled cushions. She leaned her head back with a grateful sigh and glanced sideways at a wooden Maltese cat, perched on the hearth. "I'm tired, old buddy," she murmured.

Jerry had presented the ancient copy of an Egyptian ruler's cat to her one evening before they'd left for dinner. He'd stroked the smooth wood. "Here's an appropriate present for you. But of course you're not a cat."

"I could be catty if I saw another woman after you." She'd laughed and now recalled the startled look he'd given her. Had he thought she was referring to Mandy? She'd not had a clue then. So much for hindsight!

It was all so strange. He hadn't wanted children and yet he'd left her for the paramour who was carrying his child. And had seemed pleased at the prospect of fatherhood.

She turned her head to a small end table filled with photographs in silver frames and sought the one with the handsome blond man lounging in a chair on the Dallas Country Club patio. She had taken the picture after a tennis game. Alongside it was another photo in which Jerry was standing by his Jaguar. He was dressed in a Montana jacket and slacks that fit his matador-thin body like second skin. Blond, almost white, hair, smoothed back behind the ears and clipped to just above the shirt collar framed a face with prominent brows, small grey eyes, aquiline nose. With the Van Dyke beard worn to hide a somewhat receding chin and small mouth, he had a distinguished look. The camera had caught an elegance, a kind of pride in himself, which was conveyed by his bearing.

Janelle closed her eyes and tried to examine what her attraction had been for the man. He was from one of the old-wealth families of Fort

Worth and she had met him at Southern Methodist University. He had charmed her with reserved respect, excellent manners. She'd never met a man like him. Old Texans, like her father, wore corduroys and cowboy boots and gave bear hugs and fannie pats for affection. Even on the honeymoon, he'd sought out expensive shops for sport coats, European cut suits and tasseled loafers. Janelle had questioned his extravagant taste and he'd explained that he'd always had the money to dress well and did not intend to change his habits.

She'd been reared to believe you gave to your man and then gave some more, even if his ideas were excessive. She'd shrugged off doubt when he'd come home from a buying spree flushed and fairly dancing with excitement while Timothy, the doorman, trailed behind carrying boxes of shirts, suits, shoes. "Let a man run. Don't pull the reins too tight," her father had said.

Why had she left the tormenting photos out? Did she really believe things might change and he'd come back to her? Here, her failures were framed to torment her every day. Did she focus on the past to pay the price for being a fool?

A before-Jerry conversation with her mother and a maiden aunt came to mind. They'd been discussing infidelity, quite candidly. Her very genteel aunt had surprised her when she explained, "The appetite, 'an universal wolf,' as Shakespeare defined the propensities of the male animal, is satisfied by instantaneous gratification. The appetite of the female is less subject to the need for immediacy. A woman will not usually go seeking. If this is correct, then the attitudes concerning the appropriateness and or the consequences of a sexual liaison should not be looked upon in the same way."

"Right on, Aunt Patsy," Janelle mumbled to herself. "Jerry being the male, couldn't resist Eternal Eve. I, the female, was able to resist temptation. I didn't break the vows we made at that shindig. And how should Mandy be classified?"

Janelle now surmised that she herself had become an extension of Jerry's ego. He'd loved for people to meet his ornamental wife, the daughter of John J. Jamison. She'd been dismayed at the endless feasts of excitement their schedule forced on her, but he continued to accept invitations. Probably he'd been shy of the glittering group he courted and needed her support. She was a private person and many a night had wanted to stay home. Just stay at home.

Jerry had set the pace. Jerry, the journalist: flamboyant, articulate, charismatic. What a robot she'd been. But in the business office, she'd felt in control. That's what she really was saying when her dad had told her about Jeb, but she hadn't known it.

Janelle pushed up from the deep couch and walked around the lovely room, touching the silk fabric of a marshmallow-soft lounge chair, smoothing a hand over a silver-topped tea table with its dainty glass legs. He'd decorated, with her uncertain approval, in all white on white with shining chrome and silver accents. It was as cold to her now as their love must have been for him. She walked over to the softly draped window that overlooked the park and far reaches of the city. Pulling aside the soft fabric, she did not see the lights, the golden ribbons of cars moving along the boulevard, but rather saw again her own reflection. A small, slender woman with long blond hair that framed a face, not exactly beautiful, but symmetrical. A near replica of Nell Jamison, all but for the firm mouth and large, deep-set eyes. They were like John J's.

She studied her reflection with less than approval. Even their love-making was orchestrated by Jerry and if truth be known, was never too satisfactory. There was a night, after they'd attended a banquet where he'd received an award for outstanding investigative reporting. She'd been proud of him, wanted to congratulate him. He'd pushed her praise aside. "Well sleuth-work is more exciting than wrangling with the Victorian censors for the HIDE AND SEEK show."

That night, after they were in bed, she'd snuggled up to him and ran fingers down his side. He murmured, turned his face away and readjusted the book he was reading to the bedside light.

She felt ashamed and foolish as she recalled how she tried to interest him by sliding her hand in the opening of his pajama bottom. She'd wanted him to notice her, make love to her. He'd pushed her away with a frown, and pulled the cover up over his shoulder in silent rebuke. Why had he turned from her?

Janelle felt a wave of loss sweep over her. The reflection of her tear-drenched face floated over the city scene like the ghost of her mother. "Must have been my fault . . . my fault . . . .." She laid her cheek on the sun-warmed window pane and sobbed, "Oh, Mom, I couldn't balance it all." Her dad's warning had been right! She must have seemed more like a calculating business woman than a wife to Jerry. She knew his faults—there'd been flaws in their marriage. Yet, even after eleven months, she still blamed herself. Slowly, she went back to the table for a last look at Jerry's photo then put it inside the drawer to close out the sight of the man.

A shrill peel startled her and she hurried to the telephone.

"Hello!" came a low Texas drawl. Old Texas, but who?

"I've an estimate for the damage to my car."

Him! Her eyes glanced over to the mantel clock, Seven-thirty, not much she could do about an estimate at this hour of the day! "And?" She waited.

"I believe the repairs will be about eight thousand dollars if the other two estimates I intend to get are in line."

"Well, you have my insurance and business numbers. Call me tomorrow at my office. I can't do business in the evening. And *please*," she emphasized, "Get those other two estimates before calling."

"Yes, ma'am!"

She could hear him chuckle in an almost friendly way. "Would you, . . . could I drop by your office tomorrow? At your convenience of course."

He was trying to be cooperative, maybe even apologize. She hesitated and he continued. "Would ten o'clock be all right?"

Her mind flew through her appointments. She could meet him and still get to the DPCO luncheon engagement at twelve-thirty. "Yes, ten will be fine, Mr. . . . .?"

"Tyler."

Janelle stood and stared at the phone a few seconds after she hung up. The appointment would be a good way to finish up the incident. She groaned. How could she feel so excited yet so angry? She knew how as she visualized that exasperatingly handsome man while the words "over-sexed," "over-sexed" played themselves over and over in her mind. And she wasn't?

After a skimpy meal of pot pie and salad, she washed up the few dishes in the sink. Not exactly gourmet fare. She could have gone out with that securities man who kept calling her. Malcolm Jones, one handsome face in the crowd that Jerry enjoyed seeing now and then.

Boring and predictable. Certainly not like the man she'd "bumped into" today, whoever he was. But it did show there were other men out there. She needed to make more of an effort to improve her own social life. Maybe eleven months was long enough. For the first time in almost a year, when she slipped under her down-filled comforter in the huge bed, she didn't miss Jerry.

Chapter Four

No morning light penetrated the taffeta-draped darkness. Janelle had to force herself to roll over and punch the insistent alarm. "Five AM!" she moaned. "I can get up or stay in bed until seven." Turning on her back and stretching out arms and legs, she lay motionless listening to the early morning sounds of birds, delivery trucks, and traffic, always the pulsating traffic. She considered the cheerful wakefulness that usually eluded her until she'd had her first cup of tea. There was a tingling sensation of anticipation when the face of the Maserati man flashed in her memory. Something like the Marlboro man in the cigarette ad. Too good looking? Maybe he *was* a male model.

Later, all ready but for a dress, she padded over to the closet and grabbed her favorite jacket-dress of red and white linen, and held it up in front of herself in the full length mirror. It would be just right for the DPCO meeting and, well—a wide slightly off-center grin brightened her face—for the ten o'clock meeting as well!

She pictured the man, then sobered. She was thirty years old. And just a normal woman. She quickly pulled the dress over her head to hide the grin on her face.

Finished with the usual morning rituals of watering the two green ivy plants in the hall and the small herb tray on the kitchen window sill, she rushed down to her car which an attendant had waiting. In a more peaceful frame of mind, she drove down to the fateful intersection and enjoyed the ribbons of rainbow colors made by the fast moving cars. She frowned. The man had been irritating, mannerless. Why had she felt such attraction? Soon she'd be throwing herself at semi-drivers at truck stops.

The Jamison Insurance Building, thirty stories high, played sentinel to the labyrinth of short, squatty buildings reflected in its glass exterior. The cavernous marble foyer was empty of footsteps and laughter at six-thirty in the morning. The click, clack of Janelle's heels bounced off the walls like drums announcing the charge as she briskly walked to the line of elevators and touched the express to the 25th floor.

Unlocking the door to her outer office, she stepped into the semi-light interior of her office to enjoy the layers of pink haze sprinkled with dust moats from the rising sun rays which filled the room. Surprisingly, rain had been predicted for this last day of March.

Working her way out of the jacket, she hung it up in the closet and walked over to her desk to find the DPCO proposal in three neatly arranged stacks. There was a note beside the folders:

Janelle, I'm sorry I missed the Hide and Seek student meeting yesterday. I can't go to the oil meeting with you and Jeb today. Tell me about it later.   Helen

Janelle shook her head. Could she never beat Helen in the office? She must have returned last night to get this ready. What a wonder she was. Her dad knew when he hired this woman that he had not only an excellent personal secretary, but an asset to the company. Janelle also knew she and Jeb had been right to promote Helen to be business manager of the HIDE AND SEEK Television Program. And now, her two best friends seemed to be heading toward something more beyond business. There was obviously affection between them and they'd had lunches together several times in the last two weeks.

"Hi! You're here early." As if summoned, Helen walked into the room. "Sorry I missed yesterday with you and the kids. I heard about the DPCO meeting from Jeb."

Janelle smiled at the trim figure in the soft, blue linen skirt and matching silk cardigan. Was there just a tinge of warming when she said Jeb's name? "I came back last night to get the paperwork in order."

"I don't know how you do all you do. Jeb is so proud of it"—Janelle added hesitantly, "and I've wanted to thank you for your understanding these past months during my divorce proceedings. I couldn't talk about any of it, but you accepted my odd moods, the blank days."

Helen's eyes were sympathetic. "There's nothing to thank me for. It was miserable for you."

They'd never discussed the divorce past basic information. She'd come to the office every day when the divorce proceedings were being finalized, sitting behind the door all day, overwhelmed with hopelessness, having lunch delivered, not able to talk to anyone. Word had filtered through the office that Jerry had married soon after he left her, so the office personnel could guess what she'd been through. Personal privacy was valued in the company; her father had set that standard long ago. But today, it was time to talk to her friend.

"Well, it's been almost a year, Helen, and I am feeling better about myself. I guess last night I finally faced that I'd failed somehow, but it doesn't hurt so much. I've needed the HIDE AND SEEK television program and I've felt your support and understanding. Thanks."

Helen uncrossed her slim legs and pushed herself up from the comfortable chair. "You're welcome, for what I'm not quite sure," and quickly added, "So DPCO's big boss is coming to review the package? How many copies will you need? There are eight of each there."

"We'll need four copies for Mr. Big Oil to fax to his office in San Francisco. He's bringing two of his men with him; guess we'll need two more of each section for them, and Jeb, and me. Jeb's asked me to present the proposal." She went on, excited to share and talk about the strategy of the meeting with Helen.

"I'll get the girls on it and also get the benefit diagram copies," Helen said. "By the way, is there to be a last taping of the oil segment tomorrow with the kids?"

"I guess so. Jeb is to ask the man today to appear on the show. I'll know more after the Dalton meeting. What else is going on with the student research for future shows? Yesterday when I met with the kids I thought Robyn seemed to be a little slow getting the AIDS material out. I wonder how much longer it will take?"

Helen answered over her shoulder as she quickly walked to the door, "Seems he's having a hard time getting some facts together from the hospital. I must go and get the secretaries started." She waved a hasty retreat and hurried out.

Janelle followed and headed to Jeb's office for their daily meeting. She felt the urge to tell him about the Maserati man. He seemed in a hurry to get downtown for a Kiwanis meeting so Janelle passed it by. Anyway, she didn't need to tell him everything that occurred in her life. It was enough to have to face the Texan without telling Jeb how irresponsible she'd been. With a glance at her watch, she rushed back to her office, hurried to her private lavatory to freshen her makeup and grabbed some spray to moisten her eyes. "Ouch!" she yelped as she felt a burning sensation in her eyes. Groaning, she quickly took out her contacts and dried her watering eyes with a towel. Breath freshener for moisturizing was a sure sign she was not her usual cool-in-command self.

Grabbing some tissues she rushed to her desk to answer the voice box. "Ms. Jamison, Mr. Tyler is here."

"Send him in, please," she said in a firm voice quickly stuffing the tissues in her pocket as she waited.

Three long strides brought the man to the front of Janelle's desk, where he extended a large, sun-bronzed hand in greeting. "Good morning!" Tyler's energetic greeting lit up the room and his smile, which caused tiny laugh lines at the corners of his steel blue eyes, gave him the look of one who hadn't a care in the world.

"Good morning, Mr. Tyler." Her smile was equally as bright, but her eyes hurt. His hand closed over hers in a powerful grip. They stood, grey eyes locked on blue ones for a moment before Janelle hurriedly freed her hand and started to shuffle through some papers on her desk. There it was again. This was not just any man. This one had a pull as strong as the Atlantic gulftide.

Tyler seemed to sense her nervousness and moved back from the desk. "I appreciate your seeing me this morning, Ms. Jamison. I have only today in the city and believe we both will feel better when this small altercation is behind us."

Small altercation? Tears formed in her eyes. *Damn that mouth spray!*

He noticed, looked concerned, but made no motion other than to take a handkerchief from his pocket and offer it to her.

She grabbed a tissue instead. "You said you would have the other estimates?" Best if they stuck strictly to the insurance settlement.

"The lowest bid is sixty-five hundred. Guess the car is one of those that need expensive repairs." Tyler shrugged his shoulders as if in apology, pulled back his coat and slid his hands into his pants pockets to stand, legs splayed apart, in a body stance that spoke of complete self-confidence.

Indeed! Janelle leaned over her desk and wrote some figures on a blank form while she silently assessed what he wore. A silk tweed jacket, black slacks, gold Rolex watch that showed from under the cuff of a white-on-white shirt. Custom-made grey snakeskin cowboy boots completed the portrait of Texas millionaire.

A flashy show-off? Well, that really didn't seem to be the case. Rather, he was like a self confident person who took little notice of the clothes, but certainly was noticing her. Janelle could feel his boldness as he stood motionless, completely at ease, a half-smile playing on his face. "I'm prepared to sign the statement which you have, I presume, obtained from the police and my insurance claims agent!" The words were sharp projectiles flying at a man she hardly knew, but who was ruffling her serenity.

"Well now," Tyler began with in slow, friendly way. "Considering all things, and having gone back to the spot where we bumped into each other," he attempted a feeble grin, "I believe you did have a legitimate excuse for veering into me. The glare from the sun at that time of day can be blinding." He slowly sank down into the leather chair and crossed a booted foot over his knee.

Jan could feel two bright spots of color start to form on her cheeks. Damn, he was condescending. "I'm not excusing myself and I want to pay for the damages. How much did you say it would be?"

She noted that he was seated while she remained standing. *Of all the nerve.* She sat down with a thump and held a tissue to her left eye.

She was sending mixed messages. She was attempting to be efficiently indifferent and her damn eyes were making her look like a crying idiot who was playing for sympathy.

"I have left the papers with your secretary. There's no payment necessary." Tyler spoke with a Texas accent that would have melted the cream cheese on a bagel. He cleared his throat and shifted his body in the chair. "You know, ma'am, I get the feeling that you're not quite ready to accept my apology for the way I spooked you yesterday."

He uncrossed his leg and leaned forward, hands on his knees, and gave Janelle a piercing look. "You see, I was in a rush when we bumped into each other and I hated to break my stride—costs money as well as time."

"Well, I wouldn't want to contribute to breaking your—stride. Guess we'll both be glad to put the incident behind us. I do a few business things now and then myself." Women confront, they don't nego-

.tiate. So her dad had said.

She started to say she was sorry for her remark, but before she could speak, he said, "Well, guess that about does it then. Would it be possible for me to hope we could become better acquainted over a cocktail and dinner?"

Janelle sucked in her breath. "I really believe that our small altercation can now be set aside and forgotten. I'm busy this evening. Thank you anyway." Janelle stood holding to the edge of the desk for support. They seemed to be suspended in time looking at each other. She standing with a forced smile on her face, he sitting with a studied gaze that forced her to look away.

"OK, then," Tyler shrugged and unwound from his slumped position to rise from the chair. With obvious irritation held under control, he said very slowly, "Thank you for your time."

She smoothed back her hair and looked over at him with relief written in her smile. He did not return the smile, but rather, stared back at her with blazing eyes. His jaw muscles rippled under taut skin.

Janelle's skin flushed, her heart pulsated. Here was unbridled power held in by sheer will. This man's magnetism was indeed that of an animal, possibly a civilized one, but an animal all the same. She dropped her eyes from his intent stare. Her voice softened. "I, I appreciate the dinner invitation which was certainly unnecessary." She shrugged.

His disappointment, or was it anger, was palpable, as he said in a tauntingly gruff voice, "We'll never know what we missed will we? Unless . . ." Like energy suddenly fired by white heat he moved behind the desk and with one swift motion, grabbed both her arms, lifted her from her chair away from the desk, and pulled her to his hard chest.

The seconds it took for him to move left Janelle speechless. She wiggled and turned to push away from the steel bands that held her body tightly against the length of him, but there was no escape. She stopped struggling and lifted her head to look at him with eyes wide with shock. The possessive, yet gentle, embrace felt good. Her quivers of indignation succumbed to feelings of helplessness. She became calm, aware of their heart beats as he bent his dark head and kissed the top of her blond head.

With the graceful touch of a sculptor, his fingers traced the white column of her throat to the curve of her chin, and tipped her face toward his. A thumb gently rubbed over her soft lips until they parted with an unspoken 'O.' Pulling her closer, he brought his lips to hers and softly kissed her. Seconds passed. He raised his head to look at her as if waiting for a rebuke, but she did not speak, only looked up at him with an expression of astonishment on her face.

"Goodbye, beautiful lady," he whispered in her ear, then gently released her and silently strode out of the office without a backward glance.

Janelle pressed fingers against her tingling mouth as she watched him walk out. Feelings of desire kindled by the kiss subsided and feelings of frustration ignited. She clutched her arms tightly around herself. *Of all the conceit! The nerve!* "Dear God!" she whispered aloud.

Chapter Five

A man with the body of a wrestler and kind brown eyes approached Janelle as she entered the Crimson Door Restaurant two hours later. "Hello, Oscar." She greeted the smiling man. Oscar Leoni, owner-maitre d'hotel of one of the finest Italian restaurants in Dallas, and father of Julie from the kids' show, gave Janelle a bear hug greeting much like her dad used to greet him, bless him. "Have Jeb and our clients arrived?"

"Mr. Standly and the others have not arrived, Miss Jamison." Oscar used the formal greeting even with his closest friends when they were guests in his restaurant. "Shall we?" he asked with a gesture of his hand and led Janelle through wide doors at the side of the foyer to the private dining room always reserved for Jamison business luncheons.

She nodded to Oscar in satisfaction. Polished hardwood floors and oriental rugs covered the floor of the spacious room. The glow of the overhead chandelier glinted off Sterling chafing dishes and Waterford on a sideboard. A centerpiece of pink carnations and mums added an elegant note to a round dining table, covered with a white linen cloth, and set with service for five. "Very nice," Janelle murmured as she proceeded to the lounge section and sat down in a chair which faced windows covered with floor length lace curtains.

Oscar's eyes were warm with affection, as his gaze rested on the innocently provocative woman. "You look lovely, Jaw-nee-la."

Janelle turned to look at Oscar and smiled at the older man. "It's always good to be here, in this room! I was remembering how much Dad loved to come here."

Oscar smiled his agreement. "I'll bring you a glass of Puligny-Montrachet while you wait," he said and walked across the room to the mirrored bar set behind one of the pillars in the corner of the room.

"I was with Julie yesterday morning at the studio. She's doing a great job for the videos. How are Gena and Jamie?"

"Fine, growing, spoiled." Oscar ticked off the words as he poured the wine, and returned the amber colored liquid to her. "You are Julie's ideal lady, you know. She speaks of you often. How excited she was when she got to present the HIDE AND SEEK restaurant program for you. It was Ms. Jamison this, Ms. Jamison that."

Oscar chuckled. "I remember John J. first telling me about the Three J Company and the HIDE AND SEEK program. He enjoyed getting the credit for sponsoring the program, but he let everyone know that you created it! Oh, how he liked to brag about you!"

To a point, she thought. She touched his hand affectionately. "Oh, how he liked to visit you. I never have seen two men so much alike who could argue a point into the ground. Remember when we were here going over the idea of HIDE AND SEEK? You spoke up and praised the idea."

Oscar shook his mop of sweeping black hair. "Maybe I shouldn't have been so bold."

"Oscar, you had every right to speak up. Jerry and I were trying to convince Dad of the usefulness of it all. You spoke from the heart as a friend with children and you convinced him that kids speaking to kids was a good idea."

At the mention of Jerry's name, Oscar came to Janelle and took her hand. "Please let know if you ever need help."

Voices could be heard outside the room. With a quick reassuring glance at Janelle, Oscar hurried to the door to greet Jeb Standly and the other men who were just entering the private room.

"Hello, Oscar!" Jeb greeted his friend with a clap on the arm as he introduced the three men. Turning, Jeb's eyes lit up as he saw Janelle and strolled over to greet her. "I was held up in traffic. Sorry." He ended by leaning over to give her a peck on the cheek.

Janelle accepted Jeb's kiss, and stood up. "I have been enjoying . . . " Janelle stopped in mid sentence her mouth open in surprise as she looked past Jeb. *Mr. Tyler. The Mazerati man. Why in Gods' name was he here?*

Wide-eyed, Janelle watched as he strolled over with a wide lopsided grin "Hello again!" His blue eyes gazed intently into hers, with just a hint of friendly amusement twinkling in their depths.

"You know Janelle?" Jeb asked looking from Janelle to Tyler with a puzzled expression.

Janelle closed her mouth and swallowed. "Tyler—Dalton, I see. We've . . .met." Her heart pounded.

"In traffic." Tyler finished her sentence and grinned boyishly, seeming to relish Janelle's surprise. And, not waiting for her to explain further, he turned to two men. "Before we go into explanations, may I introduce my partners who have made all the arrangements for this meeting?"

Janelle's mind was in a whirl. *Dalton Oil! Obviously he realized who I was this morning when he pulled that act, that trick. That side-winding, belly-crawling bastard!* With clenched fists at her sides, she smiled sweetly as Tyler introduced Bob Wiles, a short stocky man, definitely a Texan. "How-dee, ma'am," he said as he extended a calloused hand.

Harry Bender, the other man, looked older than Tyler and Bob but also had the mark of Texas in his mannerisms and sun-weathered face.

"Bob and Harry, my compradres, are usually my forerunners," Tyler said, his gaze riveted on Janelle.

"This time, I had a jump on you both. I met Miss Jamison yesterday and at a short meeting in her office this morning. We got a start on you talk'in about sports cars," he explained with a chuckle.

So, he's covered our little altercation, the office, the kiss very conveniently. Janelle noticed Jeb's raised eyebrows.

"Yes, I grazed his car yesterday. He came to the office today to discuss the settlement." Her cheeks blazed. She studied the wine in the glass she held.

She vaguely felt a hand touch her fingers that gripped the wine glass. She glanced at Jeb, but it was Dalton; a guarded, sober-faced man. "Miss Jamison." His eyes were glued on hers. "I was a bit familiar when we met. I should 've known not to try to rough-break a rope-shy thoroughbred. My cowboy roundup kind of joking was inappropriate. I apologize."

Jeb cleared his throat. "Well, I don't have to introduce you two anyway!" And gave Janelle's arm a pat as he added, "Let's join Janelle with a drink before we eat, shall we?" He led her to the couch indicating the others should join them.

The five sat around the coffee table and enjoyed the appetizers and the beers and one neat whiskey that the waiter had brought. The men talked of SMU football, the Dallas Cowboys, the NFL play-offs while Janelle quietly sipped her wine. When the waiter came to suggest lunch would be served, the group moved to the dining table to enjoy Oscar's choice of entree: poached salmon with creamed feta cheese pasta, mixed salad greens with a raspberry vinaigrette dressing, and warm crusted rolls.

Janelle was still unable to join in the talk with the group, trying to force down a few bites. But a jumble of confusing thoughts made each bite stick in her throat as she recalled the accident and the caustic remarks she'd thrown at Tyler in the morning meeting. She gulped a few swallows of wine and steeled herself to look at the others at the table. Tyler sat across from her, in relaxed business attire of Western style shirt, string tie, and silk tweed jacket. The slight bump on the nose and a scar on his chin seemed to add a stamp of masculinity to his features. And what she'd interpreted earlier as arrogance, seemed now to be more an air of comfortable confidence. Harry sat beside Jeb, dressed conservatively in a business suit and listening to the others talk. Bob, who sat next to Tyler, was the flamboyant extrovert of the two lieutenants. Janelle caught the tail end of an anecdote which ended "Why, after that, butter wouldn't melt in his mouth!" She saw Jeb throw back his head and laugh.

Janelle glanced at the oil men. She tried to catch any undertones which might signal how much Tyler's men knew about the raucous kissing session at the ten o'clock meeting she and Tyler had that morning. As the meal continued, she detected no leering expressions. Finally, she let herself get caught up in the easy conversation of the men.

After a question from Jeb, Tyler announced, "LLamo Sibab has set up a meeting with three of the OPEC heads. He's been a friend of mine since I was ten years old. Elbo is five years older than I and, when we first met, was at least twenty years older in experience!" He chuckled, then went on.

"I'd tag along with my dad on his trips to Saudi. We stayed in Dhahran where the Sibab family lived. Llamo's father, Llamo senior, was a good friend of Dad." Tyler hesitated, toyed with his pasta.

Jeb and the others were expecting him to continue with his story, but Tyler seemed preoccupied.

After a long pause, Janelle became impatient to hear more, "And just what did a ten-year-old do in Arabia while his father was transacting big business?" She'd tried to keep her tone mild, but her words sounded skeptical.

He paused for the briefest of moments, studying her face, then a shadow of a grin appeared and he answered. "Well, you might say, I played Gunga Din. I had adventures with my friend Elbo, riding a camel out to an oasis in the desert where we shot rattlers and brought back their tails to sell at the vending stalls in the city market. I followed Elbo like a puppy follows his master, and," Tyler breathed deeply as he wiped his mouth with his napkin, "got into some situations much too old for my years!" He stopped, took a bite of pasta and remained silent.

Jeb changed the subject. "How well is the new pipeline working?" From this topic the conversation revolved to the oil business in general, the economy, the government, and taxes until the end of the meal. The table was cleared, linen whisked off and a coffee thermos and coffee cups and saucers were added to the dining-conference table. No more was said about Saudi Arabia and Tyler's pending trip. Janelle wondered why he was going. What he would do over there? Beautiful women? Rough-breaking of fillies the old-fashioned way? The lines that edged his eyes gave his weathered face a soft touch when he laughed. He looked hard and lean with a grace in his manner and tone of voice that Janelle recognized as that of a very shrewd and intelligent man. *Male model indeed!*

The meeting began. Jeb passed out the folders on the insurance plan. Separating the folders of the proposal package, and laying out key documents not before included in any such insurance package gave Janelle a chance to calm down and center on the business at hand. She began the discussion with reference to the overall plan. "We have tried to fashion an exclusive policy for DPCO, as suggested by Mr. Dalton. I would like to point out that the $700 million policy you have in front of you has ten sections; Property, Liability, Auto/Trucking, Difference in Conditions Earthquake, Flood, and Workers Compensation and Employers Liability are separated and explained in detail. The Merchant Marine Act of 1920 (Jones Act) Coverages, and the Longshoremen's Harbor Workers Compensation Act of 1927 (USL&H Act) for over water, and Outer Continental Shelfs Land Act extends

USL &H to employees of offshore drilling platforms you have been familiar with from past policies. This applies to operations beyond the three mile limit (3 leagues) in Texas in the outer extremities of the continental shelf (200 miles). Jeb can you say a little more about this?"

He nodded. "Since offshore drilling operations pose high exposures to the above Acts, adequate amounts must be figured to protect both the owners, operators, and drilling contractors and their employees. We've tried to be consistent in just what the DPCO rigs are, so that the underwriters will have a complete list of equipment capabilities including fire deterrents and blow-out safety measures."

The men leafed through more of the proposal. Harry stopped to ask about the workman's compensation for oil drilling crews in regards to employment related accident or disease. Jeb explained that included was a disability salary for on-the-job injury based on the percentage of salary, and that percentage, as suggested by DPCO, would be figured on years of service with the company. More of the coverage was discussed with no changes until Tyler leaned toward her with a piercing look and asked what companies would be participating. Startled, she pushed back, then, considering that he was only concerned about the details of the policy and that his body language was appropriate for a multi-million-dollar deal, she determinedly suggested they all turn to the folder in question.

"As you can see, Vigrant Insurance Company will insure for $100 million, by purchasing reinsurance from one other company. Luis D. Masetto Insurance Company will insure the next $200 million, purchasing three reinsurance policies. And Lloyds of London plans to take another $200 million." She ended with, "That will leave your company with the $200 million as proposed."

He read the fine print and confirmed with a nod.

Janelle said. "I believe our eyes are glazing. Let's take a short break."

Tyler was still leafing through the proposal and looked up at Janelle's suggestion. "Before we have a break. I've looked through the workers comp and understand that your policy cannot cover outside USA and Canada because the host country, being Saudi in our case, must endorse such a policy for that country's employees. Yet, you call your plan, 'Global Coverage.' I take it that means everything has been set up for us over there?"

"Yes, the policy is for global coverage. We have obliged you by working with companies in Arabia. We'll meet you any place in the world."

"Well, that just sounds mighty fine ma'am," Tyler said in a slow Old Texas drawl with a satisfied grin. Janelle felt her face warm, the others broke out laughing, and the two hours of intent discussion ended on a comfortable note. As if on cue, Oscar himself brought over more coffee while the waiters refilled water glasses.

After the brief intermission, the others listened while Tyler and Janelle batted questions and answers at each other. "I did notice that dental was not covered. I know you've thoroughly researched what we should have, but just wondered what could be done about that."

This Texas oil man had consistently asked pertinent questions which concerned what kind of coverage his people would have with the plan, rather than how much the plan would cost him. She was more than impressed, and now used to his intentness, was actually relaxed as she answered the question on dental coverage. "We can certainly take care of further medical coverage if you wish it. There are several options to the dental cost. Also, coverage of Health Insurance, Vision, Prescription Cards, Life Insurance, 401-K Pension Plans and Profit Sharing Plans are being formulated for your approval at our April meeting that is already scheduled with Mr. Bender and Mr. Wiles—and you if you're in the city."

A smile as warm as sunshine spread over his face. "I'll be here as sure as bluebonnets bloom in spring." His look was penetrating, his powerful strength of will pulled at her as he leaned over the conference table. With what was left of her self-control, she lowered her eyes. He apparently got the silent dismissal of his secret agenda and directed his attention to Jeb.

"Jeb, these people have only me to properly provide for them. They're like my family."

Harry added in country drawl, "He shor' does care. Bob and I have to hold him down and hog tie him sometimes when he gives away pipes and Christmas trees at the top of producin' wells."

"Yep, jest like Santa Claus . . . always thinkin' of ways to make his little elves happy. Harry and me are the Grinches," Bob said. What were the Christmas trees? Janelle wondered.

Jeb nodded understandingly. "You're providing a cushion for your employees that few employers would consider. We admire that. Now, if you agree, I'd like to go through the Pension and Profit Sharing with your lieutenants here. How does that sound?"

Tyler looked at Bob and Harry who nodded. "All right, let's have a caucus right now, Bob and Harry talk to Jeb, I'll talk to Janelle." Tyler seemed pleased with the arrangement.

Janelle felt a sweet hint of fear as Tyler moved around to sit beside her at the table. "I can see your concern for your employees is sincere." Janelle gazed at him steadily. "Nobody would accuse you of playing games." Had anyone else caught the flirting undercurrents of this man's business conversation? Maybe she'd only imagined it.

With a smile, he slapped his pencil against the palm of his hand as he scrutinized her. "Well, I care and do get carried away at times, as Bob suggested. But I usually keep a firm hand on myself." As an after thought, he added. "I believe I'd been better off if Bob or Harry had been with me this morning."

If that was a form of apology, it wasn't enough. Now, business first. Jeb was calling over something to them. "Janelle, I mentioned something to Tyler about the HIDE AND SEEK program on the way over. You may want to pursue that."

Janelle nodded to Jeb, who returned to his conversation with the two men. "I don't know how much Jeb has told you about the program."

She started to continue, but Tyler interrupted. "Jeb filled me in earlier while we waited for Bob and Harry outside. Sounds like a great idea you have. Is this the first program?"

"No, we've had several others, among them one on dating, one on studying the classics, another on family involvement in sports, and one on government in Texas." She stopped to take a breath. "It takes quite a while to get programs to the point they can be shared so they come out every six weeks."

"Are the topics ever controversial? Who gives approval for all of these programs?" Tyler seemed genuinely interested.

"There's a review panel to approve all material, then another to critique the taping for moral, ethical, sociological balance, not exactly censorship, but a close second to it. I could go on, but you might get bored."

"Not likely, I need to know all I can if I'm to be involved."

"Well, the student panels change for each program and are made up of ten students who represent the public schools in Dallas School District. They are picked by their peers and faculty for their leadership qualities. I don't mean necessarily their National Honor Society membership." She grinned as she tried to pull Tyler into her kids' world. He wanted to know if the television programs could really make a substantial difference in teen attitude.

After looking over to see that the three men were still fast at work over sheets of insurance briefs, Janelle went on to assure him the kids were indeed questioning behavior attitudes because they were in charge of the subjects. "And the details of the student panel have been worked out. That was something to get done!" Janelle smiled with a shake of the head recalling the wrangling between the students who had been chosen by their peers to be a part of the HIDE AND SEEK team. "Once the serious business of organizing the kids was completed, the pecking order between the leaders had to be established. And believe me, they were as hard on themselves in picking leaders as the political parties in Washington, D.C.!

"Students from the ages of twelve to twenty are hand-picked. They come in, talk about an assignment, choose a segment of the subject for research and go out in groups of two with at least one sponsor with them to work on the research."

Tyler interrupted, "Sponsors? How are they chosen?"

Janelle explained. "That's the important part. The student picks a sponsor from the family; mother, father, older brother, sister, or friend over twenty-one. That sponsor goes out with the student to get the material needed for the particular segment of the program. That way, everybody's protected."

Tyler nodded thoughtfully, "And then, how long do they have to do the research and how long to tape the program?"

"They have a month to do the research. No one student has a big segment to cover. The shooting is done after the panel gets together and reviews what is needed to make the program factual. That's fun for them. She quickly added, "But what's really exciting, is when they put together a general script-develop idea and tape it. Nothing is canned, it's strictly ad lib when they get in front of the camera."

"That must be nervous time for you the producer." Tyler smiled, shaking his head thoughtfully.

"You sound just like the panel of school experts the first time I shared the guidelines for the programs," Janelle grinned remembering. "They asked me if we censored four letter words—expletives. I assured them that the expletives would be beeped if too blatant, but some would be aired. After all, the students would be talking to their peers and the language would, within good taste, have to be their language."

"That must have gotten a real response. My dad thought switches from the peach tree were a good censoring device."

"Quick and to the point I should imagine." His look of exaggerated pain made her pucker her lips in mock sympathy. "Anyway, after the taping, our censors have the final OK on the content of all the programs."

"And does it work?"

"Well—we've tried a lot of things. The first time we filmed, we had the students on chairs in a group like a classroom. "The kids were like zombies, mumbling in a cemetery. Oh, they had the material down well, but they couldn't seem to get together in presenting it even with card props." Janelle smiled remembering. "It took one eighteen-year-old boy to figure out what was needed. Robyn Greer suggested we forget the chairs and go to couches where there could be tables for soda cans. He also suggested that one person be the group leader to pull it together." Janelle lifted an eyebrow, "Guess who got that job?"

"The guy with the idea!" Tyler grinned, pushed back in his chair, and crossed his arms over his chest as if pleased with the guy who spoke up. His look of satisfaction told a lot about the Texan. He liked aggressiveness. Didn't she know! "Let the ten sit where they felt most comfortable, on the floor, couches, chairs, stand . . . be relaxed as if they were in a room, at home, or someplace where they were at ease."

Janelle shuffled through some papers and came up with a photograph of the students. Pointing to a boy in the photo she said, "This is the guy with the idea, Robyn Greer. He got the job for that first taping and has had that job ever since. This gal," she pointed to a tall girl next to Robyn, "Colleen Blair, is his co-anchor. Robyn is a natural and, although he's street smart with a wicked use of language at times, Colleen can settle him down." Janelle chuckled.

"What was your first program?" Tyler asked.

"'Friends and Favorites in the Schools.' It took us three full months. The kids came up with a memorable program on popular clothes, conduct, and cliques. It was a mad scramble, but we met the deadline requirements of the school officials and adult panels. Here's a copy of the *Dallas Morning News* coverage." She handed Tyler a clipping from the HIDE AND SEEK file. *Innovative HIDE AND SEEK is a challenging educational experience for Dallas students* was the headline.

Tyler leaned toward Janelle. She got a faint whiff of his cologne, something like cedar trees in a woods. "You mentioned adult panels. Who other than the censors are involved? And other than the kids' ideas, do you have help with the selection of programs?"

Janelle sat back in her chair so she could concentrate on his questions. He was a person for details—as she was. "There's an adult research panel of seven that suggests and approves programs before the kids' teams go out for information. On that panel is Jeb over there and Helen Sutton, a vice president of our company. Then there's a well-known and respected psychiatrist, a psychologist, a minister, a different one every program so all denominations have a chance to be represented, and two school officials. They rotate too." And there had been Jerry.

She stopped the thought and quickly focused on the second question he'd asked. "The censor committee I mentioned is composed of eight citizens who see the final video and, of course, there are the freelance advisors and critics—students, parents, teachers."

"What kids see the videos? I think I would've enjoyed a TV break in my school when I got tired of sending notes to the girls or going to the principal's office."

"Well, the Dallas schools present a program once a week for six weeks to students in grades six through twelve. It is shown at the low period of the day, at three o'clock, or close to it when there is a study period. Oh, and it isn't required viewing. That would get into individual rights which usually means parents' rights." Janelle sounded frustrated.

"How do they monitor that?" Tyler was skeptical.

"Good question and a continuing problem." Janelle tapped her pencil on the paper. "Each new program is getting better feedback, better attendance, and less hassle from the outside world. The students are really getting into the issues and have even started some outside groups to discuss the issues raised on the programs. I know teachers are using the program too for further study."

"Have you any hard questions to put to the viewing students?" Tyler appeared to have a purpose for his question.

Janelle smiled at him, "Well, after the subject dealing with the oil industry, we plan to do one like that." She took her pen and printed on a sheet of paper as a frown formed between her brows, the word AIDS. She pushed the sheet toward him. "The United States governmental agencies have already poured millions of dollars into materials to educate the public and alert individuals about the lethal effects of the HIV virus. But warnings of the seriousness of the disease and information about its prevention have not reduced the number of victims. People are dying—and right here. It's a subject we've wanted to get the kids to discuss. We've had a little pressure on this one and even the new panel of students who are to do the segments seem hesitant."

Tyler touched her hand for a moment then withdrew his. "The Black Plague of 1983. I understand your concern. It's a hot, catch-phrase disease. There is a real need for a documentary series that gives details of the virus." He seemed to study her for a moment then with a shake of his head spoke in a slow deliberate way. "I admire you—would never have believed it this morning."

His honest confession troubled, then pleased her. At least she thought he was trying to understand her. She quietly said. "Me too."

"I have a feeling my next question will get an interesting answer." The man leaned an arm on the table and faced her. "What program is being taped right now?"

A smile began to curve her lips as she too put her arms on the table. "The final segment on the oil industry is coming up and the students want to interview a real, live oil tycoon I think Jeb spoke to you about appearing. What do you say?"

"Miss Jamison, it will be a pleasure. When do we tape?"

They both stood. Tyler looked at her silently, intently. Janelle, with a flutter of apprehension, hoped he wouldn't try the good-bye of the morning visit. "Tomorrow at noon. It's short notice I know. But I heard you say you must go out of the country at the end of the week and the student leader, Robyn Greer, can come from his school to interview you at that time, since he's also there for the AIDS' session. Thank you." She shook his hand vigorously. With a slight nod, she quickly turned and walked over to Jeb.

Tyler followed. "How did it go over here?" he asked.

"Fine." Harry looked up and acknowledged his boss. "It's quite a spread," he gestured to all the forms. "And—paper work ready for your signature."

"OK, I'll review them tonight and take them to the Jamison Agency tomorrow." Tyler started to walk away, then turned back to Harry and Bob. "Oh, by the way, I'm going to stay over to tape a show for the HIDE AND SEEK program. Ever hear of it?"

Both men said "No" simultaneously.

"Well, I'll want some details on the offshore rigs, the employment pay scale, our union contracts—that sort of stuff— before I meet with this panel. See what you can get together before you leave today. I believe the kids will put me on the griddle and this hot dog don't want to get charred. Talk to you later." Tyler turned to Janelle and Jeb.

Janelle had started back to the table to gather up her papers. Tyler came over and said in a low voice only she could hear, "Miss Jamison, it has been a pleasure!" With a slight twinkle in his eyes, as if he could read her thoughts, Tyler leaned toward her. "You're not only beautiful, but you also have a good business mind and are one hell of a . . ." he grinned, "negotiator!" He glanced at Jeb who'd just walked up.

Tyler sobered as he took Janelle's hand into both of his and held it gently but firmly. "I believe with the few changes we will have a deal in everything." He emphasized the word everything. Still holding her hand, he turned to Jeb. "Could you two be persuaded to have dinner with a lonely bachelor this evening?" He looked at Janelle.

Janelle tried to release her hand from his, but Tyler held her hand firmly as he continued to speak to Jeb. "My lieutenants fly back to their families in south Texas this evening. Being a lonely bachelor, I can easily change my itinerary. I have delayed my flight to California until Thursday so I can appear on the HIDE AND SEEK program."

Lonely bachelor. A happy bubble welled up inside Janelle. She looked up at him, he looked down at her and the two stood holding hands with grins on their faces.

"I believe I'm free. What about you, Jan?"

Janelle started, and quickly withdrew her hand from Tyler's. "I promised Helen we would celebrate our new account or drown our sorrows in defeat, whichever this meeting dictated." She smiled at Jeb as she continued, "Helen had as much to do with the DPCO package as I." She wanted to go to dinner with this man, yet did not want to appear too eager to accept his invitation.

"Bring Helen along if it's convenient with Jeb." Tyler smiled encouragingly. "We can talk about the HIDE AND SEEK program with her."

Janelle delightedly feared she was hooked. "I can't answer for Helen."

"Of course you can," Jeb inserted. "I'd be delighted to have Helen with us. She has had a lot to do with all the plans. I'll ask her."

Janelle smiled her acceptance. Good. Get the two of them out of that office, sit them down next to each other with soft lights, a little wine, good food—let nature do the rest.

Chapter Six

Janelle returned to the office and gave Helen details about the oil company insurance plans and told her about the accident with the stranger who turned out to be the president of DPCO. "When Jeb introduced us I felt like I'd been hit by a bucking mule—the accident, his visit to the office. *That* Texan was the Dalton Petroleum president." She consciously omitted the disturbing kiss.

Helen frowned. "Well I hope that man had a purpose in surprising you like that."

Janelle quickly blamed herself. "I had the same feeling I'd had long time ago when my dad asked me to go out and bring his car from the garage. I'd been teenage indignant and asked him why Peter the gardener couldn't get it. But I did stomp out the door to get his car and found my high school graduation present in front of the house . . . a Robin's egg blue convertible."

Helen smiled wisely. "What was your present this time?"

With a grin, Janelle said "A multi-million dollar client," as she held open the door to the parking garage where they were greeted with the usual screech of tires and smell of burnt rubber as cars careened down the winding ramp. The swish of city traffic from outside the building forced Janelle to yell to be heard. "Tyler Dalton has agreed to appear on the HIDE AND SEEK oil program."

"Apparently, Mr. Dalton is well qualified to talk on all areas of the oil industry. A hunk too. Isn't that how the kids say it?" Helen yelled back just as Janelle's car appeared and stopped in front of them

"They're so right!" Janelle slid into the bucket seat calling over to Helen. "Let's wear something long."

Jan heard Helen call back, "Maybe I'll put on something glamorous for the other hunk," Helen waved.

Janelle drove in a line of evening traffic that moved and curved as if linked by an invisible chain—lock-stepped like sand pipers on Padre. The blue sky of late afternoon was patched with grey, billowing, rain-filled clouds. Nothing more than a shower had been predicted, but rain was falling steadily by the time she got to the canopied entrance of the condo complex. Timothy opened her car door, and she went up to her home so intent on memories of the afternoon meeting that she hardly remembered giving Tim her keys. Happiness filled her as walked into the shaded living room. Perhaps the feeling was because the pain about Jerry was gone. Perhaps it was because she looked forward to the evening with Tyler Dalton. Though his aggressive personality would not be her choice, he presented a challenge. What a day! She felt like a cowboy ridin' a bucking horse—scared, excited, too stubborn to fall off.

Breathing in deeply she closed her eyes and hugged her silk robe around herself as she drifted into the bathroom. In a daze of imaginings, she drew her bath then slowly sank down in the lavender-scented bubbles. Squeezing a sponge filled with the scented warm water over her body, she hazily pictured Tyler running his hands through his thick hair.

She dozed, awoke, and sat up with a splash in the cold water. The bathroom clock showed six-thirty. Tyler would be there in thirty minutes. "Probably will be on time," she muttered. Quickly stepping from the tub and drying herself, she walked out to her bedroom where she'd put out her clothes.

Dressed, she stumbled into high heeled shoes, rushed to the dresser to brush her hair and apply lipstick and a small amount of eye shadow and scrutinized herself for last minute repairs. "You're an attractive woman. Be as nice as you look," she said mumbling the well remembered words of her mother. Then, frowning as she noted the plunging neckline of the gold lamè gown that revealed the soft swell of her breast, she took from her jewel case a round diamond pin. She attached it to the deep "V" of the dress and smiled, saying out loud another of her mother's reminders, "Better in the mind's eye than publicly flaunted." The last words were punctuated by the door buzzer. She quickly dabbed perfume behind each ear, then rushed to the foyer to hear Tim's voice announce Tyler.

"Send him up please." Last minute woman moves of licking her lips and smoothing down the sides of her clinging gown were performed as she waited for the knock on the door. It came. She opened the door with a smile of greeting and silently observed the man walk toward her. The pinstripe navy suit and rep tie he wore were signs of a city gentleman, but the sun-weathered face and black, alligator-trimmed cowboy boots were the signature of an outdoorsman, Texas style.

She watched somewhat tremulously as his gaze slid from her face, to the pin nestled between her breasts and on down the clinging fabric of the gown. The appraisal took no longer than a second to send its message, neither did the feminine intuition that told her she should close the door and shut him out of her life. This was a risky man. But challenged by his look of approval, she boldly held out her hand in greeting.

"Good evening," he said huskily and took her extended hand in both of his. She grabbed her full length gold satin coat from the foyer chair, and he took it and held it for her. Lifting the collar to circle her neck, he hesitated, then smoothed her hair from under the coat holding the moment with his hand on her shoulder. "Kinda breezy outside after that little rain."

"Thank you. I'll be fine." Her prim reply smothered internal vibes that signaled *beware.*

High in the sky, like an eagle's nest at the top of a mountain, the Petroleum Club hung over the galaxy of lights in nighttime Dallas. When Janelle and Tyler entered the executive club cocktail lounge, Jeb and Helen were already standing beside each other, backs to the entrance, looking out over the city.

Tyler immediately excused himself to get them a drink. Deciding she'd not interrupt the couple who seemed deep in conversation, Janelle sat down at a table nearby. She didn't want to eavesdrop, but Jeb had a resonant voice. "It always excites me when I stand above the city, and see the changes that have been made. Why, I can remember forty years ago when that Red Flying Horse of Magnolia Oil Company, later, Mobile Oil, over there on top of that building was the highest point in the Dallas skyline!" Jeb pointed to the neon figure of Pegasus dwarfed by high-rise buildings.

Still oblivious to the arrival of Janelle and Ty, Jeb pointed to the right. "Helen, see that four lane thoroughfare?"

"Yes," Helen murmured. Janelle could tell she was preoccupied and barely listening to Jeb's on-going history of the city.

"Forty some odd years ago that was a two-way street that I drove on to get downtown. When that four-lane highway was under construction, dust was an inch thick, like Dallas in the 1870s when it was only a hamlet of 1500 people. I'm always amazed to remember that back then Galveston was bigger than Dallas and Houston. The city sure changed in a hurry when the railroad came through. It's grown to be an important transportation center, plus the third largest international trade center in the world—the second largest city in Texas, so the Chamber says. And not to brag, but insurance companies like ours helped make this city what it is, along with other giants like the oil industry."

Helen dreamily murmured, "One wonders if all those people down there really know why they're rushing."

"Guess the rushing is for the gold ring. Business people chase it." Jeb stopped, then added, "Life's pretty much a race to get someplace."

Helen laughed. "I never knew what a vibrant, electrified place I was coming to when I came to Dallas. That's been good for me. What would we do without new challenges?"

He looked out the window for a moment. "I've never needed challenges to prove myself." Janelle could imagine the scowl on Jeb's face. He could be rough as a chapped hand sometimes and you never knew when it would start.

Helen quickly stepped back as if surprised by his abruptness. The heel of her shoe caught in the thick carpeting and she grabbed at Jeb. He pulled her to him, looking questioningly at her for a moment before he released her. With an awkward pat on her shoulder, Jeb turned away, his brows raised in surprise at seeing Janelle.

Janelle rose and approached with a smile. "Have you been waiting long?"

"We've been enjoying the greatest show on earth." Jeb tilted his head to the view, thirty-six floors below. "Our city at night!"

"Jeb will have us singing the 'Yellow Rose of Texas' in a minute!" Helen laughed ruefully.

Jeb looked at Helen questioningly. The two beings Janelle loved most right now were certainly uptight. New relationships were always teetering on the brink of uncertainty. Perhaps there were undisclosed feelings that they were afraid to share. Perhaps the slight catch of Helen's foot would have been the catalyst for more intimate moments. Whatever the uncertainty, the romantic in Janelle wished they would get it together. They were right for each other. Janelle walked over to Helen, and linked arms with her. "Time to eat?"

Just then, Tyler had come up carrying a tray of drinks. Jeb still scowled, Helen was flushed, and Janelle had a forced smile. "Rekon' we'd better have drinks at the dining table. Come on, I'll carry our drinks."

"Yes, let's." With Helen beside her, she walked through the inky blackness that swallowed the hall, all but for path lighting to the dining room entrance and the hidden pinpoints of light in the ceiling that framed four large oil landscapes which hung on black walls. "Isn't the way they've illuminated these paintings interesting?" Janelle exclaimed as they walked by paintings of oil derricks, strata of earth, and oil rigs interspersed with pumping stations that dotted a desolate landscape. "Did you know I got my Kluge lighting idea for my W.A. Slaughter above my mantel from this hallway?" Janelle asked Helen.

Helen nodded. "The Kluge lights in the television studio were also your good idea as I recall."

"Speaking of the TV studio, I wonder when the kids have spring break?" Janelle and Helen discussed the TV show as Tyler and Jeb went over the merits of adding highways north of the city, until the four had been seated at a round table just off the dance floor. It was appointed with a fresh linen table cloth and napkins, heavily ornate silver flatware, wine glasses, water goblets, and a low oval bowl filled with pink roses. The waiter took their order while in the background, the orchestra started playing "Besa Me Mucho." Tyler turned to Janelle. "My rumba is not the best, but would you care to explore the floor?"

"Let's try. I've not danced to this beat since college." Smiling at the adventure they were about to experience, Janelle took his hand and they went to the dance floor. In formal rumba style, he with his one hand at her waist, she with her hand on his shoulder, they danced. At first, they were stiff and embarrassed. Finally, getting the feel of the staccato beat, they danced to the rhythmic ballad as others watched the handsome man glide the young woman around the floor. The music ended. Janelle started back to the table, but Tyler took her hand. "The food isn't there yet. Let's dance one more shall we? Maybe we can do better with a waltz." Janelle laughingly agreed.

As they waited for the music, Tyler said. "I'd like to apologize for this morning in your office. It was as if I were compelled to kiss you. You were so damn pretty, and smart, and . . ."

Janelle interrupted "And you were not about to let a female get the best of you. The only way you knew how to save face was by humiliating me."

"You're right. I was a mean bastard, was the day before too. God, how I wish we could have just met today at the restaurant meeting. Suppose we could start all over? Call a truce for now seeing as how this is my favorite song?" The orchestra had started to play, "I'll Be Seeing You." Tyler waited expectantly without touching her.

Janelle raised her eyebrows with a questioning smile. "Well, I was a *little* defensive." Tyler grinned, pulled her to him, and they danced as he hummed the tune.

Their bodies touched and parted to the tempo of the song. "I'll be looking at the moon, but I'll be seeing you." The music stopped. Warm tension held the man and woman motionless. Each was aware of the other and the silent pact they'd made to forgive and enjoy the evening.

Their Texas-style steak dinner with hash browns for the men, twice-baked potatoes for the women, peas for something green and tossed salads with the sweet and sour dressing specialty of the chef—ended with chocolate cake and ice cream for the men and a demitasse for the ladies. Conversation flowed like the Cabernet Sauvignon they kept allowing the waiter to pour into their glasses.

Before leaving, Janelle asked Helen to go to the powder room with her. As they went into the empty room, Janelle whispered. "Helen, I feel giddy. My stomach is doing turnovers like it did when I coasted down Pike's Peak on a bike." Her gold dress sparkled in the mirrors and bounced off the walls, making the room a flashing light show of brilliant gold.

She slumped to a stool. "After this day nothing can surprise me."

Helen's eyes were fixed to the mirror's shimmering gold. "He's a mighty fine specimen, ma'am, and that other gentleman is something else too. I'm enjoying Jeb, even if he can be a bit stuffy."

"You are absolutely right. Jeb is stuffy!" Janelle agreed. They walked out, down the hall to the dining room. "But he is also as honest and faithful as anyone I've ever known."

"I know that." Helen's voice was sweetly yearning.

As the four left the club and rode the elevator to the parking level, Tyler whistled the song that the band had been playing, Willie Nelson's rendition of "On The Road Again." Janelle and Helen hummed. Jeb, interestingly enough, had an excellent baritone voice and even admitted that he'd sung in his hometown Methodist Church choir when he was in high school. "I knew that speaking voice of yours had beautiful resonance and now I know why," Helen exclaimed and fell silent.

"What! No valet to bring our car?" Janelle teased.

"We stayed too long for that service, madam." Tyler threw a casual arm around Janelle's shoulders as he propelled her toward the black rental he was driving while the Maserati was being repaired. He helped Janelle in the car as he called over to Jeb and Helen. "Bye, you two."

"Bye! Thanks again for dinner!" Jeb and Helen chorused. "It's been fun," as they walked further on to Jeb's ranch wagon.

They drove out on Field Street, and, instead of going to Cedar Springs as they'd come, Tyler turned on Commerce explaining, "Harry and I drove around this section of town after our meeting today." He proceeded through a few more streets.

"I thought along here might be a good location for a corporate office." In silence, they continued onto the freeway ramp, waiting for a cluster of cars to pass. Tyler let out a "Whoopeeee," stomped on the accelerator, and with a screech of tires, turned the car onto Central Expressway. "I'm a modern gladiator with a steering wheel for reins, and a foot pedal for horses' flanks, jousting for position on a four-lane freeway. Yes, ma'am . . . here we go!"

With an exaggerated sigh, Tyler leaned back and slowed the car, pulling on the steering wheel in mock imitation of a cowboy reining in his horse. "You know a rented car always reminds me of Bob and Harry."

"Why is that, cowboy?" Janelle turned toward him with a grin. Silently she enjoyed the play of headlights on his handsome face and broad hands that confidently gripped the steering wheel as the car again gathered speed.

"Well," he explained. "Bob had a big, pretty sorry lookin' 1940s vintage Buick, 'bout the size of this one, which we three drove to get to our jobs out in east Texas. I was totally on my own then." A touch of wistfulness was in his voice. "I lost my dad when I was twenty."

Pushing back from the wheel, again slowing the car, he proceeded to tell Janelle of the three friends meeting and their oil rig days. Janelle listened with a sensitive ear to his stories of the three roughnecks, going from drill site to drill site, picking up any kind of work they could find. He tried to describe the long, muscle-aching hours they worked running pipe, changing bits, moving machinery over rough, hot, dry land.

"We gave Bob the nickname, 'Plugger,' because more than once he used his muscles to bodily shift pipe tongs. He could lift the front end of a pickup with one hand!

"Harry was our anchor man. I was the youngest, Harry the oldest. He kept us in line." He chuckled and glanced at her with a nod of the head. "Except for one time. We'd been together about three years, and were in east Texas finishing up a job. We had stopped in the local tavern for a couple of beers before we left for another job. I got in a conversation with a local farmer. I knew the location of his farm and asked him if he would lease out some land to us for a drill site." Tyler guided the smooth-riding rental to the far left lane as he passed some cars, his eyes on the road, his mind on that evening in east Texas.

"The farmer seemed interested in working out a deal with us. He explained the reason he had not signed with the big boys was because he didn't like the way they did business. He figured we poor boys were about his speed."

Ty slowed the car allowing a minibus to go around. "Hey, am I boring you?"

Janelle smiled back at him. "No. I've done business for oil people but never heard about their start in the business, their lives. What happened to the lease with the farmer?"

"Well, I got real excited at the prospect of a lease. You see, I had the feeling that the drilling site where we were finishing up was off the mark. The dry hole soon proved me right, but I had a nagging suspicion that there was oil close by. Of course,"—the speedometer hit 70—"I was no genius geologist, but in the years we had been working rigs,

Bob and Harry would bet me about the hits and misses on the oil sites we helped drill. Guess I must have had a nose for oil, because I won their hard-earned money every time! Even won that old rust-eaten car off Bob once!" He threw back his head and laughed.

Janelle sensed he was not bragging, but rather telling the facts. She liked this man, had liked him even when he'd purposely taunted her this morning. Was that only this morning? Only a man with supreme confidence and a sense of wild adventure would have tried that trick on the very person he was consummating a business deal with in an hour or so. It amazed her to admit that she'd totally forgiven him and more. Her eyes skimmed over to look at him. She had a heady urge to run a finger down the hollow of his cheek, trace the hard line of his jaw. He was powerfully beautiful. She took a deep breath. "How did the deal go with the farmer?" They'd come off the freeway onto Fitzhugh.

"I promised the farmer his advance money by pledging all of my life's savings plus Bob's and Harry's. Were they mad when they heard what I'd done!" He grinned sheepishly as they stopped for a traffic light. "The guys pumped black words at me like bullets from a Gatling gun all the way back to our camper. I finally convinced them it was the opportunity of a lifetime. We got our government permit, got backers from some fellow drillers we'd worked for, an advance from one of the larger independent oil drillers, Mackey Tanner, another who'd known my dad, bought our own rig, and planted it on the farmer's land. Bob and Harry cursed, yelled, and grumbled 'till we came up with a big tiger hand."

"A what?"

"A perfect poker hand." He took his right hand from the wheel and found hers and gave it a squeeze. "We pulled the tool for the drill stem test. There was oil. We had a hit." There was a note of disbelief in his voice as there must have been that day when the three men actually saw and smelled the oil on the test tool.

"Hey, stop!" Janelle laughed. "Just what is a drill stem test?"

Tyler shifted his eyes from the road just long enough to see the questioning look on her face. "You really don't know do you! My—e e, how one sweet little thing can be so ig-nor-ant. You're sure no Daisy Bradford." Tyler looked over at Janelle questioningly.

"Widow Daisy's farm was the first test site for the East Texas Oil Field," Janelle affirmed.

"Right. Dad Joiner's number one. 5,000 barrel a day hit back in 1927. Daisy was also an early wild cat oil driller. Women were part of that early success."

He laughed and added more seriously, "A drill stem is a steel pipe with a metal bit at the end that is augured into the ground. The bit is pulled from the end of the pipe, or pipe string as its called, at a certain depth. Then a test tool is screwed on and sunk down in the hole and pulled up, so the chambers inside the tool can be examined for the type of fluids that have been brought up from that depth. There's a Mississippian formation about 4,500 feet down that's a good depth to test. You can smell the oil in the fluid sample sometimes. Understand?"

"I guess so. What happened after your hit?"

"We four signed a JOA." He again looked questioningly over at Janelle.

"I know. That's a Joint Operating Agreement which is an agreement between the working interest owners of a property. Memorized that from a seminar on oil terms." Her smile was little smug. Tyler lifted her hand to his lips, put it down with a pat and with both hands on the wheel continued his account of those first days.

"We three became fairly independent in money matters after that. Bill got married, settled down in Dripping Springs, Texas, out of Austin. Harry invested in more wells in east Texas, married, and landed in Austin. I liked the excitement of wild cattin', going for oil that is a long shot, so continued to buy up oil leases and drill all over Texas and Oklahoma." He shrugged. "Guess I was the gambler of the three. I get excited about the next project whether it be oil, an acquisition, or an international trade assignment. New friendships, new challenges, they're my meat!"

A few cars were on the darkened street as they turned onto Turtle Creek. Rain puddles along the curbing glistened in the headlights of the car. Janelle considered what he'd just said. He was a confident Texas man who reminded her somewhat of her father, but for the loner implication.

After a few blocks of silence, Tyler straightened his shoulders and shook his head. "You know, most people see just the gravy times of the oil business . . . money, power. Lots of people think oil drilling is kinda mystical. Let me tell you it's anything but mystical! It's hard-ass work! I'd like to write a book someday about guys like Dad Joiner, Gene Potter, B.E. Hubbard, Swaney Robertson. They had to have guts and strength to dig those first wells. God, imagine," he continued to drive and talk, "makeshift pipe, small engines, hand or horse driven pipe. Not many geologists back then. No sophisticated equipment to record the earth's strata. No electric logs to tell the progress going toward the crown."

"A crown?"

"You really are a sleeping beauty!"

"Well, I do know what the Connally Hot Oil Act of 1935 is." She shrugged and looked over at him to see if he was laughing.

He seemed more impressed than amused as he gave her a steady look. "Hot oil, that's when the driller goes underground and pipes into another well that's already been set. Luckily I haven't had it happen."

"We've insured you for it. All insurance companies insure oil clients for illegal acts being performed on an active well. Jeb takes care of all such policies for our oil clients, but that's no reason I should be so dumb on other aspects of the oil business. I don't even know what the Christmas tree is that Bob spoke of this afternoon." Janelle fell silent.

"Hey, not dumb, uninformed, and I'm one hell of a teacher. A Christmas tree is an assemblage of valves, pressure gauges, and flow control devices installed at the top of the casing after there is a flowing well. It replaces the blowout preventers used during drilling operation and allows connection to the oil and gas flow lines at the surface and it got its name because . . . .." He stopped and looked at Janelle questioningly and she said with him, "it looks something like a Christmas tree."

"See, you just need some learnin' gal." Again the exaggerated drawl that made her laugh. They'd come to the condo complex and drove around the circular drive to stop just beyond the sparkling chandelier and dignified doorman at the entrance.

Tyler shifted his weight to lay an arm across the back of the seat and looked at Janelle with a serious expression on his face. "Now, a crown is where the top oil pools then drops off. It's hard to find."

He looked at her confirmed interest, so rambled on. "Why do you think Texans are so goldarn boastful?" He answered the question with pride. "They've worked hard, sweated buckets and won, gambling on weather, ownership, making barren land pay a profit."

Janelle moved to face Tyler, resting her shoulder against the soft leather. She questioningly asked, "Don't men dig oil for money? The way you talk, they dig for the fun of it."

Tyler looked out the window for a moment. "I'd guess most old-time drillers did dig for the fun of it. The excitement of the dig got in their blood just like gold diggers." He shrugged his shoulders resignedly. "Today, the challenge is different. Land must make a profit. Now-a-days, men dig oil wells for the money and for power."

He smiled over at her. "My dad was a wild cat oil man in the beginning, before the Second World War. He never went to college, but in the early days, designed pieces for drill pipes. Some of his patent designs are used today. Some say he was a genius."

"What did he design?"

"Oh, bits, tool joints—devices that made the pipes fit tighter, hold more pressure for the pumps. He'd carve the design out of wood, then that pattern would be used to make the finished piece out of metal."

"Guess you came by your love for the work from your dad."

"I learned to drill the hard way so I could be like my dad, so to speak. The deals abroad, his patents, I had no real conception of his talents until after his death."

He stopped for a moment. A jogger sprinted across the intersection in front of a car that was moving slowly south on Turtle Creek and turned into the condo drive. The copper fountains in the garden in front of where Ty was parked had stopped flowing. She knew it was time to go in, but she didn't want to.

"Dad taught me to like detail. Leave nothing to chance, he'd say. He'd always planned for me to go to college. I didn't get there until after his death, but I got my petroleum engineering degree after the boys and I hit it big." Tyler chuckled more to himself than to Janelle. "My dad's private life was hell, but his work always brought him pleasure."

He leaned both arms on the steering wheel and looked out the front window. "I've gambled, won and lost, bought out three small drilling companies to add to Dad's DPCO Oil Company. I got Bob and Harry to come back in with me. They work the domestic oil business, and I keep an eye on our overseas work and investments from an office in

San Francisco. Haven't been back here to Dallas for five years until this trip."

Janelle felt there was a sadness to his story. The financial statement he had presented to Jamison Insurance Company showed Tyler Dalton to be a very wealthy man with interests in U.S., as well as Arabian oil. And yet earlier, when he'd spoken of his father going to Saudi, he revealed their lone-wolf lives. She sensed hidden shadows and patterns of son like father. A steamy mist still curled from the rain-drenched bushes. It was late.

Tyler turned off the ignition and turned toward Janelle, his arm casually draped on the back of her seat. "I wouldn't say no to a cup of coffee." He lifted one eyebrow quizzically.

Janelle grinned, "I'll fix you a cup if you'll continue my mini-education on oil."

"Well, all that talkin' has made me powerful thirsty, but," he slid out of the car and moved around to her door, opened it, and helped her out all the time rambling on, "if you run a float shoe with automatic fillup, three centralizers and two scratchers, the casing has a good chance of staying centered in the hole. Got that?"

"There are several ways of fixing the flow of oil and gas." He took her arm and they approached the entrance. "One company cemented the long string with 500 gallons of mud flush . . . lead slurry has 230 sacks of Class H cement with 5% salt plus 3 pounds per sack of gilsonite," He explained the lingo as he ushered her to the entrance. "The tail slurry has 30 sacks of Class H cement with 5% salt plus 3 pounds of gilsonite and 10% Thixod."

"Thixod," Tyler continued after nodding to the night watchman who had let them in and they were in the elevator going up to Janelle's floor, "is a flash-set," he quickly added, "quick setting cement, to combat gas migration. Makes a good bond for the bottom of the well, but," he concentrated on her bottom then shook his head with a frown, "not for all bottoms."

Janelle had listened, at first trying hard to understand his run-on explanation of what goes on after the oil well has been drilled and there is oil, but the geological terminology, along with the chemical compounds mixed in was too much. She found herself smiling, nodding, and at last laughing helplessly.

"Don't laugh! There will be an exam on this information later and I need to qualify you for a scholarship! You must take your teacher seriously, my dear," he growled. "I can teach you many things!" Tyler put his hand on her waist and turned her to him with one arm as he flipped off the lights and gently lifted her face to receive his kiss. Their lips met and softened, bodies pressed close. For a moment, she pulled back, then eased into a world filled with touching, soothing, kissing. He sighed and she felt his hands glide down and cup her hips to press her closer to him. The pressure of his hands startled her and she took a quick step back to wiggle out of his arms and again flipped the hall light switch.

A reed-slim lamp balanced on a chrome and glass hunt table lit the foyer. Beyond, the living room was aglow with light from polished metal floor lamps, small galaxies that illuminated a white oasis of couches, chairs and tables. At one side of the chromatic white space there stood a six-foot column of Lalique crystal whose interlaced curves of glass refracted the light into splinters of gold which suffused warmth into the austere room.

Tyler walked into the room and stood silently gazing at the art de' oblique. "Amazing!" he exclaimed in a low, intense voice.

He spoke of the one object that had been her only contribution to the room's decor, the one object that had made it possible for her to stay in the apartment which had become a cold, symbolic statement of her marriage to Jerry. Her eyes warmed as she looked at Tyler, who stood arms crossed in the center of the pristine space.

The passionate moment faded as Tyler's eyes swept back to her. "This is nice. I like it."

His words were simple, clean-cut. Janelle smiled. "I'll fix that cup of coffee."

She hurried to the kitchen, shakily spooned instant coffee into two cups, splashed in hot water from the instant hot faucet tap. Grabbing spoons from a drawer, she placed all on a small tray. A final appraisal called for sugar and napkins. She smiled, pleased with herself for the quick service, and reentered the living room to find that Tyler had turned off the lights again. He stood at the large window with his back to her looking down at the scene below. The casual male stance of hands brought an unconscious sigh of appreciation from her.

He heard and turned from the window. As she walked toward him, light from outside the window turned her shadowed figure into golden curves. "Beautiful, just beautiful!" he said in a low voice.

"Yes, I love the view . . . ." Before she could finish, Tyler moved to her and, as if desperate to hold the dream he was experiencing, cupped her face in his hands and kissed her lips, then hugged her close. "*You're* beautiful," he murmured against her hair. She drew back to look up at him, then let her finger touch the pulse-beat in his throat.

As she looked into his eyes she saw the need she felt. With gentle touches he began the silent persuasion of love that had been speaking to her all evening. She sighed with pleasure, desire overcoming reason, and followed as he unerringly led her to her darkened bedroom.

Helplessly, breathlessly, she stood in front of him with eyes closed. A zipper scratched the velvet quiet of the blackened room. She flung back her head and leaned toward him in the timeless gesture of surrender.

"Afraid I'd like to take advantage of you." She heard his murmured words.

She answered with words muffled by his lips on hers. "You make me feel a need that I thought was dead." She lowered her head and clung to him, too weak to move away.

"Jan, I want you, I think you want me."

"I'm so lonely, Ty." She sighed, "I can't take advantage of you just because I'm lonely." Hesitantly she pushed away from his embrace.

He closed his eyes and weighed each word as he spoke, "I'm a man, Jan. I'm me, you are you, we are here, now, together. I've been tested for HIV and am negative." He kissed her hand. "OK?"

"Oh, I was tested a year ago and was all right, and," she answered in a strangled whisper, "I can't have children."

Doubts satisfied by confessions, he groaned his pleasure. Afterward, she breathed in the warmth of him as they lay cradled in each other's arms. After a while, he slowly rolled over and lay facing her, "Jan, you are wonderful, beautiful, sensual," His hands glided down her soft curves and stopped at her inner thigh.

She felt a tingling helplessness as she waited for him once again. There was no shame. She did not question his right to her body. He orchestrated the mating, set the tempo with his gentle persistence. Pleasing him as well as herself, she added her notes to a melody that only they could hear and share. She did not want the night to end and snuggled closer to him, gliding teasing fingers over his body, helping create new notes to their private symphony.

The night sky was tinged with grey when she awakened. "Ty, it's morning."

"Humm," he grinned sleepily as he pulled her close and kissed the tip of her nose. He held her close as he asked, "What are some of your pet peeves besides having your doorman see a man exit your home at early morning hours?"

I have a thing about dirty bathrooms."

"Um . . . me too. In fact," Ty raised up on one elbow looking down at Janelle, "Me, I like to have things clean in the house. I hate clutter."

"I love Monet and all impressionists."

"I like that painting in the hallway of the Petroleum Club. You know the one with oil wells in it. I also like dogs, big dogs. I once had a golden retriever. I believe he was my favorite." He chuckled, "I named him Chamois because he was the light tawny color of a chamois skin. About the same shade as your hair." He brushed back the hair from her face and gently kissed one eye-lid then the other.

His voice was husky. "Beautiful word. Will you be my Chamois?" He nuzzled her neck teasingly before leaning back to look at her.

"I don't bark, don't bite and in case you'd like to know, I don't heel either!" She'd turned in his arms away from his touch. "No, believe me I'd be a lousy man's-best-friend!"

"Don't heel? Or, afraid to?" Tyler flashed her a quizzical look.

She was almost honest with him when she said breathlessly, "I don't know."

"Well, I think I'll just make you my lap dog." He cuddled her closer for a moment. Then, with a sigh, he eased his hold on her. "Better go now or I never will!" He rolled over and out of bed, grabbed his clothes and headed for the bathroom.

She watched his retreating figure and the roll of his firm hips. There was a kind of boldness to his walk, like a sleek tiger walking away from the kill. The thought stabbed at her for a moment, but she pulled out the barb and arched her back in a slow catlike way, pulled the sheet up around her ears, and closed her eyes.

Tyler returned to the bedroom fully dressed. She sat on the bed with arms wrapped around her knees and blushed at the intent, almost questioning look he gave her. She smiled, but before she could inquire, he leaned over and gave her a quick peck on the cheek.

Wonderment and sadness were written on her face. Apparently he caught the look. "I . . . I'll call when I get back from my trip." He walked to the door and turned to look at her once more with a tenderness she could not mistake. "Good-bye, Chamois." He smiled and quickly walked out of the room.

Janelle heard the door close, then the hum of the elevator and at last, the familiar sound of loneliness: the tick of the bedside clock. She got out of bed to turn off lights from the night, dreamily thinking of the night before. What may have been a one night stand for him had been for her an awakening of her own sensuality. That was the way sex was, she thought. They were both adults, both unattached. She did care for him, respected him, even admired him from what she knew of him. She exclaimed aloud "That's one hell of a guy and I'm one hell of a gal," as she climbed back into bed.

Chapter Seven

The room was filled with sunshine when she again awakened. She rolled over and buried her face in the pillow Tyler had used. The male essence of the man flooded her with an overwhelming contentment so different from her feeling after love-making with Jerry. She felt a twinge of doubt when she considered the possibility of Tyler with other women, but shrugged it off. She didn't know how she'd affected him, but he'd surely pleased her.

She started at the ring of the phone.

"Hi. Wanted to see if you got home all right with Tyler." It was Jeb's voice.

The clock read almost nine. "Why, yes, we . . . just fine," Janelle stammered, feeling herself grow warm.

"Did he say he would be in to tape the show? Helen's standing here wanting to know what to set up first with the kids and the cameramen."

How could she have forgotten to remind Tyler? "Last night at the club, I did tell him we shoot at noon, and that he should be there by eleven. But, just to be sure, please have Jean call his apartment and see if he still plans to come in at eleven."

Janelle was already out of bed cradling the phone to her ear as she ran to the closet to grab some clothes. "OK. Helen says the kids will set up for the petroleum show," Jeb answered.

It was almost eleven thirty when she got to the studio. Helen stood outside the closed door where the red light flashed the signal that a program was being filmed. "They've started?"

"Yes, but Robyn Greer isn't here." Helen spoke in a hushed voice.

"What's wrong with him?" Janelle's whispered sharply. "This is the second time in a week that he said he'd be here to help. We've got to get this oil program wrapped up. He's been slow on the AIDS work too."

Helen hesitated, then answered. "He's run into some problems. Tyler Dalton is being interviewed right now. The topic chosen was 'oil prices' and the kids need you to monitor since Robyn's not here."

Janelle silently opened the door with a wave of thanks and breathlessly slipped into the studio. "Yes, well a lot of conditions contribute to what you pay at that gas station," he was saying. Janelle got to the sound booth and put on the headphones to listen and interject if some remarks were not clear or were too accusatory. The oilman was explaining at the blackboard where he was writing some sort of formula. "The money available to pay operating expense is the selling price minus the replacement cost of the gasoline. This is called the *margin*." He underlined the word and turned to see if there were any questions. Looking over at the sound booth, he saw Janelle holding up five fingers, indicating he had fine minutes to sum up his explanation and questions.

He nodded and resumed, "A low-margin item like gasoline must have a high volume, lots of cars out there at the pumps to cover the expense of the gas station owner. The struggle to maintain volume results in a gradual reduction in price to keep the business—a little price war. Finally one of the large oil companies like Exxon that monitor profit and loss discovers that the margin is so low that it's impossible to cover cost and replacement, so the price increases to a reasonable margin or somewhat above." He drew a graph showing the change in price as the volume and margin come closer together.

"A regulatory cost, which is unseen by motorists, dictates the change in the cost of gasoline. For instance, during the hot months, gasoline doesn't evaporate as easily as in the winter, which keeps vapor out of the air. This antipollution fact satisfies ecology regulations, but the refining takes longer and is more costly. And that dictates what *you* pay when you fill'er up."

Tyler could hear a groan from one of the students. "Yes?" he asked, not sure of the young man's name.

"Boy, I thought the price of gas was affected only by the price that OPEC puts on their oil!" The student was still confused.

"It is, but also, there are fees on each filling station tank: a state fee, to measure pollutants; a registration fee to transport gasoline, which is paid to the United States Department of Transportation and a state fire marshal fee to inspect stations." Tyler wrote each fee down and drew a line across the bottom.

"The point is that all of these fees cost money which must be recovered in the pricing of gasoline. Some of the fee programs are good, and some are questionable, but they all come into the formula for the price you pay for gasoline."

"I know you told us at the beginning, but would you tell in more detail what OPEC stands for?" Donna asked.

"Organization of Petroleum Exporting Countries. It's a cartel made up of the Near East oil producing countries. Saudi Arabia is the big brother of the cartel." Tyler paused a moment, then continued. "You may be too young to recall the embargo on crude oil shipments that the Arab nations imposed on the U.S. and other countries in October of 1973 during the Yon Kippur War. The Arabs learned how much price pressure they could apply to the world market by restricting the supply. We had cars here in Texas lined up at gas stations a mile long. Gasoline prices were up, supply was down, the supply/demand ratio was out of balance.

"Fuel for transportation was not the only industry affected by the scarcity. Large turbine generators for producing electricity needed gasoline, industrial power plants needed gasoline, and other combustion sources were not an option. Coal was not an option because of its pollutants. Nuclear power was developing, but environmentally questionable. The incentive for drilling domestic oil was nil as domestic price controls made drilling too costly. It was a confusing time and some of it wasn't just the cartel freeze, but also because personal interest groups, political ones included, confused the picture.

"And I believe I've confused you enough. If you want to hear more about drilling for oil, I can talk to you when I return to Dallas. Right now, I have to catch a plane." Tyler put the chalk down and returned to his seat where he waited for the chairman to close the session.

The panel chairman, Donna Meeker, dismissed the group, the cameraman called it "a wrap," and Tyler shook hands with the students, then walked over to Janelle who had come out of the booth to stand by Julie and Pete. She thanked him.

"I enjoyed it." He smiled into her eyes as he put his lips to the back of her hand, then picked up his briefcase before quickly adding, "I have to fly to San Francisco and on to Saudi. Don't want to, but had a call from my office after I got back to my apartment. I'll think of you." Tyler hurried to the door without another word, and Janelle was left not knowing if she was saddened or relieved by his hasty departure.

She talked to the students about the next program on AIDS and explained that she was expecting Robyn Greer to be back to chair the discussion.

Colleen broke in, "Hey, shouldn't we have another session and go over the written info Mr. Dalton has furnished us?"

Pete Rowenda spoke up. "I agree. I'd like to know more about the production of crude oil and maybe check on that well blowout in Oklahoma."

"Maybe we should use Mr. Dalton's notes and have one last session on oil before we shoot the last segment of the AIDS production," Julie suggested.

"What is the consensus of the group?" Janelle asked. The group voted for more oil research. She was glad she would not have to get the critical crew together just yet for the last AIDS video. It gave her a little time to go to New York for a conference she had to attend.

Helen was seated by the desk when Janelle got to her office. "Helen, I'm going a day early to the seminar in New York. Suppose you could get ready and go with me to be my back-up for some of the regulatory meetings?"

Janelle was frantic to get away from Dallas for awhile, and from the looks of the dark circles under Helen's eyes, she guessed that Helen could use a change too. "As a matter of fact," Janelle added, "why don't we go from New York to Padre Island for a few extra days? A change of scenery, no work. Sound good?"

Helen hesitated a minute, looking down at the floor, then pushed herself up from the chair in which she had been seated. Smiling, she replied, "Sounds great!"

"All right," Janelle walked over to her closet to hang up her jacket. "I'll meet you at Dallas-Fort Worth Airport at . . ." she glanced at her watch. "Seven o'clock this evening?"

Helen nodded her agreement and left the office. She'd been edgy lately. Relationship blues? They both needed a change of scenery. As an afterthought, Janelle punched the intercom to Jeb's office. "Jeb, Helen is going with me to the communications seminar in New York. We'll be at the Plaza, then go to the beach for a few days. Jean has our number if you need either of us."

"Right, to the TV seminar." Jeb's voice sounded detached. Then, in a brighter tone, he said. "You girls deserve a rest from the office. Going to Padre from New York are you?"

"How did you guess?" Janelle smiled at the machine. "Yes. We'll miss you, but, what can I say, we'll not miss the office right now." She chuckled. Jeb hated New York. He never understood when she wanted to go to the city to see a play or go shopping. Nothing was as good as what was here in Texas.

"Jean," Janelle called out to the outer office. "I need the papers for the New York conference."

Soon, she had them, stuffed the papers in her briefcase and with a, "Thanks and see you in a week!" she breezed by Jean and down to her car, and home. The feeling of release was so unexpectedly grand that she poured herself a glass of wine to drink while she got her bag packed.

Helen was asleep as soon as their plane had leveled off on its way to New York. Janelle leaned back and closed her eyes, but could not relax enough to sleep. She had packed, and picked up the phone to call Tyler to thank him for appearing on the program. Without him, the information concerning the oil industry would have been a typical informational program without focus. His knowledge and formidable presence had made the show. The phone continued to ring and Janelle continued to consider that without him, she would never have known what she could be. He had shattered the shell of mourning for a marriage that probably never should have happened.

He was not going to answer. She hung up, disappointed, especially after she had to steel herself to call him. Some kind of foolish pride told her she was demeaning herself to call first. But she had called, and he was not there, so it was ended, and she did not know if it would ever start again.

She sat listening to the drone of the heavy engines of the plane and tried to stop thinking of Ty, but finally she realized she was awake because she did not want to stop thinking about him. In slang terms, he had made her, but in reality he had helped her re-make her life. For that reason, he would be a part of her from now on.

Chapter Eight

The seminar had been enlightening. Both women were exhausted from the busy schedule that saw them popping in and out of workshops and study sessions at the conference center. Helen went to meetings relating to new video and filming permits which would be a part of the Jamison studio's future. Janelle attended communication meetings about censorship and network programing which would effect their independent studio. They'd regrouped each evening before going to a banquet or to an open house where overwhelming details of new government regulations were discussed.

The third day of the seminar finally ended at three, and Janelle and Helen took a cab back to their hotel room from the conference center and grabbed their things to go to South Padre Island, Texas. Both were convinced that their teenaged television producers had a viable product for years to come.

Janelle leaned back in the fast-moving car as they drove down Fifth Avenue, passing the high walls of grey buildings, reminders of the sophisticated city. She was not tempted to ask the cab to stop for some browsing as they passed by some of her favorite haunts. New York City always communicated such a taut, latent energy as you whizzed by, the stink of exhaust from the cars, trucks, and buses that moved along the streets, horns blowing—millions of people behind those gray walls doing millions of unknown and interesting things. And there was concentrated cultural energy here. Seeing a horse and carriage parked on Central Park West, and trees just leafing out in pale shades of shadowed green which seemed a reminder of Cezanne's impressionist paintings, gave her a pleasure that could not be compared to spending or learning. *Artists have a way of capturing the fleeting forms of beauty,* she thought, and pictured Dallas and South Padre. "Why is it that the colors of New York pale in comparison to the colors in Texas? Everything is brighter there. Helen, I'm as bad as Jeb!"

Helen looked at Janelle questioningly for a moment, then turned to the moving New York scenes with a frown on her face.

Janelle mistook Helen's frown as a question. "I'm a true Texan!"

"Pete and I lived in L.A. Somehow there's a dim quality of the light there. Maybe it's smog." Helen continued to look out the window and watched the people of the city hurrying their lives away. "It's not much different where you are—you need ties of family and friends to make the place bearable. I imagine all of those rushing people out there are just as happy as we are if they have some purpose in their lives which is more important than the next meal or the weather."

Janelle looked sideways at Helen. Purpose in life, at least on a re-lating-to-people basis, seemed to have eluded her. She'd been checking her answering machine from the hotel for the last three days to see if he'd called her in Dallas. He hadn't called.

The taxi driver pulled up at the La Guardia Airport, and the two women executives got out with luggage and headed for their next ad-venture. Helen's face fairly glowed with anticipation as she admitted it would be great to be away from Dallas for a few days. She'd not been away from the city or the office for over a year. "All I ask is that we have plenty of Gulf bay shrimp and whiting fish."

In less than six hours aboard an American Airline flight, from New York to Dallas, and on to Harlingen on an Eagle commuter plane, the view below had changed from city lights to canyons and rivers and at last brown, black and green patchwork displays of large tracks of farm-land with an occasional farmhouse and barn. This was the southern part of Texas, where ranches were big and spread out over hundreds of acres.

The Harlingen Airport lights came into view. Their plane made a smooth put-down and cruised to a halt in front of the airport termi-nal. Helen and Janelle went down the plane's steps in front of two women, a family of four and one older man. People and children were inside the airport waiting to greet their family and friends. Porters were busy pulling luggage off the moving conveyer belt. One man helped Janelle and Helen with their bags, deposited them at the rental car desk, and in less than fifteen minutes, they were in a car and on their way to Padre Island.

Their destination on the island was South Padre Village, a little slip of land north east of Port Isabel, that had a population of 1500, numbers which doubled in the winter. Like Janelle, snowbirds came to the winter resort to live in beach houses, rental houses, high rise condominiums, and hotels. All of this was nestled on a strip of sea grass and sand only one-half mile wide and seven miles long between the Gulf of Mexico and a shallow lagoon, Laguna Madre. Matamoras, Mexico, by way of the Gulf of Mexico bridge was some forty minutes from the Jamison property.

Too tired to eat dinner, they stopped at a grocery in the town to pick up sandwich fixings, orange juice, cereal and milk then drove on to Janelle's beach house. They left the car in the garage under the house on the ground floor level, and walked up to the kitchen. Helen poured them a glass of milk and made sandwiches while Janelle went on in to open the living room plantation shutters that led to the open porch. The night was black with wind and fog that blotted out all view of the Gulf, dampness penetrating. So, agreeing that it was too wet to sit outside, and weary from the city rush and seven-hour trip to South Padre, they had their snack in the kitchen and went upstairs to retire. "Tyler Dalton dazzled the kids," Helen said as she followed Jan upstairs and into Jan's room.

Janelle inwardly agreed, but aloud said, "He'll be back." After a long silence she added, "I do miss Jerry on the programs."

Helen was silent, sober, then, tentatively she said. "Jan, you know the way I feel about rumors." Janelle saw Helen's distressed look. There'd been a call in the hotel just before they'd left for the trip to Padre, but Janelle had assumed it was a private call, maybe from Jeb. "Helen, what's happened?"

There was a silence as Helen moved over to the window-seat and sat down. She spoke slowly, "I've been trying to tell you since New York. I had a call. We were so busy . . ." Her voice trailed off.

"What?"

"Well, Perhaps it's best if I just blurt it out. They say Jerry has AIDS. And he may have infected his wife with the virus." Janelle's features froze. She slowly sat down on the edge of the chaise lounge.

"Jan, listen to me," Helen said firmly "I couldn't be sure it was true. That was Jeb who called me last evening before we left the Plaza. Jeb, Jean, and I wanted to run down the story before we told you. The students on the AIDS panel had heard it from Robyn Greer, who had gone to check some research in the AIDS wing of the hospital. Robyn hadn't seen Jerry for some time, but swore he saw Jerry entering an elevator looking thin and gaunt. Robyn spoke to him, but Jerry seemed in a daze, walked past Robyn without speaking, and left on the elevator."

Janelle faced her friend. "But why wouldn't I know? Why are we just now hearing? Jerry surely would have called me." Helen said nothing. "Not that he'd want to under the circumstances." Her voice trailed off with imaginings unspoken.

Helen offered, "And as far as hearing—it wouldn't necessarily get through to you. He and Mandy had moved to Fort Worth. They've been very quiet, almost in seclusion, haven't they?"

Since Janelle said nothing, Helen went on. "Robyn knew of the confidentiality a patient has until the patient wishes to have the news of his infection announced publicly. He asked a nurse, a friend of his mother's, and the nurse said that Jerry had been in for some sort of test. It seems Robyn confided in Julie Leoni, Julie told her father, and her father called Jeb.

Janelle stared at her. "Robyn has taken it pretty hard," Helen went on. "He thinks so much of Jerry and you. He feels he somehow has let you both down." Helen's voice wound down weakly.

"No wonder he's been unable to function lately." Grim faced, Janelle turned away to pace back and forth the length of the bedroom.

"There's more, Jan." Helen swallowed and took a deep breath to keep her voice steady, "Jeb checked out the rumor by calling Jerry's wife. Of course, he was sympathetic, said he'd heard it and told her how. She told Jeb that she'd lost their baby from an AIDS-related complication, meningitis complicated by pneumonia, and that she had left Jerry. So far, her own health was stable."

Janelle looked over at Helen with horror written on her face. "My God! That poor man!" Janelle stared at Helen.

"Yes, but I worry first about you." Helen said.

Janelle nodded thoughtfully. "I was tested as a part of the research for the show. You remember. It's been over two years. Negative." Janelle finished in a hushed voice.

"And he was tested too?"

"Janelle looked over at Helen with a slight frown. "We all were.

Yes. Jerry was negative. But it was right after that when things began to change." No need for politeness now.

"What do you mean?"

"Jerry and I didn't live as man and wife for the last year of our marriage. He was out every night. Then the Mandy affair got into full swing." Janelle sat down on the bed. "And I guess there was more. I didn't know any of it," Janelle rubbed a hand across her eyes. "Or was too inattentive to notice. But maybe it saved me."

Helen went to Janelle and put her arms around her. "Ah, Janelle, I'm so sorry. Jeb has not told anyone. He suggested I tell you when we got to Padre. He said there was nothing to be done for now, and that it might be best if we stayed here as planned."

Janelle stood up and moved to the window. "That poor little baby!" Janelle could not imagine a worse grief than losing one's child.

"You're not furious with him for not calling you?"

"Of course I am. I'm scared silly, too. You know I've had unspoken feelings about Jerry's sexual preferences from time to time. That friend—can't remember his name. We had gay friends in our group." She shook her head. "Oh, why do I think it was a gay relationship that caused his infection? It could have been other exposures, needles for one. He gave blood to the Red Cross periodically. Or maybe, that time he had to have a transfusion when he had that car accident and lost so much blood."

Janelle looked out on the inky blackness of the sea and searched the past. There was more, much more about this that was awful. "I've had sex once since our divorce. What should I do, Helen?" She stood motionless and waited for the older woman to give her the answer.

Helen walked over and took Janelle in her arms and slowly rocked her back and forth in the age-old way of comforting without words. After a while, she helped Janelle to a chair. "Jan, do you want to go back to Dallas and check it out?"

Janelle was locked inside herself. The censor meeting for the AIDS show would be a nightmare now. Jerry! AIDS! Ty! And herself facing a black abyss of uncertainty. She wept silently, tears running down her face.

"Why don't you try to sleep?" Helen suggested. "I'll come back later and check on you."

After Helen had left, Janelle forced herself to get undressed and absently got in bed. She stared at the ceiling and considered how tragic the news must have been for Jerry. She knew about the virus. It did not play games once it announced itself. Jerry had to know he was dying. She pulled covers up to her neck and tried to concentrate on what matters she would have to attend to on returning to Dallas, but it was as if her mind were a blank screen refusing to tune into anything meaningful. Fatigue moved in like fog.

Much later, through her sleep she heard a whisper of movement. Someone turned off the bedroom light. The gentle roll of waves on shore soothed her and she surrendered to deep sleep.

Chapter Nine

J anelle awakened draped in golden ribbons of sunlight from shuttered windows. She snuggled under the blanket and listened to
the sea splash against the beach. The flip of the awning fringe above
her window tat-tatted like a metronome, beating in time with the
screech of white-throated gulls scolding and pecking for food on the
beach. The familiar sounds soothed her for a few moments, then
thoughts of Jerry came back. She threw back the coverlet and hurriedly
walked to the window to open shutters and view the sun, rising golden
on the horizon, fanning out in a clear blue sky, with a reflective sea
below.

She watched until the sun's circle had risen above the water and
blazed down on the Gulf of Mexico, pink-tinting the sandy beach. Tiny
birds pecked at unseen insects at the water's edge as they marched about
in lock-stepped groups through frothy foam.

She closed her eyes and for a moment blotted out everything but
the sounds and smells of the sea. A deep contentment had always filled
her when she saw sunrise at the beach, but today thoughts of Jerry, then
unwanted memories of the censor meeting on AIDS pushed in on her
mindless peace. Jerry had always been critical of the censor group.
"Bunch of hide-bound fogies with more money than human sympathy," he'd said.

Putting on a robe, Janelle quietly tip-toed by Helen's closed door,
and went down to the living room to her briefcase which she'd dumped
by the television set the night before—got out a video tape, and slipped
it into the machine. She wanted to see part of the tape where Jerry was
presenting the HIDE AND SEEK program on AIDS, to the adult committees. It was so horribly ironic. Perhaps there was some clue in his
face. But, of course, he hadn't known then.

Though they'd had it in mind from the very beginning of the show, it was just over a year ago when she and Jerry first broached the AIDS topic to the six members of the Research Review Committee: Jeb, Helen, Janelle, Dr. Ralph Hughes, a psychiatrist; Mrs. Mary White, Dean of Academic Affairs for DSS; Dr. Russell Mann, psychologist; and Dean Daugerty, a Baptist minister. This committee had sanctioned the AIDS program as she and Jerry had predicted.

The video she was going to watch was filmed the day the AIDS program was presented to the six members of the Censor Group made up of civic leaders and educators, with the Research Committee included in the meeting.

The power button flashed green; the snowstorm on the screen was replaced by the scene in the company's conference room. There was Jerry standing at the head of the table. This was the Jerry Janelle remembered, dressed in grey slacks and grey silk shirt accented by a red striped tie. An extravagantly expensive navy suede jacket was slung casually over his shoulders. Jerry was ready for the big selling job needed to convince the censor group of the importance of this series. She'd been proud of him that day.

She turned down the volume so she would not disturb Helen, but loud enough for her to hear Jerry's eloquent plea. "For two years the Jamison Insurance Company has sponsored the HIDE AND SEEK television program. It's been a series that has tried to expand the consciousness of the young people of our city. We have tried to be sensitive to their opinions as we have tried to broaden their view of the world in dealing with economics, social issues, personal responsibilities and choices. Essayist Daniel Callahan has stated, 'we need to grow to care about others in the world, to balance that independence which enables people to have a sense of controlling their own destinies, and those ties of obligation and affection which are for each an indispensable source of solace in the face of a world that has little reason to care.' Our goal is to help build that bridge between independence and societal obligation. Young people need to understand society's problems before they can be part of the process of solving them."

Jerry stopped a minute to let the group ponder his words, then he continued. "The series has been blessed with two outstandingly sensitive young people, Robyn Greer and Colleen Blair, co-anchors of the material presented by and to our youth of Dallas." There were introductions.

She fast-forwarded past the part where Jerry gave statistics of decreased delinquency and school absence which could be partially attributed to the HIDE AND SEEK educational programs. On the days of the program, absenteeism was down—and, he said, "The information given has increased the sensitivity of youth to their life style choices which affect their lives today and in the future."

Again she passed by the awards which had been received with Jerry's prediction that with PBS exposure the Jamison television material could have a major impact on the future.

Then as she began the tape again, Jerry was saying, "And it is you, the Research Review Committee and Censor Panel members who have given a moral, ethical, and sociological balance to the programs selected by the youth. We thank you!"

Janelle noted the smiles and nods of approval as the camera moved over the group. Of course the censor group was used to Jerry's charismatic ways. There was a tension between planners and censors which seemed to keep the programs meaningful yet taut, candid yet respectable. When they created a script with social responsibility, there seemed to be a delicate balance, like the edge of a razor-sharp knife that cuts through but does not draw blood.

The camera stayed on Jerry as he continued, "The AIDS virus has been likened to the bubonic plague of 1348 which killed over one-third of the European population. That plague changed Europe forever, bringing changes in religion, social life, and government authority. In this year of 1983, the AIDS virus has infected over one million in the United States and over twelve million worldwide. The forty million infections worldwide predicted by the year 2000 gives responsible citizens cause for panic. And pandemonium there will be if this virus is not stopped. The pilot ready for your critique today is on the virus and its history. It is informative and by far the least controversial of the five segments. Please watch it for style as well as information. We will discuss it and the written material which has been prepared for you." Jerry sat down and nodded for the video to begin.

A wide-lensed camera held on the adults sitting around the conference table. The student video now incorporated into a small box on the left hand side of the screen showed students coming into the room and making themselves comfortable on the floor, or in chairs which encircled a table where two students, Pete Rowenda and Julie Leoni, sat. There were eight students present for the first segment of the program—Pete and Julie who had done the research, four more students who were to listen to the findings of the researchers and ask questions, and Colleen Blair and Robyn Greer, co-anchors who would keep the discussion moving should there be any heated arguments. The two were good at their job and the student groups respected their leadership. The setup resembled an informal late-night gab session at somebody's home.

The tape ran. "We have found qualifying evidence that Human Immunodeficiency Virus, HIV, which in the final stages is referred to as Acquired Immune Deficiency Syndrome, AIDS," Julie Leoni emphasized the name of the virus, "was discovered in eastern Africa where there was copulation between man and green monkeys." The censor group on screen murmured but were attentive. "The virus first infected Americans in 1976 or 1977 when tourists vacationing in the Caribbean made contact with the virus and brought it to New York City, Miami, Los Angeles, and San Francisco. The health authorities of these four cities were the first to recognize the unknown strain of virus, and reported their findings to the Centers for Disease Control in Atlanta, Georgia, which defined the virus in June of 1981 and retroactively reported four cases in 1978, eight cases in 1979, and forty-four cases in 1980." Julie stopped and looked at Pete, who explained transmission: homosexual and heterosexual.

Janelle put the tape on pause as she thought about how much the young group had learned from a regular panel member, Adam Stapleton, a handsome six-foot-three black basketball star from Kimball High in south Dallas. His remarks succinctly defended the black population in Africa by pointing out that the virus did not necessarily start with blacks, and by suggesting it could have been anybody with less than human instincts. Andy Slade, a chubby, happy Korean guy who had been adopted by a former GI and his wife, could be counted on to get teams to work together for the good of educating, not dividing, their audience. His humor was sometimes shattering, but this time had been effective in relieving tension. His remarks had gotten the group discussing HIV.

Another, more explicitly informative video was shown, and as

Janelle fast forwarded through it, she could see in fast-motion-the arguing committee members rising from chairs, pointing at Jerry and each other in outrage, denial, and confirmation about publicly talking about condoms, sodomy, homosexual intercourse and oral sex in prostitution. In general, it had been too much for these Old Texas people who could not accept that there would be—was certainly going to be—a good deal of promiscuous sex in their town. All but one—Mrs. Hill.

She tried to find the place where the civic leader, eighty years young, spoke up for the series. She and her deceased husband had been philanthropists for the Dallas community for over fifty years. From the Dallas Women's Club to the Presbyterian Hospital Board of Directors she was known to be her own person when it came to deciding the fate of proposed city improvements, cultural issues, or land and highway improvements. She epitomized a civic leader with humility and humanity. Janelle wanted to see and hear her again.

She backed the tape up too far—Pete still had the floor. Janelle watched a little of his report. "It seems that the virus stays in the body undefined, and that as long as it is in the body, there exists the potential to infect others. The individual exposed to the HIV-positive has the possibility of being infected with the virus. We all could be victims unless we practice safe sex." Poor Jerry! The tape ran on, but Janelle forgot it for a moment, focused on Jerry and his destroyed future and, in dismay, on herself.

Donna Meeker had just asked a question and Pete was explaining. "Donna, safe sex is to be discussed in the next program. Let me just say, for those who want to start practicing it this month before we meet again, the culture breeds in the blood, semen, tears, saliva and urine; therefore, safe sex is the only preventive for sexually active individuals. And safe sex means, either no sex or, stimulation and masturbation, or, with some question as to effectiveness, the use of K-Y jelly lubricated condoms." His quick delivery took some of the embarrassment from his candid remarks. The students were struck silent at the implications. Janelle knew they were also wondering how the censor committee would accept the new information. Janelle recalled how irate the censors had been. All but one. Where was that segment about Mrs. Hill?

She fast forwarded again and stopped where Jerry smiled good humoredly as he spoke directly to Mrs. Thorngood, "Whether you like it, want it, or not, the individuals involved in this plague are a part of our world, Mrs. Thorngood. It is not a question of liking or disliking, accepting or not accepting certain behavioral styles. It is a necessity of life to understand what this virus is and what it is capable of doing. We do this by learning about the lives of those who have been affected by it."

Now there was psychologist Dr. Mann and his charts explaining the young people's quest for identity and his remarks about verbal education being preferable to written material because of the learning disabilities, problems with reading, language and cultural differences some youth may have. That was a very vital point he'd made.

She skipped ahead. Yes. This was the spot. Janelle recalled that Mr. Manion, censor committee chairman, had taken a YES-NO vote and declared the NOs had it. Mr. Manion spoke when the tape played. "Would anyone else care to give his or her opinion?"

"I . . . I believe the vote must be unanimous in our group?" a voice inquired tremulously—the camera zoomed in on a tiny, gray-haired lady whose regal posture was framed by the leather chair in which she sat. There it was at last, Mrs. Hill. Janelle knew the elderly lady had come from a small-town, was a soft-sell type of leader who could be counted on to give frank and sound opinions. She sat back in the wicker high-back to listen to the woman.

"Mrs. Hill?" Mr. Manion appeared irritated.

"I voted *yes,*" the elderly lady said in a firm but quivering voice then continued, "And Mrs. Beedon suggested if one of us voted yes we should explain our vote. I believe my vote was not recognized."

Mrs. Hill smiled. "I feel I keep abreast of the latest trends. Nothing has ever held my attention as this crisis presented today concerning the containment of the plague called AIDS."

The small woman hesitated. "I'm a product of the traditional system of the early nineteen hundreds as are you censor members, when cultural standards, social conventions, and moral values were dictated by parents, ministers, and priests with no questions asked. Progressively, through the years, there has been an erosion of God-fearing behavior. Self-restraint has been devalued by the acceptance of what has been called, 'do it if it feels good.'

"I've lived through four wars in which our country has been involved and have seen the progression of attitude toward war change from one of national pride and loyalty to one of cynicism and indifference to participation in war itself. I have asked myself why is this so?

"No longer are war heroes or literary scholars adulated but rather movie stars, musicians, and sports people are looked up to as heroes and their amoral or downright disgusting lives have become examples of what the good life should be. Depiction of outrageous behavior as the norm in books, magazines, newspapers, and movies has accelerated the changes which have taken place."

Jerry and the others were listening enrapt. "Some parents who have lived through these changes see both responsibility and the disciplining of their children differently than we did. To some parents discipline is just too much trouble. To other parents, discipline is a reminder of the rigid dos and don'ts of their own childhood."

Mrs. Hill looked around the room and smiled. "I have strayed from my original subject. The youth today are not the innocent children we were in the early nineteen hundreds, nor are they so easily led. They question our authority. They question our wisdom. They listen to our suggestions with indifference. This is because they don't believe we live in the real world.

"We, the older generation, may be the keeper of values and wisdom but without the respect of the young, our opinions and warnings will not be heard. These young people of HIDE AND SEEK are taking up the challenge of communicating real situations and real needs for change in our culture. They are youth attempting to recognize right choices."

The small woman who had stood during her remarks, now sat, put down her notes, took a sip of water, and looked steadily at each person in the room. "Let us remember that what this video series attempts to show does not come close to including what most of the young have seen in real life, or have seen on other television shows. We in this room may be innocent and wish to remain so, but we cannot hide from reality."

Mrs. Hill smiled gently at the other censor members. "I feel we must honor the young people's bright, eager minds by giving them information that may help them live, reproduce and protect this world of ours, on their terms." She sat back, folded her hands in her lap, and closed her eyes.

Janelle turned off the tape and walked back up to her bedroom. She was glad she'd looked at the tape again. Mrs. Hill's eloquent defense of the AIDS educational series gave the censor group a chance to reflect upon their personal attitudes and what had formed them: righteous indignation, refusal to accept the truth, even envy. The change of attitude of many individuals after the group discussion led to the censors' final approval of the AIDS educational programs.

Janelle lifted her face to the morning breeze that flowed through her bedroom windows absorbing all her love of Padre. Sad realization flooded her. The group was now directly involved in the terrible subject they'd researched. Robyn Greer had delayed the series because of Jerry.

Janelle considered the facts that Helen had told her the night before. Jerry had become a victim of the disease he fought. How could she face those young people and finish the last segment of the AIDS program? Janelle stared out at the sea as if she looked for answers in the vast expanse of blue and silver.

Chapter Ten

With more determination than she felt, Janelle put on a bikini and robe and again padded in bare feet down to the quiet living room. The large, open room was filled with white wicker furniture covered in soft blues, washed greens, and bright yellows which echoed colors of the large Dhurrie rug that covered one section of hardwood floor in front of the fireplace. The colors reminded her of her mother.

Her dear mother! The room was filled with memorabilia. Her eyes roamed over the framed pictures arranged on a round wicker table. One was of her dad and mother with happy smiles, arms around each other facing the camera with the glass-like sea behind them. Another was a picture of her mother and her drinking lemonade on the balcony. That picture had been taken by Nancy or Charles—the couple who were the caretakers of the property.

She walked out of the living room to stand at the porch railing of the open balcony which wrapped around the beach side of the house and overlooked the sea. Leaning out, she invited the heavy breeze to whip her hair. And, lifting her face, she breathed deeply of the salt air which smelled of moist weeds and the dried-by-the-sun crustaceans carried ashore by the sea.

Closing her eyes she had a vision of sandcastles washed away by the tide, kites soaring high above the water's edge swooping and diving like giant birds playing in the offshore breezes, her dad standing waist-high in the foamy water casting for whiting. The scenes were beautiful pictures of a fantasy life that was no longer real. How she wished she could go back, but the sandcastles had all been swept aside, washed over by the tides of time.

"The view is heavenly, Janelle!" Helen carried out two cups of steaming coffee and handed one to Janelle before sinking down on one of the white lounge chairs expelling an exaggerated sigh. "This is the life!"

"It surprises me you haven't been here before." What a weight had been put on Helen to wait until Padre to tell her the tragic news. "Somehow I thought you had." She sipped her coffee.

"I've been here. I recall once when your mother was remodeling the beach house. You must have been in school. I brought Mother with me. My, how she enjoyed the beach, this view. I loved it too. Your folks did invite me many times, but there was always something to keep me from coming. I remember your parents had invited me, I'd planned to come, but had to cancel at the last minute. It was Mother's last week at home, then the hospital, and her last days with me." They watched the gulls for a long moment.

"How blessed I was to have her with me for several years after Pete's death. She had wanted to die before she finally went, but I was selfish and prayed for her to live. I did so need her.

"Someone once described the feeling after the loss of a loved one, like floating in a parachute that's been dropped into empty space. It's lonely and frightening, but the parachute will open if we pull the cord. We all have to pull the cord, go on living."

"You've had some sad times, Helen."

Helen had been eighteen years old when she married Pete. It was near the end of World War Two and he was an enlisted man in the Navy. Shortly after their honeymoon, he was sent to the South Pacific and was gone for two years. The war ended, and Helen met Pete in San Francisco on his arrival home from overseas. They had only two months before tragedy hit. Pete had gone across the street from his office to get a newspaper. A drunk driver lost control of his car; it jumped the curb, hit and killed Pete. After Pete's death, Helen had come to Dallas to live with her mother. She'd worked for Neiman Marcus until, as she'd told Janelle, she got sick of having her hair put up in a beehive twist everyday and smiling until her face ached. That was when she'd taken a job with Jamison Insurance.

"Helen, remember the first time I met you? Was I jealous!" Janelle had come home from the University of Texas in Austin for the weekend and had breezed into the outer office of her father's suite eager to surprise him.

Helen smiled and nodded. She looked the picture of contentment as she lay on the lounge resting on the pillow of her hands. "I remember. Your dad and I were looking at a piece of jewelry for your mother's birthday. I could tell you were really upset. You opened up the conversation with a sarcastic, 'Well, am I intruding?' "

"Oh, I was awful! I thought you and Dad . . . so stupid! I was really ashamed after you explained that my mother and your sister had been in college together and you had known Mother before she ever met my dad. Helen, you were like another family member coming into the company. " She was silent, lost in thought. "That bracelet that you helped Dad pick out was always her favorite."

Helen gazed out at the blue water. "Nell Jamison was the most thoughtful person I've ever met. Your father never looked at anyone else."

"You know, Helen, that last year I should have known Jerry was living a second life. I was so involved in city activities and in the insurance business I had no time to face what was going on. I believed he loved me and I didn't want to ask any other questions."

Helen nodded. "You trusted that you were loved."

Her parents had that kind of trust. She had presumed she and Jerry had that kind of trust. Foolish naivete.

Helen handed her cup to Janelle, who took it on her way to the kitchen, then returned. "I've always wondered what Pete was like for you to remain so faithful to his memory."

"He was an easygoing man. I was a critical, judging and a very young woman when we met." Helen sat on the lounge and propped her feet on the seat, elbows on knees and looked off in the distance. "Pete said to me one time, 'Helen, never let anyone change you or your values. They make you the unique person I love. But you shouldn't insist on imposing those standards on others. You'll be disillusioned if you do.' Pete taught me to accept people at the point they existed in their lives, not where I thought they should be where I was in mine. I'm a better person for having been his wife."

Helen eyes were sad. "I believe we'd still be very much in love if he were alive today. He taught me how to accept him, not for what I thought he should be, but for what he really was. He was a real man, not a fantasy. There was a depth of mutual commitment there. We didn't need to speak of it." Helen mused for a moment then started. "I'm sorry, I talk too much."

Janelle shook her head, "No, I asked you to tell me." She felt a stab of sadness for Helen and for herself. She wanted to confide in Helen about Tyler, but how could she after listening to the kind of love Helen and Pete had shared? Her one night of passionate love with Tyler was hardly that of two who shared a lifetime commitment. And yet she couldn't get him out of her mind.

Helen lay back and covered her eyes with her arm. "Jan, sometimes I have some of those same feelings for Jeb as I had for Pete. I trust his judgment. I enjoy just seeing him, just knowing he's physically in the office. I look forward to each day knowing we'll be together there. At times, I'd like to know him better, but my old-fashioned guard is up. I don't want a fling that might end. I couldn't stand that."

Helen pushed herself up off the lounge, laughing. "Speaking of flings, I think I'll fling myself into that beautiful sea for a swim before breakfast!"

"Yes, let's!" Janelle quickly jumped up from the lounge chair, grabbed a towel, and headed for the side steps of the balcony porch. Both women ran down and through the sand to plunge into the cold, frothy salt water. They swam, then pressed back shivering, leaving a trail of oozing footprints in the wet sand.

After breakfast, they went back down to the beach. Janelle sat with arms wrapped around legs, chin on knees and studied the iridescent sea. The sun brushed the heavens with blinding shafts of golden red. A sailboat skimmed by like a gull in flight.

Lying on her towel with her face upturned to the sun, Helen remarked, "This is real luxury; a warming sun, quiet breeze, sea sounds to relax you as your skin browns up." After a brief silence, she added, "Janelle, I haven't forgotten Jerry. I thought you might not want to talk about it."

"Thanks." Janelle swallowed hard to relieve pulsating dread. The searching conversation had kept reality at bay. She lay back on her towel and covered her eyes with an arm. She wished time could stand still in this peaceful place. Finally, the swish, swish of the incoming sea lulled her to sleep.

The Gulf breeze had stiffened, spraying up a sea mist which dampened her face, and awakened her. She got up to stretch and saw her friend was no longer beside her. Looking out on the beach, she saw Helen talking to two small children at the water's edge.

Hastily she gathered up towels, newspapers and magazines to take into the house. If she kept busy and did not think past the day, she could close off the frightening tidal wave of guilt and fear that threatened to engulf her. But she couldn't fool herself. There would be no lasting peace until she went back to Dallas, found Jerry, and discovered if after all, she had the HIV virus. It could be.

Janelle was busily wiping the kitchen counter when Helen returned from the beach. "Janelle why don't we go out for dinner?" she said brightly.

Janelle turned a tearstained face to Helen. "Oh, Helen. I've got to go back, and sort things out, find out the truth!" With bowed head, she leaned on the counter in an attempt to control herself. "Would you call to make a plane reservation for me?" She looked at Helen. "Helen, you must stay. I insist." She picked up a sponge and furiously scrubbed the sink which was already clean, then turned to the stove.

Helen took her by the arm and directed her to the cane-backed chair by the table. "Sit down. Of course I'll call for you. But I wouldn't think of staying here without you. We'll go back together. I'll call right now to find out what reservations are available before we decide anything. Go on now. Get your shower," Helen urged.

The no-nonsense order calmed Janelle. "All right, but I do insist that you stay and enjoy Padre. It will add to my frustration—unhappiness —if you don't stay and enjoy it for both of us. I can give you a Padre must-see list."

Slipping out of her bathing suit, she went into the bathroom and had just taken a shower when she heard Helen call from below. "Janelle, can you hear me?"

She wrapped in a towel and opened the bathroom door. "Did you get them?"

"There are no reservations available today. This is the end of the spring break for the college kids. There was one seat—a reservation for tomorrow, Tuesday, at seven in the evening. I'll have to stay and go back on Sunday as we had originally planned. Get dressed and we can see a little of the island together, then I'll treat to dinner." Helen continued, "We'll go out for dinner and come home early for you to pack. How does that sound?"

Slowly, weighing each word, she answered Helen in a flat voice. "I guess it would be best to go out and eat. We didn't get to buy the bay shrimp we had talked about." She returned to her room and forced herself to dress.

Later, when Janelle went downstairs, she found Helen in the kitchen mixing something in the blender. "I'm making a little toddy I dreamed up. Not much alcohol, but lots of vitamins!" Helen handed Janelle a glass of the smoothie she'd prepared. Janelle sipped the drink she didn't want, but tried to sound enthused. After all, Helen had a right to a vacation. "Helen, if we hurry, we can see the jetty show."

"What is the jetty show?"

"It's a name Dad made up. Come on, I'll drive." Janelle did feel a tug of excitement as she drove them to the southern tip of the island two miles from her house and just across the causeway bridge from Port Isabel, to a parking area close by the water's edge. They got out and walked along the shore to a rock and cement harbor, Brazos Santiago Pass, where long docks with boat slots ran along both sides of the water passage.

The jetty show had just begun. An end-of-the-day parade of large and small fishing boats chugged into the harbor, while Dolphin jumped and circled in the sea foam which bubbled from the churning propellers. "Oh, I love it!" Helen exclaimed and hurried out on the dock to take some pictures of the large mammals that frolicked around the fishing boats like excited puppies.

Janelle walked to the dock railing. Screeching sea gulls dipped down to catch the scraps of fish bait and scales that fishermen threw out over the side of their boats. The birds' chatter blended with the beat of synchronized sea slaps on the dock, the sharp snapping of flags and masthead ropes. All of this created a background percussion for the shouts of fishermen and others who called back and forth from boats to shore. " . . . Got some whities!" . . . "I'll take some whities!" . . . "Need some grouper!" . . . "Biggest swordfish of the season!" . . . "How about bay shrimp?"

Closing her eyes, she breathed deeply of the sea-smells of fish, crushed sea weed, wet sand, ready to indulge in some of that fresh seafood from the Gulf. Her voice mingled with the other voices as she went to join her friend. "Helen, let's go get some grouper. I'm hungry!"

Helen nodded as she put away her camera. "I think I got a shot of the dolphins jumping out of the water. It's as if they had been trained to perform for the boat people."

Janelle steered into Canal Street and eased the rental Buick into a parking space at Blackbeard's Restaurant, known on the island as the best place for cajun black fish, hush puppies, and coleslaw. "My folks always came here on Friday nights. Mother liked to go out for dinner and, if Dad could get fresh fish to eat, he was satisfied. When mother and I were alone, we ate at home and played scrabble or our own game of S and S."

"Hello!" A voice called to them as they approached the restaurant entrance. The two women looked up and saw a young man and woman leaning out over the top-deck rail of the three-storied structure.

"Hi, you two!" Janelle waved to the couple. "It's Nancy and Don Young, my beach neighbors." She called up to the couple. "This is my friend Helen Sutton. What're you up to?"

Don called down, "We saw your car at the house earlier and were planning to call you. Want to go to the Third Coast tonight to hear some real Western music?"

For a moment, she hesitated, considering the wave of gloom which threatened to engulf the recesses of her mind. Then, firmly, she turned to Helen. "Why not? There'll be time, and it will occupy the rest of the evening. Men and their lady friends go there to dance the Texas two-step and the Cotton-eyed Joe. It's not fancy, just cowboy boots and hats, jeans and split skirts. The music is great and you just might get a chance to dance."

Helen hesitated. Janelle grabbed her arm, "Besides, I don't want to go home and think."

"OK, I'm game," Helen grunted. "It'll give me a chance to wear my jeans one more time before I go back to the corporate world."

"And the cowboy boots," Janelle added and called up to the couple to OK the trip, "We'll meet you there after dinner." With a wave, Janelle followed Helen into the restaurant. They ordered and were soon enjoying the seafood platter which included bay shrimp, white fish and grouper. Hush puppies and coleslaw with the usual baked bean accompaniment completed the filling, delicious meal.

"You'll like the Third Wave. It has some of the best fiddle players

and the biggest dance floor on the island. Lots of tables jammed together, and colorful waitresses and waiters seem to never leave your side,
keeping the drinks coming." Janelle described the dance place while
they finished off dinner with coffee. The waiter brought the bill, and
they were off down Canal Street to meet the Youngs.

Somehow the family memories seemed especially poignant this
evening. Odd, she thought, how places which have witnessed the passage of time in our lives seem to store memories in their very walls, like
artists' landscapes or photo albums that preserve the past. Driving down
Padre Boulevard recalled happier times. She went in there to buy coloring books when she was eight—and there—they all spent a rainy day
at the movies.

They met the Youngs at the entrance of the Third Wave and the
four pushed, shouldered, and shoved their way behind a waitress to a
table amid laughter, loud voices, and music. Spotlights zeroed in on
the corner of the large room to the bandstand where a cowboy with a
guitar had just started to sing.

> *Nueses don't quite seem an oasis*
> *In this Texas Kun-tur-ee*
> *I met a gal in that drinkin' corral,*
> *She taught me the Two-Step*
> *We danced 'till the moon set,*

A waitress came to their table. "I believe we have to order two drinks
at one time." Don shouted. The three women nodded, the waitress got
their orders and left just as the cowboy was finishing his song.

> *I've seen many new faces since Nueses oasis*
> *And roamed from that Ranch House Saloon.*
> *But I've never forgot*
> *That night in that spot*
> *And the gal who danced me 'till noon.*

The singer ended with groans, gyration, and Elvis Presley-like
motions of body and guitar which turned the crowd into screaming
idiots.

"Kinda busy!" Don yelled over the music and the whoops and calls of the audience and dancers. Janelle yelled back, "And it's only Monday night!" No one could hear her over the noise.

Nancy and Don hurried out on the dance floor at the beginning of the next set of dance music while Janelle and Helen sipped their drinks and watched the dancers shuffle to the Cotton-eyed Joe music. Janelle grinned at Helen. "Like it?"

"Nuesis Oasis. . . ." Helen said above the din.

"What?"

" . . . a great two-step beat!" Helen yelled to Janelle, then turned in surprise as a man dressed in fringed shirt, chaps, cowboy boots, and wide-brimmed Stetson tapped her shoulder and asked her to dance.

"Go ahead," Janelle shouted. "Here, men ask you to dance."

The man led Helen to the edge of the dance floor and after a few minutes of conversation, he sashayed her out on the floor to the Texas-two-step music.

"Helen seems to be catching on." Janelle pointed to the dance floor. Nancy and Don had come back to the table and turned to see Helen being led around in a circle by the big, barrel-chested cowboy who did the quick steps with a lightness that belied his size.

"Oh, oh," Nancy grabbed Janelle's arm. A heavy-set woman outfitted in a split-skirt, blue and white fringed blouse that matched Helen's partner's, and purple cowboy boots was walking with a firm step toward Helen and the burly man.

Helen said something, and with hands up, backed away, and hurried to the table where the three spectators were laughing so hard they almost choked on their drinks. Helen collapsed in her chair and smiled broadly at the others at the table. "Boy, but it was worth it . . . he was a might f-aw-n dancer."

Later, back at the beach house, as the two sat on the balcony, Janelle sat staring at boats—the only random spots of light on the blackened sea. Absently she remarked, "Well, now you know what we do on Padre." She took a sip of the coffee royal Helen had prepared.

"Seems innocent enough to me," Helen said. "In the forties we'd go to the local soft-drink dance halls to jitterbug and cut-in on each other's dates. Boys threw the girls up in the air, then under their legs to the tune of 'Chattanooga Choo Choo.' The next morning you could hardly move from sore muscles. But dance tunes then were nothing compared to that wild Texas two-step music and the man with the jealous wife—or better yet—that old codger you danced with. He was one of the best dancers on the floor. He looked about ninety years old. How old was he, Janelle?" Helen asked.

"He claimed he'd be thirty-six his next birthday." It was too much effort to laugh, but the memory was amusing.

Helen pushed out of her chair. "I'll sleep tonight. This evening was something out of a Saturday afternoon matinee for me. Such fun. Thanks." And, with a wave, she went upstairs.

"Me too," Janelle answered the retreating figure. "I'll put out the lights."

Janelle sat in the dark watching clouds scud over the cresent moon while furls of grey-black sea rolled into shore. The scene recalled a poem: "Dover Beach" by Matthew Arnold that she'd learned in college.

> *The sea is calm tonight.*
> *The tide is full, the moon lies fair*
> *Upon the straits—on the French coast, the light*
> *Gleams, and is gone; the cliffs of England stand,*
> *Glimmering and vast, out in the tranquil bay.*
> *. . . Listen! You hear the grating roar*
> *Of pebbles which the waves draw back and fling*
> *At their return up the high strand . . . And bring*
> *The eternal note of sadness in.*

There was a painting by Turner done about the same time that showed the relentless, bursting grey-blue waves that foamed at the shore's edge. What a wonderful honeymoon Jerry and she'd had at this place and before that—so many summers with her parents' love as a protective net. And now, the relentless sea of time and events had darkened and washed over it all. The little girl with the coloring books and shells—the new bride with the handsome husband—was gone, carried out with the tide of time. She had to pray for strength to face her future alone. She had to accept her life, yet the thought of Tyler brought back the need to be loved.

Tired, she prepared for bed. But knowing she would not sleep, she went to her writing desk to compose a list of her favorite haunts for Helen to enjoy the next few days.

1) Louis' Back Yard for dinner. The amber sky at sunset on the dining porch at Louis' looking out on the Laguna Madre Bay (Mother Warmth of the Bay). They've redefined the decor to attract sophisticates. (I really preferred it when it was less formal. I'm an inverted snob).

2) Luby's cafeteria, for a "Lube Job" (Texas lingo)—a bit farther away in Harlingen, but you must have a piece of their delicious homemade pie.

3) The Ridley Turtle Museum and Aquarium. The Turtle Lady—Ms Ila— and her environmental society have done much to protect injured and endangered species of marine life.

4) Matamoros, Mexico, is just over the Gulf of Mexico bridge. Neat place to shop for clothes and there's an open-air market for bargains.

5) Take a drive along Padre Boulevard. Specialty shops abound. Note the names of the streets; Atol, Huische, Bahama, Gardenia.

6) Did you know "bay" shrimp got the name because they are taken from the bayside of the gulf?

All in all, enjoy dear Helen. Like Rome, you'll be leaving wanting to hurry back.

As she always had.

Chapter Eleven

When Janelle entered the kitchen late the next morning, Helen greeted her holding up a carton of milk. "This carton is as cold as that lady's voice when she caught me dancing with her husband and thought I was breaking up her happy home." She put the carton back in the refrigerator.

Janelle shook her head. *Happy Home.* Thoughts of Jerry and her own possible danger clogged her throat and made the thought of food sickening. She hadn't slept, and now, couldn't eat. "Let's take a walk and breathe the sea air."

It was cool but beautifully clear on the beach. They walked past groups of college students soaking up their last rays before returning to school. Sea gulls skimmed over the beach with widespread wings, to land, legs braced for the sandy touchdown, then again soared high in the sky when Janelle and Helen walked too close. Three miles and one hour later, they sat down on towels laid out on the sand.

Janelle sipped ice water. "Mother and Dad always had a group from Dallas to the island in the fall for game fishing. It's a great sport, and the fish caught are magnificent, with trophies awarded for the biggest fish. Dad won once when he stayed long enough to enter the contest. He never stayed as long as we did—usually he had to get back to the excitement of business."

Janelle leaned over to pick up some sand and let it sift through her fingers. "I'm a living example of the end of innocence. One of the saddest things in life is to recall the safety and loving security of your childhood and realize it's gone, leaving nothing but problems in its wake."

"I know." Helen said softly, then—"What did you and your mother do to fill in the time besides lay on the beach like we're doing. Not that I'm complaining!" Helen rolled over to lay on her stomach.

"We were always too busy to get hooked on the tube." Janelle lay back down on the beach towel. "Well, each day, when we finished our suntime, Mother would pull me up by the hand and we'd go up on the veranda, get a iced-filled glass of something, and have S and S."

Helen turned her face toward Janelle, "OK, I bite. What's S and S?"

"Selective Scripture. We would pick one book from the Bible and go through it reading our favorite passages to each other."

"Your mother was a very spiritual woman, wasn't she? She had an inner grace, a peacefulness, that I could feel when I was with her. We had a lot to share in that way, though we never spoke of it."

"She was a very contented woman." Janelle stopped for a moment recalling her mother. She sat up abruptly. "I could use some S and S time right now."

"Fine with me. I'm cooked enough for one day."

They gathered up their things and went up the outside steps to the porch. Janelle went into the living room to the white wicker cupboard at the side of the room, got two Bibles, and returned to the porch. "Here's yours."

"What book should we take? What is one of your favorites?" Helen started to leaf through the Bible.

"Romantic that I am, I love the Song of Solomon. Another book Mother and I enjoyed was Ecclesiastes. It's always been attributed to Solomon."

"Is it the one where he gives all the advice to his people?" Helen asked. "I always forget who said, 'A good reputation is more valuable than the most expensive perfume.' Was it Paul or Solomon?"

"That's our boy, Solomon." Janelle opened her Bible and read, "Ecclesiastes, Chapter seven, verse number one."

Janelle flipped through the pages, "This one started quite a discussion with Mother. Turn to that same Chapter seven, verse twenty-seven and twenty-eight where the Preacher talks." She read. " 'Step by step I came to this result after researching in every direction: One tenth of one percent of the men I interviewed could be said to be wise, but not one woman.' That one made me angry." Janelle put the Bible down, put her feet up on the wicker lounge, and hugged her legs with her chin resting on her knees. She smiled softly.

"How did your mother explain that to a budding feminist?" Helen asked.

"She explained that the point was not that the Preacher could not find a wise woman, but that no one, man or woman, has true and deep spiritual wisdom." She said perhaps the Preacher did not speak of the *ignorance* of women but rather about their *innocence* because of their lack of education."

"That seems reasonable. Did that satisfy your young, rebellious mind?" Helen grinned.

"Yes. I began to understand that the Preacher was typical of his culture, a real chauvinist. History shows that some women in the past were as wise as men, but did not get the recognition. Back then it really was a man's world."

"But he spoke of more than being book-educated wise, or, even wise-to-the-ways-of-the-world. He was speaking of *wisdom,*" Helen countered.

"You sound like Mother. I've never forgotten her answer to my question about wisdom. She said in that quiet way of hers, 'Wisdom is the ability to trust in God. Nature exemplifies that trust. Watch the bird let the sea breeze guide its flight and landing.'"

Helen noticed Janelle's sad eyes. "To paraphrase what your mother might also say to you, 'Be not afraid for God is with you,' Isaiah, Chapter forty-three, verse five." Nell Jamison consoled me with that when I lost Mother. You may also wish to add Psalms 40 verses 1-3."

Janelle looked up the verse. *"A new song to sing."* She was silent for a long moment. "I haven't done this for a long while. There's such comfort here. I feel it. I believe I've been looking outside for answers —to work—to Jerry to complete me. And want got all mixed up with need. Being here where everything is so elemental makes me realize who I am."

"A child of your mother and dad?"

"Yes, but more important, a child of my Father." Helen smiled with a nod.

Janelle got up. Her eyes skimmed the smooth surface of blue water as calm as a lake. The horizon seemed close enough to swim out and touch. "Wish we could scoop all of this up and take it back to Dallas with us." She picked up her towel and Bible with a sigh.

"It's almost three. I'd better go in and dress. I have to be at the airport at six, an hour before flight time." Janelle started toward the French doors as the phone began to ring. She ran and grabbed it just at it stopped ringing. "Now why couldn't they have held on another second? It might have been important."

Helen insisted on driving when they left the house for the airport. She said she wanted to get her bearings so she could get around the island on her own for the next five days. As they went over the bridge, they admired once again the reflected, sun-bled colors of the western sky, now amber with waves of magenta and dusty pink. The two women were comfortably silent as they drove. At one point, Janelle had suggested stopping for a quick bite at a small restaurant not far from the Harlingen Airport which had advertised bay shrimp. She directed Helen and they were soon inside the eatery sipping a beer while they waited for their order. Janelle had given Helen the outline of sights to see on the island and they were in a discussion about the Ridley turtles when a deep voice called. "Janelle!"

Janelle turned questioningly and her eyes opened in surprise as she saw Tyler standing at a table not too far from where she and Helen sat.

Shock hit her like a fist. "Who is it?" Helen asked, not turning to see for herself.

"It's Tyler Dalton," Janelle said. A part of her wanted to run, but instead she sat motionless and stared. There stood the man she'd thought she might learn to love.

Helen turned in the direction Janelle had been looking. "Well, Mr. Dalton seems to be involved, from the looks of things."

Two attractive women were seated at the table where Tyler stood, looking over questioningly at Janelle and Helen.

A wave of indignation was replaced by one of dread as she watched Tyler say something to the women, then turn to walk toward Helen and her. A wide grin showed his pleasure at seeing them. Janelle attempted a weak smile and swallowed.

"Hello. Business on the island?" Tyler asked. He turned from Helen to Janelle, including both women in his question, but his eyes lingered on Janelle.

"We've had a few days off from the hectic pace your company put us through," Helen said. "How are you Mr. Dalton? You've been busy since our evening of business and pleasure. I'll always remember it."

Helen extended her hand in greeting.

Tyler leaned over to touch Helen's outstretched hand. "I do remember it too, Ms. Sutton. It is good to see you again."

"It's unbelievable how we keep bumping into each other." He chuckled and extended his hand to Janelle.

She shook his hand with a "Yes, isn't it" then quickly withdrew hers.

"I left for San Francisco right after the HIDE AND SEEK interview then was in Kuwait. I got back yesterday and called. Your secretary did mention New York and a seminar." He hesitated, "I thought I told you about my trip the night we were together."

Had Jean mentioned Padre Island? Was he the phone call? A flush of pleasure was chilled by his euphemistic reference to their erotic night.

"I'm here on business," he added. If he had come to Padre for any other reason, he wasn't acknowledging it. "Remember when we talked about hot oil?" Janelle looked up questioningly.

"Well, my men have that problem on their hands. Guess we need to reread the papers on the Hot Oil Act—part of our insurance with your company. But I understand that's Jeb's job."

Continuing silence. What was she supposed to say? The whole world had changed. "Are you going to be here long?" Tyler asked, turning to Helen as if to apologize for ignoring her.

"I can't say I'm looking forward to leaving this heavenly spot!" Helen raised her hand as if to invite Tyler to sit down.

Janelle knew she had no right to ask who the girls at his table were, but she still wanted to know. "If you have any questions concerning the theft of oil, you can call Jeb at the office tomorrow." She shrugged her shoulders in a gesture of dismissal and the slight shrug caused the slip strap of her dress to fall from one shoulder. She could feel Tyler's gaze and hastily pulled up the strap. Why doesn't he go back to whoever they are? she wondered. Her life was complicated enough.

"Better still," Ty answered, "go out with us to see the site of the theft. It's out in the Gulf, five miles over by the big barrier reef. I've got friends with me," he motioned with a nod of his head at the two women. "They've come along to enjoy some fishing while I examine the evidence. My boat is meeting us down at the Brazos Santiago Pass dock in about two hours."

"I'm sorry. I'm on my way back to Dallas. I've work I simply must attend to." Her throat closed. A part of her wanted to change the ticket, to go with Tyler and forget Jerry. Forget AIDS? Silently she scolded herself. This man had the right to take the women on a fishing trip. Why did it matter who they were? She had no claim on him to make her jealous.

Tyler looked at Janelle with hooded eyes for a second as if he was aware of her tension but was not sure what caused it, and turned to Helen. "You both could go back with a full report and have a chance for some fishing at the same time."

Janelle immediately picked up on the invitation and looked at Helen. "Why don't you go? You don't go back to Dallas until Sunday." And hastily she added, "I know Jeb would appreciate it." Her voice trailed off. She was trying to make it better, but was leaving it impossible for Helen to refuse.

Tyler seemed genuinely enthused. "Why, yes, Helen, please come. I've five people going and the boat is large enough for ten. You can fish or catch some rays for the three days we'll be out." He added with a chuckle, "There are five cabins. You can even get caught up on your rest if you wish." He looked steadily at Janelle. "I wish you would change your mind."

Janelle felt hot with embarrassment. She could not look at him. The silence spread and she struggled for breath as if she would choke on her thoughts: staterooms, seduction, AIDS.

"Thank you." Helen was accepting. "It will be an exciting experience for me. I've never been on a yacht." There was wistfulness in her voice. It was true that she'd known little but work all these years.

"Fine. Tell me how to get to your house."

"I know where the Pass is. I'll meet you there," Helen suggested.

"If you're delayed, don't worry, we're not on a schedule. Just bring sun things. It will be very casual. I'll have fishing gear, gloves, windbreakers for all the extra *work* we'll be doing." Tyler grinned.

His smile became a puzzled frown as he looked at Janelle. "I'm sorry you won't be going. Sure we can't persuade you?"

"I must get back to Dallas, but—" she glanced up at him wanting to somehow explain why she could not go. Just then, the waiter brought a tray of food to their table—"thank you anyway. I wish I could." It sounded so condescending, but there was no way she could explain what was so urgent back in Dallas.

For a moment, muscles froze under the tight skin of his jaw, then he shrugged and smiled. "See you tomorrow, Helen." He turned with a wave of the hand and walked back to his table.

Helen did most of the talking while they ate their bay shrimp. Janelle moved food around on her plate, and answered Helen with an occasional nod or "Yes," trying desperately to not look over at Tyler and his friends. Finally, unable to sit any longer, Janelle excused herself, pleading an upset stomach. Helen said she'd get the bill and meet Janelle outside.

The churning stomach was unsettling, but not urgent. She did not want to see him there, across the room, and it was something of a relief to sit on the veranda and watch people flow in and out of the restaurant as she waited for Helen. Some women were dressed in elegant flowing silk pants, others in jeans; men in sport coats and ties, others in casual golf attire. The dress of the people was as varied as were the houses from which they'd come. South Padre people were unpretentious like the dwellings: beautifully groomed, but laid back; rustic yet sophisticated.

Helen came out. "Are you all right?"

"A little squeamish, maybe from my fear of flying. I get nervous when it's about time to board a plane." At her friend's suggestion, Janelle waited on the open porch and watched Helen hurry down the steps to get the car.

She could see the running lights and blinking signals at the airport just a short distance away. "Jan?" Tyler had walked out and approached where she sat. "I was glad to see you, but you weren't happy to see me. What's wrong?" His voice was gentle. He gravely inspected her face as he waited for a reply.

His concern touched her and a desire to turn and rest her head on his shoulder was almost more than she could bear. "Tyler, I'm so sorry. I must have seemed rude." She stood.

He smiled and turned her face up to his. "No." Janelle stepped back and placed her hands on his chest to hold him away from her.

"What's the matter Jan? Did I leave you too quickly that morning in your home? It was a wonderful night. I felt as awkward as a schoolboy, but . . ." He didn't finish.

What had she done to this man? "I . . .I enjoyed our night together. It seemed so right at the time, but I've regretted my weakness since then. It all seems so self-indulgent on my part." Her voice trailed off to a whisper before she could add, *and probably, yours too. Pleasure wasn't enough.*

"Jan, I've thought about that night too." He waited a second then, "What's the matter? Are you sorry? Do you feel some kind of guilt? Hey, look at me." He turned her to face him "You said you were lonely; I was there. You made me less lonely too." His voice was gentle.

Janelle shook her head sadly.

"Jan, I do respect your feelings." He smoothed back her hair, wiped a tear, and cupped her face between his hands, looking deeply into her eyes." I want to know you better, be with you. What's wrong with that?" His voice was urgent, almost a plea.

Janelle saw the gentleness in his eyes and turned her face away from him. "There's nothing wrong. Please, just leave it at that."

He reached out to put his arms around her.

"No," Janelle said firmly. "I must go. Helen's driving me to the airport and will then go back to the island so she can meet you for the trip." In a softer voice she whispered, "It was kind of you to ask her." He dropped his arms to his sides. She rushed down the steps into the waiting car ignoring the tears that streamed down her face. "Please go quickly, Helen." Janelle urged. And the last sight she had of the place was a man standing, hands in pockets, staring after their car in bewilderment.

Chapter Twelve

Janelle sighed, feeling the thrust of the plane push her back against the seat as it climbed up and away from Harlingen. The lady sitting beside her looked over from her book. Janelle avoided eye contact, pulled a magazine from the rack in front of her, and started leafing through the pages of *Newsweek*. What she'd felt for Tyler could have been real love. At least she knew she'd cared enough for him to let him go. She sighed again as she turned the pages without seeing words or pictures.

S and S, Scriptural Selections. More like Spiritual Strength. Padre had been a blast of ocean air in more ways than one. There'd been shocking jolts, but also uplifting insight. She'd have to call Jerry right away and she didn't know how she could face it. She'd prayed for help. Maybe it was time to let go of her mother's hand and put her own in Somebody Else's. There wasn't much alternative. She closed her eyes until the stewardess announced their arrival at Love Field.

"Love Field—what a name for an airport!" Janelle mumbled aloud in disgust as she hurried through the terminal and out to the parking lot and her car. She'd go in to the office early tomorrow.

Jeb smiled as he came into Janelle's office the next morning and perched on the arm of the leather chair. "You look tan. And where is the other traveler? Did you lose her in the shops down there?"

"Well, Helen had such a good time, she decided to stay over for a few days with Tyler Dalton and friends to deep sea fish." She noted his slight frown, but didn't add the pleasure trip would include checking out an insurance claim.

"What in the world would Helen do with a fishing pole?" Jeb asked. "She's with the DPCO president, Tyler Dalton?"

"Yes, we saw him at a restaurant near the airport yesterday and he invited her to come on the boat. She'll be gone until Monday."

"Found you, did he? Jeb asked.

"Who?"

"Tyler Dalton. He called here and got your address on Padre from Penny, the temporary secretary Jean needed while you were gone." So he had sought her out after all.

He cleared his throat as he stood up from the chair. "About Jerry. I will help in anyway I can, Jani." His look of concern said more.

"Thank you, Jeb."

Jeb walked toward the office door, then stopped. "How about dinner tomorrow evening? I'd like to hear what my girls did."

My girls indeed! Old Texas—it could be forgiven in Jeb. "I'd like to have dinner but could we postpone it until Saturday night?"

"Fine. I'll pick you up at seven on Saturday." Before Jeb opened the door he added, "Jani, does Helen really like to fish?"

"No, but it beats coming back too soon to the office. Besides, she's going to check on a claim Tyler intends to present to us."

Janelle could see relief and something like pride in the smile Jeb gave her. "That's my girl, Helen," he said and walked out.

Janelle shut the door and picked up the phone. She'd learned from Jean that Jerry had moved into a Dallas apartment soon after Mandy left him and sued for divorce. The location of the apartment was not too far from the Baylor Hospital. Perhaps he had to be close to the facility for treatment.

She dialed Jerry's number. He answered and asked her to come over the next day. "What time?"

After a pause, then a rasping cough, Jerry answered, "Elevenish?" His habit of defining the time loosely reminded Janelle of former times, meeting for lunch at 'one-ish, two-ish.' The expression had always embarrassed her. But it showed some of the old "cosmopolitan man" still lurked in what had to be a shell of the former Jerry.

Chapter Thirteen

At exactly ten forty-five the next morning, Janelle entered the elevator of Jerry's apartment house. As the door closed behind her, she hesitated, took a deep breath and touched the penthouse number of the high-rise apartment. The elevator began to move slowly toward the nightmare Jerry had created. As she walked slowly to the apartment door, she steeled herself for the truth she did not want to see.

It was surreal, as if a time capsule had dumped her in the middle of some bazaar, Freudian play. She recalled Jerry saying, "Let the student groups seek out the truth and decide how to present it to the rest of the young people. If the student panel sees the results of unwise choices, they may be able to avoid trouble for themselves and for other young people in the future." Now, the pep-talk seemed as worthless as flotsam on the shore of Padre beach.

She jabbed at the doorbell, hearing at the same time a spasm of coughing behind the door. The door knob slowly turned and the door swung open. *Please God, help me,* she thought.

She was stunned to silence by the person who stood at the open door. This was not a man but rather a starving scarecrow with tilted head perched above a sunken frame hung on shoulder blades. Dry, pink-rimmed eyes looked back at her. She sucked in a deep breath, "Hello, Jerry."

"Come in Jani." She smiled wanly as they went through the foyer and into the living room .

The surroundings were new to her, but the same white walls, white carpeting, white linen upholstery as in her own apartment marked it as Jerry's place. Realization, then dismay, overshadowed her thoughts of Jerry and his condition. Why had she not changed or added colors to her apartment? She'd been grieving for this bastard and she vowed, whatever happened, she was going to get her home in order and relieve the starkness of chromatic color that was Jerry's signature, not hers. She stopped a moment, hand on the back of a high-backed chair. How could she be thinking about decorating when her formerly loved husband was dying? Loved? She didn't believe she'd ever loved this man. The fun, the shallow existence of glamour they had shared, had been inherently false. The only thing of her marriage that had been real and she could remember with pride was HIDE AND SEEK. It was the only legacy of value in four years. They'd shared illusive dreams of marriage and now had to share horrible reality.

His stooped form shuffled into the living room and stopped for a moment to look up at her through slitted eyes. A short, raspy laugh ended in a series of coughs, that seemed to wrack his entire body. "Well, Jani, I'm something to behold," he said simply. He motioned her to a chair while he slowly proceeded to a large white leather chair and sat down.

There was a round table beside him where reading glasses, water decanter, television remote control, and prescription bottles were clustered. Janelle recalled reading glasses and television remotes on tables in every room of Jerry's and her home, the bathroom included. In those days, Scotch whiskey was his only prescription. No doctors for Jerry.

"I'm in bad shape, Jani."

She cleared her throat. "I had heard about—that you were ill. I'm sorry." She saw his eyes follow her to the couch opposite his chair and felt the discomfort of his scrutiny.

"My God, isn't it ironic! The very thing I was helping to research for HIDE AND SEEK." His voice broke as he began to cough. He leaned forward, elbows resting on his knees, hands covering his mouth until the coughing stopped.

Finally, he took a sip of water. He leaned back in his chair and closed his eyes. "I'm OK. These spasms pass and the coughs help clear my air passages."

Her eyes darted around the room, trying to find something to concentrate on so she would not have to focus on this pitiful virus victim. She licked dry lips and asked. "Could I get you some tea?"

He smiled with a slow shake of the head. "No, Jani. Nothing will help. I must talk to you quickly before I choke again." He sat up a little straighter, arranged the silk ascot at his throat, smoothed back the wisps of hair from his forehead and straightened the sleeve of his grey silk smoking jacket. Examining claw-like fingers, without looking at her, he whispered. "You haven't changed. You're still a beautiful woman." And with a gasping sigh, "Oh, how much I've missed you."

Janelle grimaced. She didn't want him to be humble because she didn't want to feel pity for this man who'd caused her so much grief. With eyes downcast, she sat silently.

"Jani, my baby died. I guess I was the cause. Mandy thought so. She left me two days after our little boy died. He was born one month premature of a lung condition, possible AIDS related phenomena caused by the HIV-positive virus."

"But Jerry *when?* I'm scared for myself."

The shrill sound of a siren, the hollow roar of moving cars sifted up. Small sounds of a motor running, a clock ticking filled the silence. Jerry sipped some water and look questioningly at Janelle. "Remember when we had ourselves tested right after we started the AIDS project for television?"

Janelle nodded. She'd rather not hear, bury it along with all the other hurt, but she'd asked. She had to listen. They must finish what he had started, like unwinding thread from a spool.

"Well, my HIV test was negative at that time; and yours. You probably needn't worry."

"Why?" She looked up in surprise.

"Jani, the last year of our marriage, I must have been hell to live with. I was moody, couldn't, . . . Turned my back on you physically. So I went outside the marriage, had a lover, yes a man at first—must have contacted the virus from him."

Janelle's mind was a jumble. Thinking of the past in light of his confession, they'd practiced safe sex without knowing the reason.

"I was confused and felt guilty. Then I got caught up in the affair with Mandy. I was obsessed with her, could not talk to you. But I still cared for you." He choked, cleared his throat, and shook his head from side to side.

"He's the only one outside you and Mandy and she . . .," He had to stop what he was about to say as another spasm of coughing hit him. Janelle couldn't look at him.

"Jani," again the word she hated to hear him say.

"Don't call me that!" she cried. It was her Dad's pet name for her and Jeb called her that. They were the only ones.

"Janelle, look at me. You must be tested immediately." Jerry's voice was firm "Immediately."

"But you just said we didn't live as husband and wife the last year."

"We slept in the same bed. You lay next to me. Touched me."

"I did. And I kissed you." She remembered.

"Yes, and in the glass, our toothbrushes touched—you helped clean my razor cuts."

"Of course I'll be tested." Janelle's voice faltered. "Jerry I can't imagine—fathom how hard this has hit you. Why have you waited until now to tell me about this?" The last words were only a whisper.

He raised a quivering hand. "Janelle listen to me. I know this is a shock. I have a rampant case, and its going to kill me. It worsened before the baby's death last month. I was unable to contact you at first because of the baby . . . Mandy's leaving me . . ." He ended with a whining voice that brought back memories. Jerry didn't admit blame well.

She looked directly at Jerry and asked, "What do you intend to do now?"

"I don't know. I have no insurance." He smiled, "Ironic to admit to you, the heir apparent, First Vice President of the John J. Jamison Insurance Company."

He sounded bitter. Had he been jealous? The thought evoked her dad's presence. Thank God he and Mother were not alive to see this moment. And yet they'd been understanding people. She was the one who was falling apart, and a good part of that was because she depended on them too much—and then on Jerry.

"Did you hear Robyn saw me at the hospital? Did he tell you?"

Janelle did not answer, only shook her bowed head, remembering how she had put off talking to Robyn.

"Well, I brushed him aside. I had just come from my baby boy's autopsy. Mandy thought our son died from AIDS complications even though his autopsy showed he died of respiratory distress and shock. She knew I'd been diagnosed HIV positive and she had to be rechecked for possible HIV infection. It was too much for her to accept. She left me." He shook his head as if he had forgotten Janelle was there. "I've destroyed so many people!" He shielded his eyes with his hands. Sobs like long, wrenching hisses shook his body.

Janelle rushed over and leaned over to touch him but recoiled when he screamed an agonizing, "No!" and motioned her away. His blotched face took on a purplish hue.

To see Jerry like this, and not be able to help him left her wordless. No one, certainly not the student researchers, could visualize this real scene from hell as they read abstract articles about AIDS. She sank back on the couch cushions and while she waited for Jerry to get his breath, she recalled scenes from the last two years of their life together and was ashamed to recall her dependence.

"Janelle," Jerry was sitting up straighter, the blotched red of his skin had again turned to a dull gray. "As difficult as this is, I want you to think about our relationship. We didn't have intimate sex in the last year of our marriage." He hesitated and looked to see if she was listening, then continued, "My affair with Roger was during that time frame. I . . ." He stopped to catch his breath, cleared his throat, "I've hoped, really have prayed, that you're free from my contamination."

Janelle sat with her head bowed. She had heard him, wanted to believe him. She felt disgust for herself, for their life together, for their leadership roll in the education of the young people. All that last year he had been a fraud. It was one thing to sink into the quagmire of self-gratification, but to disguise it while promoting humanitarianism was beyond her understanding, yet she'd been a part of it.

"Janelle, are you listening?"

"Yes. I don't know what to say. I feel . . ."

Jerry let out a rasping, mirthless laugh, "Janelle, you don't have to say anything. You've always been the ideal lady."

"What do you mean?" She looked at him questioningly. Did he imply she was too good to become involved?

"Oh Janelle, I would like for just once to have you be the heavy. But you aren't, never were. I've enjoyed my life the way I've wanted to, with no burden of guilt on you for my choices. Choices which I've made, I've since regretted. I lost control of my own reason. Never trust sex to take away the pain of inadequacy, it only prolongs the agony. Look at me." He thrust purple-blotched arms up and out of their silk sleeves where they trembled like thin branches of reed. Then helplessly, he slumped over and allowed his arms to drop in his lap.

"Jerry, I have to go, but before I do, what can I do for you?"

"Could I come and stay with you for awhile?"

The faint smile of sympathetic compassion froze on Janelle's face. "What?" She slowly rose from the chair and faced him.

Circles of dull burgundy colored the stark bones of his sunken cheeks. "I can't afford this place—must move by the end of April." Again, a thin edged whine.

Janelle felt herself stiffen. "I can't do that," she said firmly.

"Janelle, listen to me. I'm desperate. How else do you think I would have the nerve to ask you? My friends are afraid of me." He hesitated then added, "And you?"

Afraid of him? Janelle was taken by surprise at his candid question. Jerry was not known for his honest communication and she found it as surprising as his request. She slowly turned back to him holding tightly to her purse. With head flung back as if in defiance, "Yes, I am afraid of you and yet, if I don't already have the virus, I know I can't get it except by direct contact of some kind and that will never happen!" Her voice had gotten steadily louder until the end of her exclamation was almost a shout. She leaned over to retrieve her purse which had slipped from her hands, straightened, and said, "I must leave. I will see what I can do for you, but, to live with me . . .it's too much responsibility." She did not finish.

"Do you have someone?" Jerry asked softly.

Janelle flinched. "No, there is no one. I just need some time to see how best to help you. Exactly how long can you stay here?"

Jerry looked somewhat relieved. Was it because of her admitted loneliness or because of her offer of help? "I can stay here until the first of the month. It will be about three more weeks, I guess."

"I'll call you before you have to move. Please see about going to the hospital, Jerry, if you can't stay alone."

"No, I have had the last of hospitals. I want to die at home."

Death? Jerry? It made her want to laugh, to cry, to scream.

A key turned in the lock and footsteps came across the foyer. Janelle looked at Jerry questioningly.

"I have a housekeeper for the time being."

There was still some money even though Jeb had said rumor had it that Mandy had taken him for everything—even old money could succumb to adversity. It was so like Jerry not to tell the whole story, Janelle thought and ruefully smiled as she looked toward the entrance where an older man approached. He had a sack of groceries; when he saw Janelle he turned to Jerry. "Do you want me to leave?"

Jerry shook his head and the man merely nodded and went through a door to another part of the apartment.

"He is from the AIDS Concern Center. I can have him stay with me until I move. I don't believe I will be able to keep him after that." Jerry had slumped back into the cushions.

Janelle merely nodded, using the communication technique they had used so often in the past. "I'll call." She walked out, left the apartment and ran to the elevator to get away, afraid she might be called back.

The elevator door closed. She concentrated on the downward pull of the elevator as her emotions sank to the pit of her stomach. She knew now Jerry was near death from AIDS. Saying it to herself made her feel more in control of the situation. She would have to help him, but how? Really, could she let him be homeless, alone? She wouldn't ignore anyone who asked her for help, let alone the man she'd loved for most of the years of their marriage. She was asking for Divine help in one breath and shutting the door on a dying man with the next. Somehow she got the idea that wasn't going to work.

Chapter Fourteen

Doctor Kindell, the Jamison family doctor, ushered Janelle into his office. She had called when she left Jerry's and had asked to see the doctor right away. "What brings you in?"

"I have a request. I want to be tested for HIV."

The abruptness of her statement, the tremulous lips that tried to smile, were uncharacteristic. "For AIDS?" the doctor said evenly. Still, he stared at her.

"My ex-husband has AIDS." Janelle swallowed hard to keep her voice from breaking. "We were divorced several months ago. I'm hopeful that our marital celibacy practice during the last of our marriage has been enough for me to have escaped. It may not have been." Janelle leaned back in the chair and closed her eyes.

The doctor came slowly around the desk, took the seat beside her, then leaned toward her and took her hand. "I will schedule one right away. Janelle, look at me. How long has it been since you've had sexual contact with Jerry?"

"Not for close to two years."

"Janelle, I know your educational television program covered the procedures used to test an individual." Dr. Kindell patted Janelle's hand and waited for her to reply.

"Yes, but they're finding more about the virus each day, and right now it is a jumble of facts to me. Please tell me what I should expect."

"It's a good idea to be tested right away. There are new drugs which have been found effective in treating HIV infection and delaying the onset of AIDS. Early intervention can be critical. After you've had the test, we can inform you of the findings in two ways. You can be directly counseled by your doctor and that doctor-patient relationship will dictate if it is to be put into you medical record. Or you can have anonymous test results," the grey-haired gentleman added. "In the case of anonymous testing, numbers are assigned in place of names, and test results cannot be entered into the client's medical record."

An inter-office buzz interrupted for a moment. She waited. When he finished with the message, she looked steadily at the doctor. "If I have it, then I will sign the necessary papers to give you permission to use the information in my medical file."

He smiled, nodded, and after a slight pause, added, "Post-counseling follows a positive test result, and the counselor reviews the importance of notifying the partners of the potential risk of infection. I don't understand why you were not notified, Janelle."

"Jerry's sickness came on suddenly. He had pneumonia and in his hospital tests they discovered he had AIDS." For the first time she wondered aloud, "I wonder where he went for testing? One of the students on the research team for AIDS saw Jerry at the hospital when Jerry was there for the baby's autopsy. The baby seems to have died from respiratory distress and shock not necessarily from AIDS."

"A bacterial infection," Dr. Kindell said with a nod.

"Apparently the mother, Mandy, tested negative too," Janelle added. Then, after a pause asked, "If Jerry had gone to the hospital and was diagnosed, how do others exposed learn about his condition and their exposure?" She couldn't imagine why she had not been informed.

"The PN, partner notification, service is offered to individuals with HIV infection at the time of post-test counseling or at a later counseling session. Apparently, Jerry did not get that far in his own counseling." The doctor slowly shook his head looking down at the carpet. "I wonder if Jerry has notified everyone exposed."

Janelle shared details of the news about the baby and Mandy's leaving. "He is all alone and has to leave his apartment." Janelle knew as she talked to the doctor that her decision was being made. "And he'll be moving in with me until he dies." Tears came to her eyes as she wept for Jerry, for herself, for the situation which seemed as hopeless as Jerry's disease.

"You can't decide to take him just yet. What if you're ill?" The doctor stood and walked to his desk. "Let's get you an appointment. Don't make any decision until you know your test results. We'll talk after that."

"What will my examination include?"

"A thorough physical examination, the oral cavity, skin, nails, lymph nodes, liver, spleen, perirectal area, and pelvic examination are included in HIV testing. The circulating antibodies formed in response to unique HIV proteins form the basis for the current screening tests to detect the presence of HIV. The ELISA, enzyme-linked immunosorbent assay, is the newest screening test; it detects serum antibodies directed against HIV. It is an extremely sensitive test and is capable of detecting HIV antibodies in nearly all HIV-infected patients." The doctor looked up from some notes he had taken while speaking to Janelle. "Is this too detailed?"

"No, please! We should have had you on the scientific segment of our program!" Janelle's rueful smile was not lost on the doctor. "Jerry must have had some indication that he was not well. I don't understand why he never shared his condition with Mandy until the baby . . ." Janelle sighed and was quiet.

The doctor frowned as he looked through a book he'd pulled from a bookcase. "Although HIV antibodies are usually detectable nine to twelve weeks after acute infection, antibody response to initial infection may be absent for up to a year or more in a very small proportion of HIV-infected individuals." He looked over at Janelle. "Jerry may have been one of the latter. He didn't know he was infected even though the antibodies were in his body."

"We could go on and on, but for now, let me say your test is necessary and the sooner the better." He held up the paper upon which he had been scribbling. "Let's call."

Janelle nodded resignedly and the doctor picked up the phone.

It was almost four o'clock when she got to her office. She opened the door, noticing a faint scent of roses which came from a bouquet of yellow roses on her desk. Puzzled, she walked over to enjoy the fragrance before she discovered a card propped up on the answering machine. "The color of Chamois." She blushed with pleasure and reread the card several times.

"Excuse me. The roses came this morning." Jean was standing in the door expectantly waiting.

Janelle smiled softly. "From an admirer," she said as Jean left. Janelle sat looking at the roses, thinking of Tyler, Jerry, her decision to have Jerry in her home. She pulled a rose from the bouquet and slowly turned it in her hand enjoying its sweet fragrance while she observed the overcast sky of the city. She suddenly remembered the last of the Matthew Arnold poem

> *The Sea of Faith*
> *Was once, too, at the full, and round earth's shore*
> *Lay like the folds of a bright girdle furled*
> *But now I only hear*
> *Its melancholy, long, withdrawing roar,*
> *Retreating . . . And we are here as on a darkling plain . . .*
> *Where ignorant armies clash by night.*

The poet had lost his religious faith. That was not going to happen to her. The days could be dark, but she was not going to allow herself to be lost on a darkling plain.

Chapter Fifteen

Early Monday, four days after her meeting with Jerry, Janelle sat at her dining table in the breakfast nook with a slightly faded yellow rose in a bud vase for company. She sipped a cup of tea while she skimmed the *Dallas News*. The business section had an article concerning the DPCO Cartel and U.S. oil interests. The company was being stripped of some of its contracts in the Near East. DPCO, servicing the largest contract in Saudi, was being accused of monopoly. She thought of Ty, then checked herself when she considered her resolve to keep him out of her mind and her life.

Saturday night when Jeb took her to dinner, the subject of Tyler and his father Ted Dalton had come up when she'd asked Jeb how the company's DPCO package covered hot-oil scams. They'd discussed the details of coverage for a while. "You know, Ted Dalton was a good friend, a shrewd business man and the best story teller you'd ever meet. I like his son too. I believe he's a lot like his dad.

"Remember week-ago Wednesday when Tyler talked about his friend Elbo? Well, Elbo's father, Llamo Senior, was a personal friend of Ted Dalton. They'd met early on when Ted was wild cattin'. Talk about timely happenings. Ted got into the oil tanker business after World War II. He'd been a telecommunications officer in the United States Navy, and was in on the after-war U.S./Arabian meeting between Roosevelt and King Ibn Saud that concerned the development of secure reserves of oil in the Persian Gulf. Ted Dalton's rise in the oil tanker business was a Cinderella story in itself."

The waitress came; they studied the menu, ordered, and Janelle encouraged Jeb to continue. "I'm still not sure how his father got into the international oil business."

"Well, as he told me . . . In 1945, on his way home from the Yalta conference, President Roosevelt stopped off at the Suez Canal for a personal meeting with the King of Saudi Arabia, Ibn Saud, who'd come from Jiddah to rendezvous as a guest of Roosevelt. The King was welcomed aboard the cruiser *Quincy* and carried to the destroyer *Murphy* where he was greeted by the President of the United States.

"Ted Dalton had been on board the *Murphy* when the royal dinner table was prepared, and when forty-eight hirelings pitched the royal tent on the warship's deck and prepared a feast for the two heads of state and their retinue."

The escargot arrived and Jeb ate with relish for a while, wiped his mouth, took a sip of Chablis and picked up on the story. Janelle continued to nibble at the snails, more interested in the story unfolding than in eating.

"Ted told me stories about the fabulous gifts that were exchanged by the two men after that dinner. There were swords and daggers set in precious stones for the President, an airplane for the King, and a wheelchair as a personal gift from Roosevelt to Ibn Saud, who was also lame. Many deals were negotiated that were made public. But the one deal that changed the life of First Class Seaman Ted Dalton was the agreement that concerned 100 war surplus T2 tankers that would be coming up for sale when the management of American-controlled Middle East oil deposits was put in the hands of private international companies.

"Ted figured if he could get his hands on at least two of the tankers, he could be a carrier for some of the big independent oil companies. He came back to Texas and convinced some of the independent oil-well owners to diversify by buying carriers for oil. Their income from oil sales could be hurt by the international agreements going on between Britain, the United States, and Saudi Arabia. This was before Truman's Marshall Plan, that guaranteed U.S. would be one of the suppliers of Arab crude oil for Europe."

The main meal had come. Jeb ate and talked between bites about his own life in those days. Janelle nodded, hardly noticing what she ate except that it was salmon, her favorite fish, and some kind of sauteed vegetables she ate without tasting. Jeb finished his meal, wiped his mouth with a napkin, then settled back to tell the rest of the Dalton story.

"Three Texas oil companies decided they would invest in two tankers with Ted and authorized him to be the intermediary in negotiating the delivery deal. Ted had many contacts in Arabia as a result of his wildcat days in Texas and the Near East. He was known and respected in the Arabian oil circles and he had a personal friend, Llamo Sibab, who was a member of OPEC's governing body. Sibab would be one of the cartel officers who would choose what independent carriers got transport contracts. His negotiating skills and Ted's team money were a winning combination. That's how he got a recognized license for transporting Middle Eastern oil from the port of Sudom, by the way of the Suez Canal to western European markets, and for transporting supplies back to the Middle East. He made lots of money for himself, and for his investors."

Janelle too had finished with the meal, but to hold Jeb in this story-mode, she ordered coffee. Jeb ordered a Drambuie. "What happened? You said the money days ended?"

"In 1967, during the Arab-Israeli war, the Suez Canal was blocked by Egypt, which meant seventy percent of Europe's oil was blocked from delivery. The oil delivery system had to free itself from dependence on the Suez and began delivering oil by way of Africa's Cape of Good Hope with supertankers. These ships had the capacity for carrying 250,000 gallons of oil in one trip."

Jeb slowly shook his head as he poured the liqueur into his cup of coffee. "As I said, that was the end of the small tankers. They couldn't compete. They were little fish surrounded by whales in the oil transport business.

"I can remember stories of Tyler, always at his father's side—in on European deals where bids, performance, and politics were discussed, and acted upon. He was known as "The DPCO Kid" who had a quick mind and a smart lip. The tanker business, hard work, international deals, European travels all came to an end in 1968 when Ted and the others were forced to sell their contracts to the big boys in the business.

"Ted died of a massive stroke that year. Tyler, only nineteen years old, inherited his home, a good name, some scrubbed oil tankers, an interest in some Saudi wells, which have grown I might add, and a love for the oil business that led him to the oil fields of east Texas. He sure skipped a lot of just being a kid." Jeb shook his head.

There was a soft smile on her lips as she thought about Jeb's story. Both she and Tyler had sacrificed play for adult pursuits.

On the way home that evening, as they'd driven back to Janelle's, Jeb was silent for along while, then said, "I don't know why Helen had to go out on that boat with Tyler. Flitting about like a Greek tycoon's girl friend on a yacht."

"Jeb, that's a little exaggerated. Helen loves her work, but she needs time away from it too. We all do, except you apparently. And anyway— aren't you objecting to a co-worker's private life a bit too much? Or is she more than that to you? If so, you may want to do something more about it than just griping."

Perhaps she'd been too abrupt, a little ungracious to him after he'd taken her out for a nice dinner. But he seemed to be wrestling with this thing with Helen, unable to define his feelings, hesitant. She'd said goodnight before she'd probably have blundered further into territory she had no right to explore.

Janelle got up from the kitchen table, freshened her cup of tea, and moved to the living room to watch the slowly changing sky turn to magenta, pink, then to an orange glow with sprays of yellow spiking from the edges of the sun—the color of her roses. For one brief moment God's wondrous light show gave her the peace she was praying for . . . a brief repose from pain.

She had not talked to Jeb about Jerry, nor had she wanted to talk about the test whose results would not be known for at least another five days. Right now, business as usual in the office was what she needed. Appointments, telephone calls, meetings—all good therapy.

With anticipation, Janelle went through morning ritual, put on white linen in anticipation of a hot day, grabbed her briefcase, hurried out into a rather warm April day and drove to the office. Her first stop was to see Jeb who looked surprised to see her coming into his office. "Hello. How are things? You look worried about something."

"I'm ashamed." Janelle walked to Jeb and leaned on his desk. "Saturday night, I was wrong to the point of rudeness to talk to you about Helen the way I did. Your life is yours and I had no right to force my opinions on you. I apologize."

She walked to the door as Jeb called to her, "Jani, I did some thinking after I got home." He chuckled as he slowly walked to her side and laid a hand on her shoulder as if to hold her there for moment. She looked up at him questioningly. "Janelle, you made good sense. I've been dubious about Helen. I have always hated office romance. And in this case I haven't been sure I wasn't just a lonely old geezer taking advantage of someone who trusts the boss.

"She's smarter than that."

"I know. I was pretty skittish after Sonya. It hurt my pride most of all. I needed your blunt words to give me a push. I've started to remedy my inattentiveness toward a certain person. I need to forget my past fall. Get on the horse I fell off before." He patted her arm and walked back to his desk.

"I think you're trying to say one mistake shouldn't keep us from trying again when something genuine comes along." Not waiting for a reply, Janelle exited with a wave.

Good. She wished other worries that picked at her could be so easily resolved. Walking into Helen's office, she noticed a bright red bouquet on the desk. Roses from Jeb. *He just jumped the first hurdle of the courting race.* Janelle smiled. *And now, I'm going to stay out of it!* Leaving a note for Helen to call when she came in, she proceeded to her own office.

Penny stopped her as she was going into her office and handed Janelle a slip with a message about a call that had come in the week before. Tyler's call! Janelle listened to the confession of the young woman who explained why she had given Janelle's address and phone number to the gentleman. "He was insistent and I didn't know." Penny looked pleadingly at Janelle. Behind the girl stood Jean who shrugged her shoulders as if to say, "I'm sorry but what could I do?"

Janelle reassured the new girl and took the message sheet Penny handed her. As she walked into her office she wadded the sheet up to toss in the wastebasket, hesitated, and smoothed the paper out on her desk top and shoved it under a paperweight. Well, he did try! She recalled the telephone ringing that day at the beach house when she had not picked up in time. Sitting down, she rubbed a dull throb at her temples. He'd tried. It would be five days until her blood test report came back. She prayed for direction. Even if she tested negative, how in the world was she to tell him about Jerry. AIDS was a grim ghost stalking their lives. What lasting shadows would it cast?

She breathed in deeply of the perfume of the yellow roses he'd sent, then pulled a rose from the bouquet and smoothed the fading petals. Even with her life full of mergers, insurance claims, new accounts, Jerry, she still had time to think about Ty. Like a sneak thief, she would open her memory bank and re-live their few hours together before their relationship so drastically changed.

The intercom light caught her eye and she leaned over to punch the button. "Yes?"

"Ms. Jamison, Mr. Dalton is on the line."

Janelle grabbed the chair arms, slowly sat down and with a deep breath picked up the phone, "Hello?"

"Hello, can you hear me?" It was Tyler's voice, far away, with an echo following his words as if he were in a tunnel.

"Yes, I can hear you." Stunned with happiness, she could not get any more words out.

"Jan?" Again his voice came from far away as if a dream.

"Ty, where are you? You sound as if you are in Outer Mongolia!"

She could hear a chuckle then his low, easy voice, "Not quite, but I am at the airport in Delhi, India, on my way to Jeddah, Saudi Arabia. It's 9:30 PM here."

"10 AM, Monday here. What in the world are you doing there? More fishing?"

"Yeah, of a different kind." He laughed. It was the way he'd laughed that night. "I had to fly out after I left Helen at the airport. My office called and told me there were some problems at this site so I flew straight from the airport here." There was a pause, then, "Hey, did you get my roses?"

"Oh yes, they're lovely. Thank you." How proper . . . a brilliant remark! Her throat muscles tensed.

"It was a hell of a way to get you to think about me, but damn it, I was thinking about you!"

Apparently, he had forgiven her cool departure on Padre. Warm pleasure spread through her. "They were here to greet me when I returned from Padre. How was the fishing?"

"Not many fish, but fine weather, good company, wish you had been with us. Did Helen get back OK?"

"She will be in before lunch. I . . . I'm sorry too I couldn't go with you."

"What did you say? Hey, have to run, my plane will leave without me. I'll be gone six or eight weeks." She could hear him laugh. "The roses will have to do until I can get there. Bye, Chamois!"

"Ty," she tried to pull him to her through the phone, "The roses won't be necessary. I . . . I'll think of you," she swallowed hard to keep back the tears. "Have a good trip."

"Right, see you when I get back to Dallas!" Click, he was gone. Janelle sagged back in her chair, and covered her face with her hands. Where was this all going?

Helen entered the outer office. Janelle saw her and went out to greet her friend. "Did you catch anything? Jeb was worried about you." Helen looked refreshed, but her smile faded at Janelle's remark. "It was fine. The Californians aboard were not too much for fishing, but neither was I." Helen looked at Janelle with a serious expression. "Tyler Dalton is a fine man, Janelle. Wish you had gotten to know him better."

Janelle grimaced to herself. Get to know him better! Janelle squeezed her eyes shut, then quickly opened them to see if Jean or Penny were back from coffee break time. Helen and she were alone.

"He was a gentleman to this older woman, and to the two young women on board." She teased Jan with the remark for a moment. "You do remember the two charming girls at the restaurant? They were the wives of the men fishing with Tyler." Helen had a wicked grin on her face.

"Oh? Helen, I'm sorry. I knew he would be a gentleman to you." Giving Helen a hug, she explained. "Worry over Jerry and the AIDS problem has me up tight."

"You've had the test?"

"Yes. I'm waiting for the results. Helen, I've seen Jerry, decided to take him in." Helen said nothing. What could be said? "What's on your agenda today?" Janelle asked.

"I have to turn in the report on the Dalton insurance hot oil scam claim. Tyler showed me the location and gave me detailed diagrams to show Jeb. Oh, and the plans came in for Mr. Bloom's Houston firm.

We've a month to set up the outline for the Houston business, do the insurance prospectus and present the plan for review. I suppose Jeb will want some input into that plan."

Helen's face was flushed. She hurried on to say, "I had a feeling if I stayed away long enough, you would have me up to my elbows in work!" She sighed resignedly, "Golly, I could have stayed for another month!" She turned away from Janelle and moved to the filing cabinet behind Jean's desk. "When will Jean be back? I can never find the kids' stuff."

"She's down the hall. You'd better fill Jeb in on the Dalton report. I'll take care of the Houston thing."

Jeb walked in. Eyes downcast, frowning over some papers he was scrutinizing, he looked up and saw Helen.

A small smile played on Janelle's lips as she noticed Jeb's delight. Go for it, Cowboy! She slipped into her office unobserved by the two who stood looking at each other. Looking back over her shoulder, she saw Jeb take Helen's hand.

Chapter Sixteeen

It was weeks later, an unusually hot day for the third week in May. Janelle had returned to the building after lunch with an insurance executive. As she walked into her office, she noticed a thick manila envelope on her desk The name "DPCO Oil" leaped out at her. Quickly, she pulled the desk calender around to discover it had been two months almost to the day since the meeting Jeb and she'd had with Tyler. She'd gone over in her mind what she would say when she finally had to see the man. So much had happened.

It had been five weeks since she had gotten the negative results of her HIV test with the warning that she should be tested again in six months to make sure the HIV infection was not dormant in her system.

Jerry had settled in her home three weeks ago. He was to stay with her until the weather improved, and then move to her beach house on South Padre. She had employed a male nurse to look after him for now, who would also accompany Jerry to Padre. So far, there had not been too much time to be with him, so there'd been no serious conversations since that day in Jerry's apartment. Janelle worked long hours. The insurance man she'd had lunch with, Bob Knowles, was in the group of friends she'd had since college at SMU. Betty Carter and Sue Stone with husbands and Elsie Mae James, divorced like Janelle, had season tickets for the opera or enjoyed after-golf suppers. Her decision to entertain made the lifestyle more interesting. There was something going on three or four times a week. Jerry watched television, played gin rummy with the male nurse and seemed reasonably content. His condition seemed to be in remission at the moment.

Having Jerry live in her home was not as bad as Janelle had imagined and above all, she felt good about her decision even though she had many duties to perform to protect herself from the virus. Cleanliness and sterilization of all dinnerware utensils was essential. Jerry's bath was separate from hers and his needs were maintained by the nurse. Janelle's cleaning woman, Mrs. Rhodes, had been given an outline of ways to clean. She'd explained, if everyone washed their hands thoroughly and did not use Jerry's water glass, dental supplies or anything else he used orally, the virus would not contaminate their bodies. Mrs. Rhodes was a kind person who understood the seriousness of the disease, yet was willing to continue working for Janelle.

She was at peace with herself until she thought of Tyler and what she would have to tell him. "Jean, would you call Mr. Dalton's office in California and see if he wants the entire plan to be mailed there or sent to his office here in Dallas?" Odd, he hadn't called.

A few minutes later, Jean peeked her head in Janelle's office. "Mr. Dalton's secretary said he had left word with her when the Jamison Insurance Company called to tell them he would be in Dallas on the twenty-third and would stop by."

Again that sweet hint of fear that had her heart racing from joy and tension. Her eyes jumped to the calendar. Today's May 20! He'll be here in three days! "I'll not be here, but put it on the calender and tell Jeb's secretary the date. I'll be in Houston." She hated herself for acting from guilt and fear.

She could not see Jean's knowing smile. "But, Ms. Jamison, Helen already sent the last draft to Houston as you suggested." Jean did not suggest that the trip was unnecessary. Her explanation and tone of voice were enough.

"Yes, well, I forgot one part of the proposal." Janelle frowned as she glanced about for some sort of physical evidence of forgotten papers. "I will be in Houston!" She was not ready to see him.

The clack of Janelle's computer keys drowned out the sound of the office door being opened, but sensing something, Janelle turned from the screen. Tyler Dalton stood leaning against the door-frame. He looked at her with one raised eyebrow and an amused smile on his face. "Miss me?"

Her nerves did loops that tightened on her chest, strangling her breath. "You're not supposed to be here for three days," she said lamely with her eyes glued to his smiling face. Was it a satisfied smirk?

"I couldn't wait after hearing the papers were ready. Yes 'um I shore've been in-ter-ested in this deal!" Slowly he approached the desk never dropping his eyes from Janelle's intent scrutiny. She dared not look away. He seemed determined to crowd her. She had to be strong— had to act uninterested—stick to business.

"Yes, . . . well, . . . I'll ring for Jeb and Helen." Janelle reached for the intercom button just as a big hand grabbed her wrist and held her hand away from the phone.

Tyler stood leaning over the desk pulling her toward him so that their faces almost touched. He held her eyes daringly. "You still can't tell a compliment can you? I came back from half way around the world, got a message that the papers were ready, and headed for Dallas before I even got out of the airport in San Francisco. No, damn it! Stop wiggling." He moved around the side of the desk still holding her wrist in a firm grip. "I came here not to sign papers but to see you." He ground out the last words. His eyes blazed.

Relaxing his hold on her, he breathed deeply and said in a softer, yet firm voice. "I couldn't wait to see you. Satisfied?" His smouldering eyes flicked over her.

She touched the side of his face. "I missed you too."

The deep warmth of his hypnotic eyes drew her to him. She unconsciously leaned toward him inviting his touch. He mumbled, "You feel good!" as he pulled her against him holding her bottom with one firm hand while the other played on her back keeping her body pressed against the hard length of him. She watched his mouth come closer and laid one hand on his chest, turning her head away as she made a weak attempt to push away. With his hand on her back, he eased her close and nuzzled her cheek with warm kisses as the other hand on her back molded her to the curve of his body.

Sliding her arms up and around his neck, she laid her head on his chest. He felt so good. She couldn't do this. It was dangerously wrong. His eyes dark with passion filled her vision. She felt his breath on her face, smelled a scent of lemon and cedar trees, "Tyler I can't. Someone could come in at any moment." His lips implored—she arched her neck to receive the trail of kisses he feathered down to the hollow of her neck where his warm mouth rested on the rapid pulse beat in her throat. She closed her eyes and indulged herself for a moment of wishing.

"No. . . " he murmured. "I locked the door."

The shrill tone of the intercom jarred them back to the room. Ty released her slowly holding on to one of her arms with gentle fingers as she leaned over to punch the speaker. "Mr. Bloom is on line two," Jean said.

"Yes, all right." Janelle moved away from Tyler just far enough to reach the phone. He stood close and smoothed her hair back as he kissed the corner of her mouth. Her hand trembled when she picked up the phone. "Yes, Mr. Bloom. Yes. Fine. We'll get the new contract ready and send it right out." She blushed as she looked sideways at Ty. "But I won't be coming to Houston tomorrow. Thank you. Good bye."

Ty seemed to read her mind, "Going to leave before the 23rd? Good thing I got here early isn't it?" Ty moved with panther-like grace to gather her to him.

Janelle felt helpless. How could she avoid his kisses? It was not safe. She did not want to tell him. He was waiting to overpower her again and she would have to stop him. "Ty, I do have a business to run and this is not exactly how I go about it!" She wiggled out of his arms and turned to face him, arms up to keep him from devouring her. She could not help but smile at his roguish expression.

"Have dinner with me!"

Just then, there was a knock on the door and the knob turned. Janelle rushed over to unlock it. Helen peered in. "Well, Mr. Dalton," Helen said with a wise smile on her face. "I thought we wouldn't see you 'till the 23rd. Business demands change your schedule? Or has Dallas a real attraction for you?" She laughed airily.

"Among other things," he cast a meaningful glance toward Janelle who stood by the door as if in a trance. He moved to the front of the desk. "I've come to sign the final papers for the new insurance claim. Bob must have sent the info about the Galveston rig?" he asked of Janelle.

Helen hesitated, "Would you rather I came back?"

"No, stay, Helen." Janelle's gesture almost pleaded as she answered Tyler. "We do have the adjuster's information. Helen, please have Jean call Jeb, and we three will go on to the conference room. Oh, and ask Jean for the support papers please." She could feel Ty's eyes watch her as she walked to her desk.

He silently followed after her from the office to the conference room. After the meeting, Tyler stood, coffee cup in hand, idly chatting with Helen and Jeb about sailfish, high winds, the size of his boat. Jeb's stories about past fishing expeditions filtered toward Janelle as she slipped out to return to her office and close the door after her. She walked to her desk and grabbed at it with both hands as a dizziness hit her.

How in the world was she going to tell this vibrant man the brutal reality? She was not HIV-positive, but neither did she have a clean bill of health. No one would want to hear such a message from a lover; it was frightening, even disgusting. And talk about Chamois, might as well say it the way he pronounced it, Sham-my—a sham. He would think she'd deceived him. "Dear God, please help me know how to tell him. I want to see him, want to be with him, but I'm afraid!"

"Jan, you didn't answer my question. Dinner this evening?"

Tyler had once again entered her room, after a slight knock that she had not heard. Her face drained of color.

"He went to her and took hold of her arms. "What's the matter?"

His hands were warm, comforting. "I'm fine. You startled me. But Tyler, I can't go to dinner with you."

"Jan, I've been crazy to see you. The damn business has kept me away for too long, granted, but you've been with me in Jeddah, when I've been in conference in California, when I talk to Bob and Harry. I see your face like a photo in my mind—have wondered how you are, what you're doing." He tried to draw her to him. "Please, won't you come to dinner with me?"

Janelle moved behind her desk, instinctively braced herself, and lifted her chin to a haughty angle. There was something true she could tell him. "Ty, you know the evening we had together was not a basis for a relationship and it puts an uncomfortable edge to our being together." She hesitated, "As for the scene that just occurred here in my office." Janelle looked steadily into Tyler's questioning blue eyes. "It shouldn't happen again."

Tyler listened to her words and, apparently, from the quizzical look on his face, did not understand what she was trying to say. "I thought we had settled all of that. I respect your viewpoint." Her face showed her distress. He went on with a lowered, reflective voice not looking at her but rather at the desk that separated them. "Still, I should think we could enjoy something beautiful together as adults without it seeming ugly or sordid.

"Believe me, Jan" he looked over at her again, "what we had was wonderful. It went beyond passion. I think you know that. I'm glad to have shared it with you." His low voice was as forceful as his steady gaze that held Jan's.

She looked away and turned from him to gather papers from her desk. "I . . .I'm not used to such evenings."

"Weren't you married?" Ty hurled the question at her in a voice that came out a low growl. He jammed hands into his back pockets and walked to the large window where he stood with his back to her.

She caught the jab about herself and Jerry. She thought it cruel, unknowingly cruel in her case. "I need more in my life than extended passion. Somehow I get the feeling that's all you want from me. If we could get to know each other on some other basis." There was an opening here to say something about Jerry. No, not at all the right moment.

Tyler turned slowly from the window with a look of resignation. "It's true we fell into bed the first day we met. It's a little odd. I can understand your hesitancy. But I suspect that we have a good deal more in common than mutual lust." He shrugged as he walked toward the door. "Hell, Jan, I've put it badly. Let me take you to dinner just as a friend. I cherish your company."

Oh, my dear, if I could be with you. I'd never ever want you to leave! Aloud Janelle heard herself say, "All right, on that basis, let's go." She smiled warmly. He had understood part of what was confusing her. The rest would have to wait.

He said. "Fine, I'll pick you up at eight." From the low, controlled tone of voice, Janelle thought she sensed puzzled anger. He stalked out of the office without looking back.

Helen was coming from her office as Tyler left the outer office for the elevator. "My, he left in a hurry." She looked back at the exit as she entered Janelle's office.

Janelle stood at her desk. "He's a busy man."

"Are you all right?" Helen asked

"I haven't slept well lately. I'm a little tired. I believe I'll go home early before Ty picks me up this evening."

"Good idea. Jean and I will go over some of the material for the kids' show and go home too. Go on, now, you leave."

Janelle watched Helen leave and smilingly shook her head. Helen could be so motherly at times and she had almost decided she'd not lean on anyone again. Still it was a comforting feeling to have such a friend. She got her briefcase, told the secretaries good night, and went to her car.

Arriving home, she eased the door of the foyer closed and slowly walked into the living room. She could hear television rumbling in another room, so knew Jerry must be in his bedroom or in the kitchen. Dropping on her bed, physically drained from her time with Tyler, she worried about the evening ahead. Burying her head in the pillow, she smothered sobs, until at last blessed sleep came.

Two hours later, bathed and in her robe, Janelle headed to the kitchen where she'd heard talking and knew Jerry was in his favorite room. There was a smell of garlic and basil as she walked in to find Jerry slumped on one of the sofa chairs they'd brought to the kitchen for him to use watching television. Grant Deeter, the male nurse, was preparing their spaghetti dinner. Jerry greeted Janelle.

"I'm going out for dinner. I wonder, could you hide—or something? I'd rather not have to explain." Janelle smiled and shrugged her shoulders as if to apologize for her implied suggestion.

Jerry nodded to indicate he understood. "I'll go to my room before they arrive."

A glance at her watch showed that Tyler would be coming in less than an hour. She smiled her thanks to the two men and rushed to her bedroom to finish dressing. When she returned to the kitchen, she found Jerry still seated in front of the television.

"Janelle, what would you say if I said I would like to appear on HIDE AND SEEK?" She looked at him in amazement. He held up his hand. "No, I mean it. I thought before I go to Padre, we might have a taping and I could be on the show." His thin slit of a mouth stretched to a grin made his face resemble one of gargoyles in a William Blake etching.

"Oh, Jerry, why?" Janelle exclaimed.

"Grant, maybe we'd better be alone for this conversation." The male nurse nodded and left. "Janelle, I'm in a wrestling match with an opponent who intends to finish me off. I want to win at least one round before the match is over."

Janelle recoiled from the request. Jerry had recovered from the pneumonia that had him in the hospital just before he'd moved in with her. He was in the last stage of the HIV virus—AIDS. He was too weak to think of it—his shocking appearance—his dignity.

As if in answer to her, he said, "There is no way for me to win my fight against AIDS. I gave up the right to win when I made wrong choices in the past. I would like to help some others avoid the trip I'm on. Especially kids. You know how much I cared for the kids and their shows. I even enjoyed the bantering with Old Texas." He had to stop to get his breath.

His name for the censor group made her smile. She knew he'd cared and felt obliged to hear him out even though she still wondered if it was a good idea for him to display his misery to all the world. "What would you want to be asked?"

"Anything the students would want to know. I'm not too proud of the way I look but the shock of seeing me this way might be a deterrent to casual behavior." Jerry actually seemed happy with his idea.

"Oh, Jerry, it's brave of you, but might it be too much for your weakened condition?"

"Janelle, I am going to die—soon. That is as real as I can say it. Reality has come full circle." He cleared his throat. "I no longer fear death, but I do fear leaving the world unproductive in my last days." He looked away from her. What was it someone said about eye contact showing sincerity? Sometimes looking away showed it more.

"You know, I always told you I didn't want children. And that's the way I felt when that kind of responsibility was too threatening to my freedom. I wanted fun, excitement, adventure. I also felt quite a lot was missing in our relationship. We both knew it wasn't working." He waited a few moments. Janelle stood by the sink listening, as he struggled with the words. So he too had felt the shallowness of their marriage.

He motioned for her to come closer, and she moved a chair to sit beside him. His voice was weak. "If my child had lived, I would leave a part of me behind to be here, to be a part of this wonderful world. I do love it, you know." His watery eyes were shuttered as he gazed at her. "I loved you too, but I was unwilling to give up my own desires for our mutual desires. I have been completely selfish, but didn't count on this." He chuckled derisively. She smiled at him.

Love which had stumbled, faltered, and then all but died, reawakened. He seemed now more like a brother who needed her help. "Jerry, I've thought often about us, about my parents too. Two couples so different in their relationships."

Janelle pulled her chair around so that she sat in front of him. "My mother and father were a very devoted couple. Their respect and love for each other was shown in everything they did for others. I believed their marriage was what love was all about. I thought we could be a mirror image of that marriage. I guess some things can't be duplicated hard as we may try. And once a mirror is broken, the pieces are too sharp to put back together."

Jerry held up a hand and opened his mouth to speak.

"No, please." Janelle took his hand and continued. "At first, I had no idea how I'd live through the pain of losing you. I felt powerless. Then the day came when I found out that you had positive HIV virus and I might too, and my world crashed. My hands were tied, helpless. It was then I put everything in the hands of God.

"Surprised?" Janelle smiled softly at Jerry. "Me too. I had never taken the time for God. My mother believed in God and while I was growing up, I went through the motions, was touched at Christmas and Easter, and went to church but never relied on His power. When my parents died, I relied on you to give me strength. I think I never really grew up. I was a dependent child. When you left, there was no one I could turn to. But that day at Padre when my world seemed to end, I reached out for God's help."

Jerry leaned back for a moment as if to rest, then lifted his head. "You know me. I've never given God the time of day. I've believed he's out there somewhere, but I filled up my day with an ever-changing movie scene of people, places, accomplishments. Maybe I thought you would take care of God for me. You and your mother seemed to know Him well."

His voice was so weak Janelle had to lean forward to hear. "I've felt some comfort during my illness. I no longer feel the need to control. I can't explain it, but I've let go. Something, God maybe, seems now to control my life."

Janelle answered. "You and I were an item, but never a union. I believe you said that once." Janelle looked away for a moment. "We had a happy friendship, but not a loving marriage, in which two people learn to share and not be self-serving and to consider the other person. Marriage is not about happiness, it's about mutual growth throughout life . . . it's a kind of salvation if you will." She stopped, then added. "Pretty heavy?" It surprised her that he was listening. Before, when they'd been together, she would never have considered talking this way. They'd never talked about feelings.

Jerry looked puzzled. "You and I shared love. Wasn't that enough?"

"That wasn't the marriage kind of love; affection, maybe; meals and bed, shared interests of the job. But we both were involved in our own agendas. I loved you, Jerry. We loved each other, but it was not enough for the demands of marriage."

"Demands?" Jerry asked.

"Marriage takes work, giving on a consistent basis. It isn't just about occupying a decorated apartment and attending parties together. It demands that the couple be responsible for each other—be unselfishly concerned." Janelle leaned forward and look steadily at Jerry as she continued. "Neither you nor I took that responsibility. We played at marriage. We had a beautiful wedding but no true marriage. There's a difference. We worked together on outside things, but we never took the time to know each other. I can understand why you left me. You were more honest than I was."

Tears that rolled down Jerry's dry cheeks seemed to bring freshness to his brittle skin. His eyes were deeply sad. "I didn't understand. I was seeking a deeper companionship, and maybe all along we could have had it together."

Janelle leaned back and sat quietly. It was a relief to talk this way. She had needed to tell him she had cared and that the divorce no longer hurt. She was no longer dependent on him. The thought brought back the conversation she'd had with Helen on the beach about wisdom and being dependent on a higher source for true independence.

At the ring of the doorbell, Janelle jumped up. "That's my friend. I must go."

"Janelle, we should talk some more. It gives me strength." Jerry said.

Janelle took a step toward him. "I can have him wait if . . . "

"No, go." Jerry's sucked in air and whispered. "There are still a few tomorrows." She gave him a hug.

She still had the smile on her face from the talk with Jerry when she opened the door to Tyler. "Hello!"

Tyler stood looking at her. The tight smile on his lips softened as he looked at her glowing face. "Hello yourself. Ready? Great!" He took the coat she handed him then held the door for her. They went down to the lobby and on outside. As Tyler helped her on with her coat, his hands lingered on her shoulders for a moment. Then they walked around the circular drive to where his brown Cadillac was parked.

"My, this is impressive!" Janelle looked at the luxurious interior, the pleated leather seats, as she got in.

Tyler came around and slid into the driver's seat. "I decided I needed a more sedate car than the Maserati. Besides, it was not in mint condition anymore." A sly smile played on his lips. "Do you like it?"

Janelle was trying hard not to laugh, but seeing the complicated computerized dashboard, she exploded into peels of laughter. "Sedate! You're a real Texan." She breathed in deeply and exclaimed, "Oh, I don't believe this," as with wide eyes she watched the entire roof of the car slide out of sight revealing a clear night sky filled with stars. "A convertible!"

"The stars come extra," he said as he pulled away from the curb.

Over a wine and a scotch in the dimly lit lounge of the Mansion, a small exclusive hotel on Turtle Creek Boulevard not far from Janelle's home, they listened to the soft piano music of the traditional ballad, "Send In The Clowns." "I like this." Tyler held Jan's hand and gently stroked her fingers with both of his hands in time to the music. "You come here often?"

"Well, yes . . . I used to." She liked the feel of Tyler's hands on hers. She relaxed as they listened to the melody. "Jerry and I used to come here now and then." She glanced over and saw he was intently studying her.

"I've heard about him from Jeb."

"Have you?" She could feel her confidence slip, then took up the challenge. "He was my husband."

"I know." Tyler gripped her hands with his strong fingers and rolled his thumb over the palms. "Tell me about him." He raised her hand to his lips as he continued his gentle scrutiny of Janelle's shadowed face.

"I, we were divorced when he left me for another woman who was going to have their child." Janelle stopped afraid to go on with the rest of the story of Jerry's life.

Tyler broke into the silence, "Were you glad or sad?"

Janelle looked at him in surprise. "Surprised, sad. I felt unloved, unwanted. I was unaware at the time that we had problems, but we did, I know that now." She hesitated, the words dangled like an unfinished rosary. She was silent as she gazed at their intertwined hands. She felt him squeeze her hand.

"Hey! There ought to be clowns! No sad memories tonight." Tyler pulled her up and whisked her out and away from the Turtle Creek Boulevard dining spot. In the car he turned for a moment and said, "One brief comment. I could kill that son-of-a-bitch for what he did to you. But I'm sure as hell glad you're single!" He grinned boyishly as he turned the car on to Preston Road. "Our next stop is Café Pacific."

His attention made her feel protected. The sudden realization that she liked the feeling frightened her. No! That wasn't going to happen again. She wouldn't, couldn't, need him for her own fulfillment in life. That was it, had to be the reason for her own discomfort with their one night of passion.

The Café Pacific, located in the shopping circle of the Highland Park Village, was a gourmet dining spot that Jerry had never liked. Janelle was glad that the intimate tables did not evoke memories. The Rack of Lamb with Dauphinois potatoes, haricot vert and wild currant demi-glacé—was beautifully served. The 1975 Chateau Margaus Tyler had chosen was heady and not too sweet.

She'd dropped her napkin and they'd bumped heads trying to retrieve it. "Suppose it's the lights?" He apparently was going to refer to their accident. She silenced him with a finger on his lips before he could finish the bad pun on the times they had "bumped into" each other. Instead, he added, "It's the man's duty to pick up napkins for women."

She replied with exaggerated surprise. "Is that why the Victorian lady dropped her handkerchief?"

"It's the little things that makes a man feel needed."

"Or could it be called control, defined chauvinistic?" Their bantering was easy and natural.

The pianist was playing, "Quiet Nights," as Janelle and Tyler left the cafe, and drove slowly along the boulevard. Quiet nights. Was there even a remote possibility there could be quiet nights with this man?

"This night doesn't have to end. We can go to a club where the jazz is loud and good and the band is inspired to try new things. I know one. Want to go?"

"Yes," Janelle quietly answered. She hoped she wasn't using him to shore up her own sagging ego, another dependency ploy, grabbing at straws to put the broken pieces of her shattered life back together. But he'd said there had to be more to it than that. Of course there had. She turned and smiled at Tyler.

Tyler saw the look and grinned back at her. "You can be so doggoned agreeable at times!"

"And you can be so doggoned self-assured at times," Janelle teased. "Why, I bet you never let your mother tie your shoes!"

Ty gave her a sidelong glance, a frown on his face. "Maybe not," he said brusquely.

Janelle could see the muscles of his jaw tighten at his own remark. She asked, "You've spoken of your dad a lot. But what about your mother?"

"That's a story that's as long and twisting as a Texas hill country trail. I'll tell you another time." The clipped words left no opening for further discussion. They finished the drive to the jazz spot in silence until Tyler turned the long car into a parking lot off Lemmon Avenue. "Musicians from SMU are to sit in with the regulars tonight," he said looking at a poster in the vestibule of the night spot they were entering.

He'd opened the door of Ta Bu Jazz night spot as he spoke. "What? I can't hear you!" She had to yell over the brass section blasting out notes in a repetitive triple beat. The jazz was great, but too loud for conversation. Unable to get a table, they stood at the bar of the crowded room.

Tyler put his lips close to her ear. "Let's stay to hear this guy from SMU play, then go." A kiss on the ear punctuated the suggestion. Janelle's affirmative nod covered a shiver of response. The jazz spot was known for giving unknown musicians a chance for a "gig" and the young student who was playing his trumpet had the attention of the club. With a background of fast-moving fingers on a piano carrying the theme of "Sweet Georgia Brown" and a snare drum beating out rhythm patterns, the boy played his horn with musical runs that left the crowd breathless. At the end of the sliding, syncopated number, single pure notes climbed the scale one by one, and each trumpet flourish got a response from the listeners until, at last, the musician reached the final high C and held it in a resounding peal for several seconds. The crowd's exclamations and whistles were deafening.

During the after-wave of claps and shouts, Janelle and Tyler slipped out of the nightclub. "What a trumpet player! Loud, but not an ear-buster," Tyler yelled, then lowered his voice with a laugh. "This is refreshing air after that fog of cigarette smoke in there." Inhaling deeply, Tyler stretched tall, then casually draped his arm over her shoulders as they walked to the car.

As they drove slowly along Turtle Creek, Janelle enjoyed the creek view, with its garden lights defining paths down to the water's edge. It was enough to ride beside this man so full of life and exuberance—she felt like a limp geranium left too long in the hot sun. The evening was wonderful, but the undercurrent of need-to-tell had her subdued and quiet. Tyler was saying, "I've got to go back to Saudi tomorrow. My deal over there has turned sour and I must get out. Also, my friend Elbo is missing right now and I have to check on that report. I'll be back in a couple of months."

They had arrived at her apartment and Tyler switched off the engine to turn toward her an expectant look on his face. "Well, I have one question." Tyler leaned over and lifted a lock of her hair and tucked it behind her ear. Such a simple gesture, done with so much thoughtfulness, moved her.

He hadn't noticed as he'd turned to study the hood of his car with a worried look. "Do you think I should get some longhorns mounted on this he'ah heap? Ah want people to know ah'm a Texan!" He looked sideways at her with an innocent, eyes-wide-open look.

The wonderfully carefree remark, his way of making the trivial gloriously funny, had her fumbling for a joking comeback, but none came. "Thank you, Ty, for a wonderful evening. I haven't been so happy in a long time." Her face showed all the joy she felt. No need for words of "always" and "forever," it was enough to be with him in the present moment.

His finger lightly touched her cheek. "You're lovely when you smile like that. If I could help you keep that look, banish sadness and fear from your eyes, I'd never stop trying." Ty brushed her lips with his thumb. "You're important to me, Chamois." He cleared his throat and turned from her to climb out of the car.

"Wait!" Janelle grabbed his arm. "I want to tell you something. I didn't tell you earlier because, I wanted this evening with you. But before we go in, you need to know."

He'd gotten back in the car and now turned to face her, a frown formed between his eyes. "What is it?"

"Ty, Jerry is back, living with me."

There was silence for a few seconds then the sound of a hand hitting the wheel like the snap of a whip. "What the hell!"

Janelle hurried on to explain, her voice devoid of emotion. She could imagine how her news affected him. But she had to be honest.

"He has AIDS. His wife has left him. His baby died. He's alone." She hesitated—did not say, and waiting to die, but added, "I had to help him."

There was a long moment of silence. "That leaves no us, doesn't it?" His words were clipped—had a mocking tone.

"I guess so, for now."

"For now? You take him in, after he goes on, or dies then you'll think about us. Is that it?" Tyler's voice was loud—his face a mask of grim lines suffused with red.

Silence touched them for a moment, then was broken by a deep intake of breath. "What about you? Are you HIV-positive? Were you when we were together? All that story about not being able to have babies, negative virus. All lies?" Cold blue eyes, unblinking, stared at her. His face muscles rippled with strain as he ground out the harsh words to hurt her—or was it to hurt himself.

Janelle sat in numbed silence. She had anticipated surprise, even anger, but she hadn't known how much his anger would hurt. Had she hoped that he might love her enough to understand? She picked up her purse and jacket, then looked over at him as if to find some sign of forgiveness. He sat looking straight ahead out the window, his profile set as if in stone.

"Ty, believe me, there are no words to tell you how agonized I am over this. I did not know any of this when we were together, hard as that may be to believe. I've been checked since, and am negative as far as I know. Jerry left me for another lifestyle. It was at that time he contracted the HIV virus—and you are free. A test has reaffirmed it for me and it would for you."

"And I suppose I have to believe you."

She watched him for a moment. He sat looking straight ahead out the front window—his body stiff, his chin thrust forward with a rigid set to his jaw. The large, white knuckled hands gripping the steering wheel showed the strength of will he exerted to control himself. She slowly pulled open the door. Bitterness edged her voice. "Please don't say any more. I can stand pain, but not cruelty." She shut the door, walked to the entrance past the night watchman, and on to the elevator with no backward glance.

Without turning on lights she stumbled into her bedroom and collapsed on her bed. Dry-eyed, she stared at the ceiling.

Early in the morning, the shrill ring of the phone stirred Janelle from her lethargic sleep. With some effort she picked up the receiver.

A somber voice said, "This is Tyler." A hesitation—a deep breath, "Janelle, last night I didn't listen to your explanation. Obviously what you're doing shows compassion for a dying man. Forgive me."

She was stunned by his words. She was the one who should ask forgiveness, not him.

"Tyler, I deserved your anger. I should have told you about Jerry, everything, before we went out." After a slight pause, Janelle added, "I was afraid. I wanted the evening with you before I shared the news."

"Thank you. Enough said I guess." She could hear him sigh. "I leave this morning at seven, I couldn't go without apologizing to you."

She glanced at the bedside clock. Five AM! She wanted to see him, but what would it solve? He was leaving. She had Jerry to care for. It was too complicated to solve in two hours. "I understand. I'm glad you called."

"I'll remember you, Chamois."

"Janelle. What a surprise. You're usually gone before I get out of bed." Jerry had shuffled into the kitchen wearing his pajamas, robe and slippers to find Janelle seated at the table having tea.

"I didn't sleep well last night. I decided to sleep in this morning." Janelle didn't add that she'd gotten up to write a letter to Tyler. She'd written an apology, tried to express something of her feelings for the short, intense moments they'd had together. "Unique," "unforgettable," "soul-bending," no words seemed quite right but she had tried.

Janelle watched the feeble man sink into his chair which was faced toward the television and swivel it around to look at her. "Maybe you could use some of my sleeping pills." He grinned ruefully. He had told Janelle that sleep was the one time he could get away from himself and he needed help getting that relief. "Janelle, have you thought any more about my appearing on the program?"

Janelle looked over at him and noticed his anxious look. "Jerry, you have already put a lot of yourself into that program. You need to decide. If you want to . . ."

"I do."

"All right we'll set it up for a week from Friday, if that's convenient with the staff, students, and you too," she added.

"Hmm. That gives me ten days to have Grant get me a decent pair of slacks, a shirt, some shoes, a few things to wear."

He was still interested in clothes—that was something. "You'll need some money for those 'few things.'" Janelle grinned. "You know, the program will pay you for appearing." Jerry did have some income from testing he agreed to do for AIDS research, but he was using that money for his nurse and other medical expenses. Thank God he could still maintain a little of his dignity. Dignity had always been as important to him as dressing well.

Chapter Seventeen

The ten days went by in a flurry of plans for the television show. Janelle had made arrangements with the staff of technicians and students to have the taping of Jerry on Friday. The studio was set up for the interview. Refreshments were ordered for a post-taping reception in honor of Jerry which would include all the students who'd appeared on the programs, plus their sponsors, the five leaders, and the two adult panels.

Friday, two o'clock arrived. The large studio room was full to overflowing with everyone involved in the educational programs. Jerry's black turtle neck and slacks accentuated the slim, skeletal figure's paleness. Still, Janelle thought, he appeared much healthier on screen due to make-up and some good camera effects. At the very beginning of the short interview, Robyn asked Jerry what he would like to say to the viewing audience and Jerry had said quite simply, "I unknowingly was exposed to the HIV virus two years ago when I had a homosexual adventure. Though I was aware of the implications of such a virus, I tempered my fears, believing that the law of averages was with me. My optimism proved wrong." Jerry smoothed back strands of thin hair. "I have AIDS."

Janelle sat tensely behind one of the cameras as she listened to his statement. She sat up to catch every word Jerry was saying—his voice was weak and she didn't have on the video earphones.

"I realize the implications of my infection. I will die before I'm forty years old. I must endure pain and, yes, I've met rejection from some people. I had no idea that I would be on this program in this condition when I was first involved in the production of this television series on AIDS which is for you young people. It's all the more painful for me because of that. I'm a hypocrite."

The kids were silent, but they had to feel a lot of conflicting emotions. Adam Stapleton who had defended the blacks so well was helping with the lighting. Colleen and Julie sat on the couch facing Jerry while Pete sat in a bean bag at the side of the couch. Robyn sat on Jerry's left ready to help if needed. Andy, in charge of cue cards, sat near Jerry's right. The cue cards were on the floor. Jerry was not using them. Donna sat by Andy. Silent tears ran down her cheeks as she listened.

The cameraman zoomed in for a close-up, shading Jerry's face just a little to soften the features of the AIDS victim.

"I've been self-indulgent in my life style. I didn't consider the consequences of my actions. The medical world has not caught up with all of nature's secret surprises." Jerry cleared his throat, took a sip of water from the table beside his chair and continued, surprisingly able to talk without the racking cough. Every last bit of his energy and willpower was going into this message for the students in the studio and to the viewing audience.

"I believe I've accepted the consequences of my own irresponsibilities. I will die. I know I can suffer: I am suffering." He cleared his throat and wiped his mouth before he continued. "I also know that to live as I used to, with not a thought of tomorrow, just the pleasures and experiences of the day will never again be for me. Neither will a more meaningful life. I forfeited some deep, maybe lasting, pleasures for short term ones." Jerry leaned up in his chair and looked directly into the camera. "Does that sound a little like you?" The confession of the specter-like person with hollow, red eyes rimmed in black left the viewers in the studio shocked with the blunt honesty.

There were muffled comments and some movement from the students who stood in clusters around the edge of the room. The cameraman panned their sober faces. The panel: Robyn, Andy, Colleen, Donna, Julie, and Pete were silent. Jerry leaned back in his chair, cleared his throat causing a spasm of coughs, and closed his eyes a moment. Robyn, knelt beside Jerry. "Do you want to stop?"

"No." Jerry replied. He smiled and held his hand up and slowly gestured for the cameras to continue taping.

"I knew the boundaries that were laid out by my parents, most of my peers, my society. I crossed the line of safety. I took chances, which were outside those boundaries."

Jerry's voice was getting weaker and his hands visibly shook when he wiped his mouth. Moisture glistened in the crevices of his eyes. "This may sound like a sermon. Maybe you think this is some sort of penance—my sack cloth and ashes. Maybe it is. Take it as you will. But if I can move just one of you out there to stop and consider life for the precious gift that it is and live responsibly with careful choices, then I will not have lived and died without leaving something of lasting good." His sad face stared into the camera steadily. Robyn motioned the cameraman to stop the tape.

The students, the cameramen and their crew surrounded Jerry with words of congratulations and thanks. Jeb, Helen, and Dr. Mann of the Review Panel stood in a group exclaiming over the impact of Jerry's remarks. While Mrs. Thorngood explained to fellow censors that Jerry was truly a martyr, Mr. Manion hesitantly agreed. Robyn leaned over and gave Jerry a hug; others joined Robyn. Finally, there was a daisy chain of arms surrounding Jerry. Janelle watched from a distance and, at one point, caught Jerry's attention and held her clasped hands up in a gesture of triumph, job well done. He nodded to her.

The students were good therapy. Jerry smiled broadly. Colleen got in front of the group and began, "Gim'me a J, Gim'me an E." When their rousing cheer started, Janelle could not hold back the tears. She was not ashamed of crying for this man who had so much to give and so little time left. She was the only one who knew that the doctors had just told Jerry he did not have enough time left to move to South Padre. He had to be close to an AIDS medical facility in the Dallas area. This interview could be his last creative act before he went into the hospice to die.

They all moved to a long table where there was a huge sheet cake decorated with a miniature camera and crew. There were soft drinks which Helen and Jeb helped serve. The party ended on a high note when Jerry raised his hand to tell them the news that Janelle had learned that afternoon. "This show is to get a Merit Award for contribution to the cultural and moral improvement of the city. We all deserve a big hand!" Jerry's announcement took his last ounce of energy and between spasms of coughing, he motioned to Grant who helped him up from the chair and the two left.

Helen and Jeb were going to dinner with some of the review members and had asked Janelle to go. She had declined, saying she wanted to get home after the kids' reception to say good-by to Jerry.

"I think the quality of what you said surprised us all," Janelle said as she walked over to Jerry's chair in the far corner of the living room. He was resting while Grant finished packing books and keepsakes and a few clothes. Most of Jerry's things had already been moved to the AIDS hospice.

"I never realized how much I cared for those kids, Janelle. Robyn gave me his school yearbook and he wrote in it, 'Mr. Taylor You are the coolest of cool dudes and as tough as any Dallas Cowboys quarterback.' They cared."

It was almost a question and Janelle quickly answered, "You've been the person who gave them the spark they needed for these programs."

"I really did upstage myself today, didn't I?" Jerry chuckled as he looked up at Janelle who stood by the window watching him.

"It worked as nothing else could." *And the spark of self-confidence still burns dimly in you, Jerry,* she thought.

"Janelle, thank you. I love you. But I could never have grown enough to be your equal."

"Oh, Jerry!" She ran to kneel by his side and took the rough hands in hers. "I loved you. But it wasn't a contest."

"Tell me about Tyler."

Janelle stood. "I'd rather not."

"Why?"

"There won't be anything between us again." Janelle walked away and stood at the window looking down on the boulevard.

"Do you love him?" Jerry's voice was stronger.

"I don't know."

"Janelle, look at me." She slowly turned. "If you love him, tell him. Remember, we were an item! Perhaps you have something beyond that now. You'll never know unless you give it a chance."

She had no answer for his suggestion. Quickly, she returned to his side to ask if he'd like a glass of water, or some tea. "No, we're ready to go." Grant had come into the living room with the luggage.

Janelle leaned over to take his hand. "Jerry, I'll come and see you."

"Please, my dear, do not. I mean it. I want you to remember me with what's left of my dignity still intact. Let's end it this way, caring about each other." She raised up, nodded, pushed his wheelchair to the open door where Grant waited, then slowly shut the door behind them.

The soft, diffused light of evening after the sun had set was now Janelle's favorite time of day. How sad the twilight time had seemed just a short time ago! She pulled Jerry's picture from the drawer in the end table and studied the man's face. He'd become a real person to her in the past few weeks. Just as shading gives depth to a portrait, their conversations had opened nuances for her in Jerry's personality. She understood him better, and herself even more.

She switched on lights and went to find her Bible. It was gone from the bedside table. She'd forgotten that she'd slipped it into Jerry's suitcase. She'd written down a few Selective Scriptures passages for Jerry and had put them in his book. One she recalled was First Corinthians, second chapter verses eleven and twelve—where Paul tries to explain to his fellowmen about the wonderful gifts of grace and blessings God has given us—all of us.

The morning light shimmered through the blinds, throwing a haze like a silken canopy above her bed. She lazily stretched, got out of bed, and felt the room whirl. Her stomach churned as she started for the bathroom, then had to stop to grab the door frame for support until the wave of dizziness passed. Lately, it seemed she'd not had much appetite. Being around Jerry—the sights, the smells of sickness and medicine had made her physically ill—she knew it.

She got to the kitchen and the smell of the coffee in the cannister made her feel giddy again. Slowly easing herself down to sit in a chair, she braced her arms on the table top and held her head between her hands. She'd have to call the office. Even though it was Saturday, Jeb was expecting her to come in for a while to do some long-range planning. Forcing herself to sit up, she pulled the phone to her and dialed the office. "Jeb, I won't be in today. I feel a little under the weather."

"Are you all right?" Jeb sounded concerned.

"Yes, just a little squeamish. I think I ate too much rich food at the kids' party. Serves me right!" She laughed into the phone, hung up, and groped her way back to the bed. Little black dots danced in front of her eyes and a tight coolness pinched at the corners of her eyes. "I'm not going to faint! What's wrong?" She squeezed her eyes shut, then opened them wide with wonder, and sat up with a jerk. "Tyler—over two months—I can't be pregnant." Her menses had always been irregular. That was one reason why doctors had said she would have great difficulty in getting pregnant. But not impossible.

She dialed the doctor's office. "Could I please have an appointment with Dr. Kindell sometime today?" She pushed damp hair from her face. "Two o'clock. I'll be there."

She finally got up to take a shower then went out to meet Mrs. Rhodes, who had come to clean. There was a lot to do now that Jerry was gone. She could work alongside the cleaning lady. There was no better therapy than cleaning the kitchen and bathrooms when one wanted to blot out worry.

Chapter Eighteen

Janelle looked speechlessly at Dr. Kendall when he said, "You're over two months pregnant, Janelle." Then he had given her some printouts, a vitamin prescription and suggested she come back in a week or so to have the baby tested for HIV. Janelle left the medical building and was driving around in the steamy heat of the last day of May, trying to grasp the doctor's words. Thoughts like scattered leaves in a windstorm tossed in her mind. What would she do? Who could she talk to? She drove about mindlessly, thought about going to sit in the Turtle Creek Park, but told herself it was too hot. She considered going to a drive-through for a cola; the thought was gagging. She finally decided to drive to Helen's house.

Helen, too, had been cleaning. The sweeper was in the middle of the living room floor. Helen rushed to move it out of the way and carried some papers and magazines to another chair to give Janelle space to sit down on one of the loveseats by the fireplace.

Janelle was calm as she looked at her friend. "I've never before taken advantage of your offer to come over anytime!" she said with a faint smile.

"And I know it would have to be pretty important for you to do so. How can I help?"

"Remember the night you, Jeb, Tyler Dalton, and I went to the Petroleum Club?" Helen nodded without speaking. "We went home in separate cars? Ty drove me to my apartment and we became passionately involved after our first kiss."

Before Helen could comment, Janelle continued. "I've been very mixed up since Jerry left me. I've gone over and over in my mind why I would jump in bed with the first man I was out with after the divorce was final. I thought maybe it was some kind of celebration that I was free of Jerry. Or was I searching for some sort of affirmation that

I was a desirable woman? Partially that was it, and I've talked to Tyler about that dependency and tried to put our relationship on a different basis. But there was another answer. Tyler seemed wonderful to me from the very first time I met him. Call it love at first sight. We were so attuned, so comfortable with each other I don't even apologize for going to bed with him. It seemed so right somehow." She was silent.

"You're pregnant? Is that it?" Helen's voice held nothing but understanding.

For a moment neither spoke, then Helen gently asked, "Do you love Tyler?"

"I don't know. Maybe. I know that what I feel for him is far more than I ever had for Jerry. It may be just a great loneliness that he comforted. Like a friend. I've been much too willing to lean on others."

Helen said, "Janelle, my mother once explained love to me. It was shortly after Pete's death when I was missing him so desperately." Helen hesitated.

Janelle nodded. "Tell me. I need anything that will help."

"My mother told me that marrying love leads to marriage. That marrying love is made up of two emotions: passion and concern." Helen spoke softly remembering her mother's words.

"She explained that passion is a personal emotion stimulated and fulfilled by an *act* with another person. Gratification comes from completion of the sex act and is wonderfully selfish!" Helen laughed. "She told it like it really was!" In a gentler tone, she continued. "My mother said that concern in love is also a personal emotion stimulated and fulfilled by *interest* in the other person. When you're concerned you think of the needs of the other one before yourself. That kind of love comes from seeing the other in the love-match satisfied and happy. It is unselfish." What Helen just said was what she'd said to Jerry— another's interest before your own.

"I guess my mother thought Pete and I had that kind of love, and after Pete's death, she wanted me to remember the concern I had for the man. Her remarks helped me understand that by having concern and love for others, I would remember the good feelings I'd had for Pete, expand on them, and I'd have a permanent memory of him. I do too."

"And you're wondering if I have that sort of love for Tyler."

"And he for you, which is just as important."

"I don't know. I think so, but we've been together so little. I need to see him more. But with this . . . "

Helen stood up. "Let me get some tea, maybe some soda crackers? I hear they help the sick feeling." She'd already headed for the kitchen without waiting for a reply.

Janelle rose and went to Helen's Steinway and pecked out, "Send In The Clowns" with one finger. She could hear Helen moving around in the kitchen, the whistle of a teakettle, a rattle of cups, then Helen's footsteps as she returned to the living room. Janelle walked back to her chair. "I'm glad you said what you did. I believe we are friends, at least he has tried to be a friend of mine. And if our love is the kind of unselfishness you've described, perhaps we can succeed even with the baby to think of."

"I know what its like to not be sure of who and what is lasting. You can't ask for more than you're willing to give, Janelle. Remember the game S and S? And you said you liked Song of Solomon. I think of that verse 'This is my lover and this is my friend.'" Helen offered soda crackers.

For the first time since they had started to talk, there was a glimmer of the old sparkle in Janelle's eyes. "I remember. Thank you."

"If it helped, it was well worth it, my dear. We're not family by blood, but I feel we are a family through the heart." Helen stood up and set her tea cup down on the side table and slanted Janelle a look. "Janelle, Do you intend to keep the baby?"

"Yes, I want the baby. I've always believed I could not have a child. This may be my only chance. Isn't that ironic?" She turned to look at the lady who was so like her mother. With a sigh, she leaned back in the deep chair and closed her eyes. "If I must raise the child alone, it's not going to be easy.

"Helen, remember when we went to the Dallas Museum of Art a few months ago to see the sculpture of Claudia Reese entitled, 'The Red Shoe Collection?' " Janelle sat up and directed her gaze to Helen. Helen nodded.

"Remember the sculpted piece of a woman in Reese's collection, so different, so imaginative?" Janelle frowned as she focused inwardly on the memory of the art piece "The woman wore a headdress of vegetables and had on a back-sling with a baby in it. The baby's little head peeped over the figure's shoulder. The woman held some kind of container, wore slacks and had on red work boots. Remember?"

Helen nodded and added, "It was entitled, 'Conflicts/Mother and Provider.'"

"And the artist described the piece as a conflict with balance." She stood and walked over to the apartment window overlooking the terrace lawn. "I feel the conflict of wanting to keep my own identity, my job. I will have to learn how to balance the child, my job, my single life."

"Then, you honestly do want this child?"

Janelle whirled around, "Do I want my arms? My legs? Helen, this," she patted her abdomen, "is not me but is someone God has given me to carry. I didn't plan to be a mother. Heaven only knows I didn't think I could carry a child." There was a half-shy flicker of hope in her eye as she added, "It is a miracle in a way, and this miracle is going to have a chance to be a person. I do not need the father to decide that."

Helen voice was calm as she asked, "You may not be alone. When you tell Tyler—"

"I will not be like that woman who trapped Jerry!"

Helen ignored the outburst. "Janelle, you're a strong woman, an independent woman. I would not dare tell you what to do in your circumstances. But Tyler has a right to know. You know that, and you're already talking about lifetime love with him. But whatever happens, whether he's in your life or not, you can count on me."

Janelle pulled Helen to her feet and gave her a gentle hug. She walked over to an end table to pick up her purse. "I must go. And, Helen, it's helped just talking to you about this. I've needed to say some things aloud." Janelle gazed at her friend for a moment then started out the door. She hesitated when Helen spoke.

"Remember the other sculpture of Ms. Reese's titled 'Metamophoseries?' It was a figure lying in repose representing the passage between life and death. Your road seems almost that difficult. It won't be easy, Jani." Janelle acknowledged her friend's remark with a smile and walked down the steps to her car. Suddenly ravenous, she headed for a Wendy's. As she waited in the long line at the drive-through restaurant she considered the letter she would have to write to Tyler. It would be short, to the point. She'd written many business letters. She'd approach this Tyler letter as if she were writing a proposal.

She could not bear the thought that he might marry her out of obligation. Come home every night, his independent life ruined. After all, he had made absolutely no commitment to her.

She drove up the circular drive, stopped in front of the condominium, left the keys with the doorman, still intently considering how to write the letter. Finally, inside her home, shoving aside papers on her favorite chair, she sank back into the soft pillows, and closed her eyes. The one glimmer of peace she felt deep down within herself was in the spot where this baby was beginning to form its life. *Isn't it strange,* she thought. *I've tried to live a good life and have had no desire to step out of 'boundaries,' as Jerry called them, set by my parents and by my own values. My choice of Jerry as a long-term husband, was one time my emotions got in front of my logical self. I was concerned for myself and married out of loneliness instead of waiting for God to help me with right choices.* She considered another of her mother's sayings. "If we are patient, God will help us make right choices for our lives. 'In patience possess ye your soul.'"

Later, in her bed, sifting through the conversation with Helen, the day with Jerry, and Tyler, suddenly all of the worry stopped and there was a sudden rush of peace. She knew what she must do. She'd tell Tyler and would know from his reaction if he wanted to be with her and their baby. And it didn't actually matter whatever his choice might be, the miracle child would have all the love she could give.

Awakening, at six, refreshed, with determination in her step, she fixed tea and toast, ate, then went to her desk to write the letter. It was, of course, the second one he'd had from her in the last week—she'd written in detail about Jerry's situation just after he'd left.

Dear Tyler,
   It's June and Dallas is hot, in the usual blistering summertime. I wonder what it must have been like before air conditioning.

Two hours, and three pages later she put a stamped envelope addressed to Saudi Arabia in the mail. Janelle went in to the Jamison office.

She hadn't used the word love once throughout the letter, even when she recalled moments of their time together. It seemed too coercive. She did say she wished she could see the beautiful coastline of the Red Sea with him. With an upbeat note suggesting a modern woman like herself could very well manage the balance having a child would demand she ended with, "Call when you're in Dallas." It was not quite a business letter; neither was it a love letter. *Finè obligè.*

"This is it!" Janelle took a deep breath and like a diver going down to the thirty-foot level of the sea, opened Jeb's office door. It had been several days since her visit to Helen's. Now she would tell the other good friend. She did not intend to go into any detail. She would defend Tyler's part in this complicated situation if necessary. She saw that Jeb was on the phone, so quickly walked to a chair opposite his desk and sat down to wait. She counted the squares in the patterned carpet and continued to rehearse what she wanted to say. Helen had been understanding. Looking over at the portrait of her father, studying his strong features, she had a hunch Jeb would understand, just as her father would have.

"All right, Jani, what do you want to tell me?" He came around and sat on the edge of the desk and waited.

She avoided looking at the silent man as she repeated her rehearsed words without any of the details. When finished, she looked steadily at her friend. "I am the one who is taking the responsibility for this."

Jeb slid off the desk and walked toward her, his face inscrutable. He stopped in front of her and a smile started, as swift as a shadow. "So you are going to have a baby?" He sounded pleased, almost excited. He lowered himself into the plaid chair facing Janelle and leaned back. "What do you know, a baby!" There was a comfortable stillness between them broken by the intermittent muffled ring of a phone in the outer office as each silently waited for the other to speak.

"I plan to leave in about a month to relocate."

His face grew firm and he turned to face her squarely. "For God's sake, Jani, do you think this is the 1940s and you're to be shipped off to the St. Katherine's Home for Unwed Mothers? You can't leave!" Jeb's words exploded as he jumped up from the chair. "You belong here. We're your friends, your family now and we need you here. Take some time off, take a vacation, but come back here. Everyone in this place will understand and support you!"

Jeb held out his arms in a gesture of comfort. Janelle rose, went to him, laid her head on his chest. With a bear hug, he kissed the top of her head, and gently held her. "Jani, please talk to Helen before you make your final decision."

Janelle looked up at him. "Helen? She didn't tell you I talked to her?" She gently pushed away from him and walked over to stand by her father's picture. "No, of course she wouldn't. That's Helen."

"Helen and I have been seeing each other a lot, but I can't imagine that as a topic of conversation." Jeb spoke somewhat defensively.

"Oh, Jeb, I'm glad you're seeing Helen."

Jeb walked over. He looked resigned and concerned. "Promise me you'll let us help you during these months until the baby is born. We need you here and you need us."

Janelle smiled, she caught the word, *us*. Tyler's answer to her letter would make a difference, but she still would need her friends. "Oh yes, I'd like for you and Helen to go through this pregnancy with me. I'd like that very much!"

Chapter Nineteen

October, one of the nicest months in Texas, had been a miserable time for Janelle. She was heavy with child, plagued with swollen ankles, tired of maternity clothes. She wanted to stay at home in a mumu and let the world slide by, but she got up and went to work. Even the fateful day she had received the letter, she still went out for dinner with Sue Stone and Betty Carter. Elsie Mae had a new love interest so had neglected her college buddies lately.

She'd come home from a grueling day, exhausted, and had changed to her robe, went into the kitchen, thankful that Mrs. Rhodes had left a chicken casserole in the oven with a note about a chilled lettuce and mandarin salad in the refrigerator. The mail was on the table. Sorting through, a foreign stamp caught her eye. Saudi Arabia

It had been four months since her announcement of the baby to Tyler. Sadly, she had heard nothing. She hesitated to open it. Instead, she poured herself a glass of milk, took a sip and sat down heavily on the padded kitchen chair looking at the letter as if it were a snake about to strike. She did not know Tyler's handwriting well, but something about the writing on the envelope did not register as his slanting scrawl. She opened and pulled the letter from the envelope. It was from Harry Bender. What had happened? Why was Tyler's friend writing to her?

September 12, 1983—Jeddah, Saudi Arabia

Dear Janelle,
I know this letter will come as a surprise, but I felt I had to let you know about Tyler and why he has not written to you. He's been in Saudi Arabia, received word his friend LLamo Sibab is living somewhere in France, and in July left to find his friend. I've stayed on here to finish up work so I was here when a second

letter came from you. It had been delayed in transit. Ty had burned your first letter after reading it. I did not read that letter and am concerned that you will not get an answer from this one for I do not have an address to forward your second letter to Tyler in France.

I've known Ty since he was four years old. He's a complicated man with a staggering amount of pride and an empathetic understanding of others. He had a traumatic childhood that left him sensitive and very aloof. His mother left his father and him when he was only six years old. Did you know that? He was raised by a housekeeper and a very embittered father who believed all women were no good. I know Tyler never had the hatred for women his father had, but had been told enough times not to trust a woman that he was skittish as a lizard laying eggs. He was afraid to become involved in anything remotely suggesting a lasting commitment. He plays the part of a macho, independent man, but inside he is a scared little boy who lost a mother, never was nurtured by a father, and was not sure of what love for a woman could be.

He told me he really cared for you.

Still, he seemed to shut the door on all of the wonderful memories you two must have shared. Before he went to France, he closed off all conversation about you. I believe all the pent up hurt his mother had left him with resurfaced with your first letter. Some way he grew suspicious and the old syndrome started.

I'm sorry you are not hearing from him but believe me it's predictable. I thought I'd let you know. I've enclosed your unopened letter. Sorry its been so long.

Sincerely,

Harry Bender.

Janelle crushed the letter in her hand, and stared blindly at the table top. Too much to absorb, too much to try and read between the lines, but definitely no more Tyler. She slowly eased herself up out of the chair and moved to the window that overlooked the back of Turtle Creek Park. Waves of heat seemed to float like shadows in the air.

Jeb and Helen had married in August and had been asking her to move in with them for the last months before the baby came. She'd been hedging, afraid to slip back in a dependent mode. She now realized she would never be dependent on anyone again. She could live with them, get a good start with the child, then move out on her own when the time seemed right. She had the rest of her life to live and she might as well make it as pleasant as possible.

Janelle moved into the couple's home in Highland Park on Windsor Parkway and continued to live with them until December came, when she bought a house, two blocks from the Standlys. It was the former home of Mrs. Hill, who had recently died. Janelle loved the house as soon as she had heard it had belonged to that dear lady who had stood up to the censor group and led the vote that finally approved the AIDS program.

HIDE AND SEEK had been the spearhead for a new educational approach of honesty and openness that permeated every educational program produced by the Jamison group. Public broadcasting had accepted most of segments, which in turn had opened up national viewing of the programs. Janelle knew that without Jerry and Mrs. Hill, the HIDE AND SEEK television videos would not have had that thrust of honesty that undergirded every program. So they'd made a mark, probably far more than they had expected.

And, near Christmas, after a tiring twelve-hour labor she'd undergone with Helen at her side, there had been Teddy. He had a thatch of rich brown hair with a cowlick, just like Tyler's, that let a lock fall down in his eyes. He was a big boy, nine pounds at birth, strong features, and big eyes that had such long eyelashes that Janelle had to smooth them to keep them from tucking under when his little fist rubbed his eyes.

And now another year had passed and Christmas was coming. Thankfully, life was achieving some of the balance she'd seen in the museum sculpture. She had a nurse who came in for special days, but most work days, Teddy went to work with Janelle and stayed in the company nursery until time for her to go home The feeding schedule and the playtime were all factored in for Janelle, like the other people who worked for Jamison and who used the new facility. It was beginning to be one of the most satisfying perks some members of the staff could have, and Jeb had been the one to insist upon it. His words on the subject had been, "How can we have the senior vice president running home every three hours to feed that hungry boy?"

She did think about Tyler and wondered about his life. The entire brief romance had been tarnished, really destroyed, by the touch of AIDS and her care of her former husband. It was probably far too much to ask any romance to endure.

Janelle looked at the sleeping baby boy. It was John Theodore Jamison's first birthday. Janelle had not planned a party, so was surprised when Jean, Helen, Penny, and Jeb came into the nursery with cards and gifts for baby Teddy. A clown came to entertain all of the day nursery toddlers. Hats and whistles and birthday cake were passed out to all of the children, then the nurse and two attendants in charge of the group herded the other toddlers to one side of the bright room where the children could play with toys. Janelle's staff helped Teddy open packages. All of her friends and staff exclaimed over and, in turn, picked up the smiling birthday boy. Their support throughout the year had been steady with no questions asked or explanations needed. Only Jeb and Helen knew Tyler was Teddy's father. The happy day ended with dinner at the Standly's, and then home to bed.

Janelle took another peek at her sleeping child, tiptoed out of his bedroom and quietly walked to the kitchen. She turned on the intercom to hear him breathe. That sound of breathing was the only balm she needed for business tension!

Janelle looked around her sleek white kitchen. Chrome and white—Jerry's colors. But this time, she'd added a blue trim on the counters and a border of blue on the curtains which she thought softened the sterile look. She fixed herself some hot chocolate and thought about Jerry. She could still see him sitting by the television in the kitchen. In a way she missed those days, but mostly she missed their revealing conversations that had been so long in coming to them both.

Barely breathing, not talking but seeing all who came to visit with him, Jerry was, remarkably, still alive. He'd had pneumonia again, barely recovering this time. The doctors in charge of his case said it was a miracle he was still breathing, but being attuned to holistic healing they believed the visits from the students, their sharing HIDE AND SEEK programs, kept him alive. Even though he could not talk, his gestures and weak smiles told them how much their visits meant to him. And she had gone. His request that she stay away had been impossible to keep and he had not really wished it. She'd even taken Teddy with her once, but the nurse suggested it was emotionally too much for him, so she no longer took the child.

Janelle had dinners with her old college friends, and had seen Elsie Mae James through a couple of love affairs. She had an occasional drink after work with a male friend, but no dating. She was content to stay at home with Teddy and read, work, and play with her son.

She had named John Theodore for Tyler's and her father. It wasn't that she hoped that Tyler would come back and the three of them would ride off into the sunset. She did not even want that anymore. She was content with the way things were and only occasionally, as at Teddy's birthday today when she was feeling particularly vulnerable, did she wish him here.

The next day, Janelle hurried through the house checking lights and getting bottles and baby food in the kitchen. Teddy waited on the living room carpet. He was bundled up in a down-filled snowsuit that hampered his wish to get to the end-table where pictures with shining frames attracted him. He pushed one padded leg forward then tumbled to the side, rolled up, and pushed the other leg forward and tumbled over. His gurgles of delight followed each tumble and roll.

For a moment, Janelle stood and watched, fascinated by his perseverance as he rolled and bobbed like a round bottomed top across the room toward the table. She smiled as she picked him up and took him to the pictures he was going for. "See, this is a picture of your daddy and me." The photograph in a silver frame was a picture of Tyler and her seated at a table in the Café Pacific. It was all she had to remember that evening, and other happy moments, except for this marvelous, bright, joy-of-her-life chunk on the rug.

"Come on, we've got to get to work!" With a grunt, Janelle picked Teddy up and went through the pantry to the garage. Strapping the heavily clothed child into the car seat with a snap, she closed the car door. She stopped in her driveway to enjoy looking at her brick home with its turret-covered entrance. The deep slate roof was spackled with the remains of the snow flurries from the night before. Fresh snow glistened on the snow-covered hedge rows of dormant azaleas, making them resemble huge mounds of cotton-candy.

The blue spruce can have outdoor lights for Christmas, Janelle thought as she drove away from the house, by Helen's and Jeb's home and with a turn to the right, onto Preston. She drove her chattering little passenger past snow-laden trees, wrought iron fences, roof tops. Gossamer webs of smoke floated from chimneys and drifted through a grey sky. Traffic moved sluggishly along the sanded street, evidence of nervous drivers unaccustomed to the hazards of slick roads.

Janelle breathed deeply. It was December and the snow an unusual happening in Texas. It was wet to be sure, as all Dallas snows were, but created enough white to make it look like a New England Christmas for awhile. She grinned as she caught a glimpse of Teddy in the rear vision mirror. He was staring out the window at moving shapes. She started to sing, "Dashing through the snow . . . ," Teddy did his own rendition with gurgles and baby language until they got to the Jamison Building. "We're here, Teddy," she told him as she swung the car into the underground parking lot.

As soon as they got to the nursery, Teddy wiggled in her arms and gave Janelle a quick kiss before she sat him down by some other children sitting in a circle listening to an animal song. With a wave to the nurse on duty, she left.

A three-minute walk took Janelle from the day-care center to her office. If Teddy needed her, she could get to him quickly. The success of the day-care program at the work site for mother and child was significantly evident in her relaxed work performance and in Teddy's eagerness to be with other preschoolers.

Passing Jean with a smile, Janelle proceeded on into her own office. "Janelle!" Janelle turned questioningly. Jean stood in the doorway of the office. "An old acquaintance of yours is to be in this morning."

Janelle had a puzzled expression on her face. "Who?"

"Tyler Dalton. His secretary called, said Mr. Dalton just got back to the states. She told me that he has been in Saudi Arabia and France for almost two years. Can you imagine that guy?" Jean grinned and added, "She said Mr. Dalton intends to stop in to check on things, and people." Jean winked knowingly as she turned to go then abruptly stopped. A big man stood in her path.

"You're right, Jean," a deep voice said, a voice that Janelle had not heard for almost two years. With wide, questioning eyes, Janelle looked past Jean and saw Tyler standing beside the entrance. A secret thrill went up her spine. She braced herself with hands on the desk top as she feasted on the sight of the handsome man.

"Hello, Janelle," Tyler said quietly, staring at her flushed face. "You haven't changed a bit, beautiful as ever." His voice was husky. They stood looking at each other.

"Excuse me." Jean backed out of the door and closed it.

But soon the office door burst open again. Jeb Standly rushed in. "Hello, Tyler!" Jeb greeted as he took long strides over to Tyler with an outstretched hand. "Good to see you! When did you get back?"

Jeb was talking rapidly, which gave Janelle time to collect herself. The two men shook hands and started to talk to each other. Janelle stood speechless and stared. Tyler's jacket stretched across his wide shoulders, but hung loosely at the waist accentuating his thinness. His face was gaunt, with deeply etched lines by the eyes and mouth. That mouth! Janelle's heart leaped. He'd changed a little. There were more sun lines at the edge of his deep, serious eyes. The lines around his mouth were grim-etched.

This man, with his air of hesitant confusion, had fathered a child he didn't know about. He'd been angry, had never even written. There was as much drama here as in one of those soap operas Helen sometimes tuned in on. But she wasn't about to let herself be one of those women in the stories, even though the moment he had spoken her name all the barriers had come down and she felt vulnerably in love again!

He turned toward her and the flash of those eyes reminded her of Teddy. She smiled dreamily, thinking of her son.

"It is good to see you, Tyler." Her smile was tremulous.

He looked grim as he directed his comment to Janelle. "I might have written, but I didn't. I was out of touch even with my company executives half the time." He didn't know of his friend's letter. She felt a little angry. A petulant child, he had shut her out. Dignity returned. She had done all this alone, and with her "hand in the hand of the man who walked on water." She now had a lot of freedom in her life.

Jeb cleared his throat and took Janelle's arm to steady her. "Why don't we three go to lunch? There's a new little French restaurant right here in our building."

Janelle stiffened, "I, . . .can't." She finished lamely as she thought of Teddy, his bottle. She looked pleadingly at Jeb. "You two go on."

"Come on Jan, just something light. Helen will take care of little things," Jeb emphasized the reference to Teddy, "that need to be attended to."

Tyler stood, in that confident way he had, arms folded over chest, legs apart, head tilted to one side, a stiff smile on his face as if to challenge her to come. His eyes swept Janelle. "Come on. You look like you could use a full meal."

"All right, I'll tell Helen we're going."

Of course, Jeb wouldn't say anything about Teddy. He'd already turned to Tyler and was telling him about Helen, " . . . and we were married a year ago August."

Janelle listened to Tyler congratulate Jeb. And Jeb made some excuse for Helen not joining them for lunch as she grabbed her jacket and rushed out and on to Helen's office. "Helen!" Breathlessly, she got Helen's attention away from the computer.

"Yes?"

"Tyler Dalton is here!" Janelle hissed barely above a whisper looking over her shoulder as if Tyler would appear at any minute. "Jeb and I are to go to lunch with him. Will you feed Teddy?"

Helen nodded and frowned, "Lunch—do you think that's a good idea?" Janelle could only shake her head. How could she know?

Jeb and Tyler were already in the hall when Janelle came from Helen's office. "You two go along," Jeb said. I'll see if I can help Helen and I'll join you. See you there." And Jeb disappeared into Helen's office, leaving her to look after him as if her life-line had just slipped away.

They got off the elevator and walked into the restaurant, where the waiter led them to a table for four in a small side room. In embarrassed silence, they both went through the motions of preparing for the meal. They sipped water, unfolded napkins, looked at menus, then finally looked up over the top of the gold printed pages at each other. They both grinned and lowered their menus. He leaned forward, elbows on the table, "I like your hair. It's shorter isn't it?"

Janelle brushed at her short cap of hair. "Yes."

Are you married?"

"No."

Tyler leaned back and looked at the napkin he smoothed over his knees. "Anyone you're interested in?"

"Yes." She thought of Teddy and felt a glimmer of guilty satisfaction as she noted his hesitation as he took a drink of water.

She relieved the awkward pause by asking, "And what's your answer to those two questions?"

"I . . I've been on the go pretty much." Tyler looked around the room as if to find something to change the subject.

She laughed ruefully.

"What are you laughing at?" Tyler smiled quizzically.

"You." She shook her head. "You reminded me of you by my car door after I hit your car. You were frustrated that you had been delayed by the accident. And today?" She hesitated and sobered somewhat, then continued somewhat harshly. "Probably frustrated because you don't like to talk about your private life. Right?" She dipped her eyes so he could not see the depth of her feeling in spite of her deep reservations.

"Jan, do you remember what I asked you the last time we were together?" He leaned his arms on the table, challenging her to look at him.

Do I remember? Janelle thought as she observed the yellow rose in the small bud vase. A rose like those sent so long ago. She remembered all right. "You were angry about Jerry coming to live with me. But, you did call, and I did understand how it must have seemed to you. I wrote you in more detail." *And you never answered.* Janelle stroked a velvet petal of the rose.

Tyler grunted. "Yes. I know I apologized, but I was still stinking mad. There are a lot of things involved." *I know, Harry told me,* she thought. Janelle looked at him questioningly.

Tyler stood, but continued to look at Janelle. "Jan, could we have dinner tonight? I have to explain to you."

This time the pleading was not lost on Janelle. She said softly, "Yes, dinner."

"Well, where do we start with what has been going on in your life?"

Jeb smiled as he vigorously shook Tyler's hand, then sat down beside the man, and turned to Janelle. Did you find out all about this young man?"

"No, but I'm sure you will." Janelle laughed at her friend. "Jeb has just gotten used to not seeing you, and now, here you are in the flesh. He told me your office memorandums were adequate, but he would like to see the real boss."

"And did you wonder about me too?" Tyler asked with a questioning raise of an eyebrow and his little boy Teddy's grin.

"Yes, I did." All the time; as she grew as large as a circus tent, lumbered around eight months pregnant and watched in the delivery room, when they held up a small squalling replica of him for her to see.

Janelle slipped out after they had eaten, and left Jeb and Ty at the restaurant chatting about old friends and changes in the city. She had to get back to the office on business, she said, but it was really to go to Teddy. When she got to the nursery Helen had fed him and he was napping. He lay on his stomach with knees tucked under him, leaving his rounded bottom higher than his head. Janelle lightly touched his cheek and slipped out of the sleeping room of the day nursery with a wave to the attending nurse. Other children were in the main room playing and chasing each other, but their noises didn't disturb her sleeping son.

She walked on to Helen's office and told her of the plans for dinner. "I'll be glad to keep Teddy for you. Do you want me to come over there?" Helen hesitated.

She knew Helen wanted to know how Tyler was to be told about Teddy. How could she tell Helen when she didn't know herself? "No, I can bring him to your house."

Chapter Twenty

The business day had finally come to an end and Janelle hurried home to gather up Teddy, his night clothes, and favorite cuddle bear. They went to Helen's and Jeb's where she heard Jeb speak again of how much he thought of Tyler. Jeb seemed unashamed of his affection for the man, and so was Helen for that matter. Somehow, their admiration for Tyler made Janelle feel as if she were guilty of something. Well, let them stand in her shoes, telling a man in a romance already on the rocks about a son he wouldn't want to know about.

Back at her house, as Janelle waited for Tyler's arrival, she worried over her clothes. She tightened her earring, grimaced, loosened, then tightened it again with a sigh that was punctuated by the peel of the doorbell. Slowly, she scrutinized the woman in the mirror. A thin blond, with enormous grey eyes gazed back at her. They said that the mirror reflects your inner-self. This one would have to be Snow White's stepmother's to know what was within her!

She wore no jewelry at her throat. The only accent was the satin edge on the "V" neckline of her black lace cocktail gown. She knew she looked splendid when she opened the door and saw Ty's face light up. New rules, Janelle silently pleaded to herself. Honest friendship. "Hi." Two shy greetings were exchanged as they stood in the doorway looking at each other.

"Jan!" With one swift movement, Tyler gathered her into his arms and gave her an affectionate bear hug that lifted her off the floor.

Jan could not resist his strength, so clung to him for a few moments with eyes closed and enjoyed the feel of him. She gasped as she pushed away. "Let a girl breathe!" Her laugh stuck in her throat when she looked into his eyes.

"Want to come in for a minute? I've made some changes." She led him into her living room. She'd chosen cool, leafy shades, sea blues and hot pink and bright orange pillows for accents. The colors of her home on Padre, her Dallas office, and her new emerging self filled the room with energy. The only thing missing this evening were Teddy's toys, which were usually scattered about on the carpeting, but now were stowed upstairs in his bedroom with the door closed.

"The Lalique oblique is the same. Still beautiful." He grinned at her over his shoulder where he stood studying the art piece. "It's taken on the colors of the room.

"I've something for you." He reached in his coat pocket and took out a small package wrapped in gold and tied with a silver ribbon.

Janelle opened it expectantly. The box contained an *objet d'Art*, a replica of her Lalique sculpture. Only instead of being solid, the center of the pointed Lalique design with the sharp edges that glistened in the light was hollow. It was a bud vase. "It's lovely, Ty. I love it," Janelle exclaimed holding the tiny crystal vase up to see the prisms dance and sparkle, with the colors of the room.

From his other pocket Tyler silently handed her one single yellow rose carefully wrapped in waxed tissue and kept moist in its own small vial of water.

She smiled sadly. What was she to do with the guy? She reached up and gave him a kiss on his cheek. He accepted the kiss and smiled broadly as if very pleased with the whole scene. "We'd best go now."

She nodded agreement though she really didn't want this moment to end. While he placed her red velvet coat around her shoulders, she felt his warm breath on her cheek and put her hand over the spot.

Tyler drove them to Café Pacific where they'd had their last dinner together. They visited, teased, talked about changes in the city, mutual friends. Their conversation was light and easy. Janelle leaned back and absorbed all the joy she felt. *In patience posess ye your soul.* Patience does give contentment. He was here and that was all she could ask for. She told him about the company's new projects.

After their dinner, while they were having an after-dinner liqueur, Janelle said, "Let's talk about you."

Tyler leaned back and his voice took on a serious tone. "Well, my company is doing well." Remember my lieutenants, Bob and Harry? They're still with me, only the Lord knows why. Harry went with me to the Near East to sell oil contracts and we left Bob with heavy duties here. Harry finally came back to Texas by-way-of the California office and I ended up in France with my old friend Llamo Sibab."

Janelle was immediately alert waiting for his next remarks. Did he know about the letter Harry sent to her?

He cleared his throat and brushed a hand over his eyes for a moment. "Jan, Elbo died of AIDS. No one knew. He wanted it that way. I stayed with him for fourteen months, until he died. I had to. He was my brother."

Janelle was stunned to silence. A brother, as Jerry had been to her. What a way the patterns of life seemed to move and intertwine. She reached across the table and squeezed his hand. There were no words to express her sympathy.

"Janelle, I've learned a lot about myself in the past two years. I finally understand why you took Jerry in." He released her hand and slowly rubbed the back of his neck. "I've never been good about letting anyone get too close to me."

"I have the same trouble," Janelle quietly answered. The piano was playing a soft melody. Laughter, a rumble of voices surrounded them, but Tyler's voice crowded out all other sound.

He took a drink of scotch then looked at her. "Janelle, I tore up that letter you sent about Jerry, and you, and me. Hell, you'd written about the two of us, our night together as if it were an after dinner cocktail aphrodisiac. And what the hell did I care about Jerry—all those details. It shut me out." He hesitated. His eyes showed more than words could ever convey.

Janelle wanted to tell him she understood. She'd been too shy to write and share her feelings of that night. Somehow some things were better remembered than expressed aloud. "Jan, that letter took two months to reach me. I was disillusioned, disappointed. Before the letter, I'd thought of you every day, had dreams of you coming with me to see that beautifully different land.

"I burned that letter, buried those dreams." He looked at the glass he held. "After the letter I tried to shut you out of my life."

"I know, Harry wrote me. I hope you'll forgive him."

"Harry?"

"I sent another letter trying to track you down. But he had seen you burn the first one and felt he owed it to me to write. He said you were wary—burnt—because your own mom had left you."

He gave her a searching, half-angry look and then was silent for a long moment. "Remember you said something about Moms tying shoes?" She nodded. He continued, "My mom left dad and me when I was six. We never heard from her again." His words had a bitter tone. He grunted and said almost as if he had forgotten Janelle was listening. "I can hear Dad saying, 'Always chasing after her own pleasure, thinking of herself . . .' I missed her even though Dad said we were better off without her."

Janelle could feel the sadness and ached for his loss. He had mentioned going on wild catting adventures with his dad. A six-year-old, no mother, raised by a housekeeper, an embittered father—what an uphill battle he'd had to understand his own feelings. She studied the man. He seemed lost in memories. Instinctively, she knew that Ty needed to talk about this and held her breath, afraid to interrupt his reverie.

"I learned history, math, English, Arabic in different schools." He shrugged with a smile looking at her with clouded eyes. "I learned about drilling oil and gambling with options from my dad. He never gave me much good advice about lovin'."

Ty chuckled. "But I learned about girls. Another thing I learned, was never talk to my dad about being out with girls. He beat me once when I tried to talk about one pretty little high school cheerleader who asked me to her home for dinner. Sometimes, I'd get extra duty mucking out horse barns or taking an extra watch at a well sight because I'd gone over the divid'n line between right and wrong. He was one tough cowboy. He believed in hard work, almost to the expense of any home life." Tyler sighed leaned back in the chair. "Other than times of discipline, Dad let me do pretty much what I wanted to do."

Ty ran a hand over his mouth and stared out into the room. "I guess some might say I was almost an abused child." He smiled and shook his head, as he looked at Janelle with hooded eyes. "Don't get me wrong, I loved my father, even if he was mean at times. I got so I understood. It was women he hated, not me. He just didn't want me to get hurt like he'd been hurt." There was a long moment of silence.

"She drove off in her little red convertible. I looked for that car to drive down our dusty road many times, but she never came back. I kept unasked questions bottled up inside because of Dad, but I missed her, it hurt. I can still feel that same hurt at times, mostly when I feel rejected." He feebly grinned. Leaning forward, he touched her hand.

"I guess I've always had my work to cover up my feelings. I had a hard time of it after your letter, with all my bent-out-of-shape feelings. I guess I felt you were rejecting me—hadn't really cared all along. So I went to France to find Elbo, found him ill, and knew I'd stay in France with him until he died. Thinking about him, his illness, got me out of thinking about myself. After he died, I stayed on. Seemed like there wasn't much to come back to here." Looking up at her, his face softened, his eyes searched hers as if for understanding, then shuttered. He again studied the amber liquid in his glass. "What about Jerry?"

"He's still alive, but barely. I moved him into a hospice over a year ago."

"That's sad news, I'm sorry. I know now what a sacrifice it must have been."

"Ty." She waited until he looked at her. "That letter I sent—that Harry wrote me about wasn't the only one. I wrote twice more. I called to get another address. I had only the one in Jeddah. Your office couldn't give me anywhere to write. I got the message. I stopped trying to locate you."

"I'm sorry. I wanted to get lost. Harry, Bob, my California office too. I shut all of them out. Only sent correspondence through my lawyers. Finally sold my oil contracts over there, all but one that the government has seen fit to take over." He grinned as if happy to be rid of some of the load. "I tried to cover up, smother past memories, start a new life in France where I'd found Llamo. He lived in Les Andelys, France, a village on the Seine River. Nice place. I was satisfied there until after he died. I did pretty well with forgetting, everything but you. Never you." He shook his head.

The waiter brought Janelle a coffee, Tyler a Chevis, and then left.

She'd felt Ty's pain from reading Harry's letter over and over again, but having Tyler tell her made it so much more poignant. Janelle said quietly, "Have you ever seen your mother?"

"Yes. I learned she came to Dallas straight from our home outside Tyler, Texas. I came to see her before she died. She was in the hospital. I visited her several times. Of course, it never was the same as when I was a kid."

"You didn't understand why your mother left. It's made you fear women."

"Yes. I've enjoyed being a ship that passes in the night. Until I met you. No matter how much I tried over there to rid myself of my love, I couldn't. I need to be with you, Jan. As a friend first. And I need an anchor. I'm moving back to Dallas. I sold my apartment, and closed the California office. I've decided I want to be in Dallas, Texas." He grinned, leaned back and crossed his arms.

Janelle flicked a glance at other diners in an attempt to ignore the shadowed eyes which revealed much more than words. His honesty shamed her. "Guess you're a true Texan after all!" Janelle looked off toward the other diners trying to ease her own tension.

"Yup, pretty lady," he drawled. A muscle twitched in his tightly-set jaw. "I was afraid of you, you know." He grinned sheepishly.

Her stone-cold resolve melted.

"Ty, there's something . . ."

He leaned forward and stopped her protest with the gentle touch of a finger on her lips. "Guess you think I'm pretty messed up?" He took a deep drink of his scotch.

A soft smile touched her lips as she looked at the man. "I understand a little boy was hurt in a dreadful way; no mother to love him, and a father who tried, but could not give the child the kind of love he needed. No, I don't think you're messed up. You couldn't talk so openly about it if you were."

"Well, bluebonnets have bloomed twice since I said I'd return. Still friends?" Tyler sat up and extended his hand to her.

Jan raised startled eyes to his. A sob clutched at her throat. She swallowed hard and said aloud, "Still friends." She took his outstretched hand.

A relieved smile softened his features, as he pulled up straight in his chair. "Well, friend, how's the HIDE AND SEEK group doing? What's happening?"

It was no good confessing now. She'd wait until they were going home to talk about Teddy. Aloud she said. "Remember Robyn Greer? He got his high-school diploma and is now taking courses in telecommunications at Southern Methodist while holding down the editor's job for all HIDE AND SEEK programing. He's a natural. A new crew has come on.

"Our last program was on sports ethics. The kids had groups in some schools suggesting that the salaries of professional athletes were sending false messages of hope to younger athletes. Remember Donna Meeker—the outspoken one? She's still with us—she even suggested that values were becoming the zeros that followed dollar numbers." She added emphatically, "That comment got a lot of adults thinking—objecting too!"

Tyler seemed impressed. "When can I be interviewed again? I've got more material on the cartels and the foreign oil policy. Texans, especially, might be interested in what I have to say."

He shook his head with a scowl. "The game of high finance, whether sports, insurance, or oil is not always played on a smooth surface. Big government tries to be the score keeper of the game, but it really gets down to personal responsibility on the field. As they say in football, a guy has to hit the creases to get through the defensive line of the opponents. No one can do it for him."

"Are you suggesting that big business is not always ethical? Must everything be regulated by the central government?" Janelle recalled that government regulations stuffed with bureaucratic ideas to control the masses had been a favorite topic of her father and Oscar Leoni.

Tyler looked seriously grim. "There're times that values take a nose dive when the golden path of success opens wide ahead! Thank God, I'm off that trail! And, yes, I do believe we must look forward to a future of government controls and regulations if each citizen doesn't take responsibility for his own life."

Tyler leaned back to stretch out his legs under the table. "God knows, I have the desire to help people in need, but it seems the government doesn't trust those with plenty to help those with little. The power network is getting too big to notice how the small pieces of existence fit together. Most appointed officials feel more comfortable if they keep score; take the money and disperse it. But who watches the scorekeepers?"

There was a lull in their conversation. She had a dull ache which had to be released. "Tyler there's something . . ." She looked around to see if anyone was near.

Tyler's smile was tender as he waited, hesitated when he too looked around. They both had noticed they were the last of the diners. Their waiter, and the *maitre de haute* stood visiting in the archway of the entrance. "Sorry to interrupt, but don't you think we'd better get out of here? Those guys look like they're ready to go home."

Janelle nodded. He helped her with her chair and, after thanking the staff for their patience, and getting their coats, they went out into the cold night where their breath fogged and their feet slushed through wet snow to Tyler's car. "Looks as if Dallas is in for some winter," Tyler offered as he helped her in the car.

Janelle eased back on the soft leather seat of Tyler's latest car, a convertible with a burled wood dashboard that rivaled the Odyssey Two. Again, she had not shared the news which concerned them both so intimately. How in the world would he take it?

Tyler drove as aggressively as ever. He dodged cars, rammed down on the accelerator, slowed for a police car with sirens blaring and blinkers twirling like strobe lights at a dance hall. They had driven up to the corner of her former home before she realized she should have suggested he stay on Preston to get to Windsor Parkway. He turned off on Windsor and stopped the car a few doors from her house in front of Standley's, but Tyler didn't know it was Jeb's and Helen's home.

He turned to face Janelle and draped one arm on the back of the car seat. Janelle felt a moment of panic as she recalled another night in a car with this man. "Tyler . . ." she began, but he interrupted.

"Jan, I have missed nights like tonight. I have missed you." He leaned over as if to kiss her, but instead, only touched her hair with his lips. "You always smell clean and fresh! I think I'm in love with you. I've never thought I'd say that to any woman." Ty was whispering close to her ear.

Janelle moved slightly away so she could see his face. She looked pleadingly at him. "Ty, you are just now understanding yourself. Let that grow."

"I do understand myself, and I love you." He moved closer. "We can go slow and get to know each other if that's what you want."

Her heart stopped for a moment. If she'd learned anything, it was that marriage wasn't glamorous restaurants and flowers. It was a strong hand on yours in the labor room, and somebody to help sweep when you move into a new house. And to share dismay when the basement floods or to understand and forgive you when you make stupid mistakes. And bring you chicken noodle soup and jello when you're sick. This man had missed a year of his son's life: his first steps, his birthday. Aloud she answered him. "We'll see."

"Will this help?" he growled deep in his throat as he pulled her to him, and gently pressed his lips on hers. She resisted for a moment, then relaxed, and with a moan, kissed him back with all the longing of the many times she'd needed him.

"Was that a kiss of just a good friend?" Tyler smiled softly as he looked deep into Janelle's troubled eyes. He smoothed away her frown and gently rubbed a thumb over her swollen lips.

"You always bring out that part of me." Janelle pulled away from him, brushing her lips as if to cancel the warmth of his mouth. "I'm not the woman for you. You've dreamed up someone like your mother was or, like you would have liked your mother to be. I don't know what you want, but it's not the real life me who works, who doesn't like to cook, who . . . "

"Jan," he interrupted. "Why make something complicated out of a feeling? Attraction needs to come first."

Sure, but as Helen said, true concern must follow. She knew she had it, but did he?

He kept a hand on her shoulder as he studied her. "Either I have the feeling or I don't and all the unmade beds, dirty dishes, and carry-in food will not change that feeling!" Tyler turned and leaned an arm on the steering wheel. "I've decided not to travel the world on hell-bent deals. I want to stay in Dallas, have you in my life for good and bad times." He leaned over to turn her face to his once more. "I don't want you to give up your independence. We'd share our lives, ourselves."

"You may not want. . . ."

"Janelle!" A voice called out suddenly, and a man came hurrying down the long walk toward their parked car. Janelle jumped out of the car and ran to him before Jeb could get to the car. She was torn by urgency to know what was wrong. Like watching a scene from a movie in black and white, the strip of light from the house fanned out on the snow and caught the sparkles of ice and the frozen expression on Jeb's face as she approached him. Teddy was crying from within the lighted house where Helen stood in the open doorway. Was he sick?

No one moved for a moment, then Janelle quickly walked to the house as she heard Ty ask, "Jeb? What's wrong?"

"Janelle had a call," Jeb answered and had turned to follow Janelle. The baby wailed at the door.

"You live here? What baby is crying? Jeb, do you have a baby?" Tyler had walked halfway up the walk, then stopped looking after the two.

"No. Teddy is Janelle's," Jeb called over his shoulder and hurried in the house after Janelle, leaving the stunned man standing alone.

Janelle considered going back out to explain, but Helen insisted it was an emergency, about Jerry. On her way to the phone, she glanced out the window to see Tyler get into his car and speed away.

The nurse told Janelle that Jerry's advanced AIDS complicated by the opportunistic infection, P Carinii pneumonia, was too much for his weak system to fight. She knew Janelle had wanted to be with him, but he'd had a seizure and died before she could call Janelle. Janelle slowly put the receiver back in the cradle. The suffering was over. "God bless you, Jerry," she whispered. Teddy was still crying and she went in to see what was wrong. His favorite teddy bear had fallen out of his crib. She picked it up from the floor, gave it back to the little boy, then picked him up to rock him back to sleep. She was needed by her child. His unhappiness was something she could help.

Chapter Twenty-one

Jeb was driving Helen and Janelle home from the memorial service for Jerry. They'd agreed that Jerry would have liked the students' eulogies, would have been proud of the tribute the superintendent of schools had given. The cremation had been the day before as Jerry had planned. He had no family, only Dallas friends who had cared about him, and they'd been there to say good-by. "I don't want a long mourning period, Jan. They might talk about me too long," he'd kidded one day when she'd visited him.

Janelle sighed, leaned back in the car and closed her eyes. Jerry had squeezed out of her so many emotions in just seven years time: love, hate, pity, regret, sorrow. She felt the car slow down and opened her eyes just as Jeb drove into her driveway. She was surprised to see another car in the drive in front of Jeb's. Tyler's?

Embarrassment brought a flush to her cheeks. He had left abruptly two nights ago without saying good bye. She had tried to call him, but there was no answer. Then, she got busy with the arrangements for Jerry's internment which, as his executor, had been left to her. She hadn't even talked to Jeb and Helen until today. She took a deep breath and opened the door of the car.

Jeb looked at Janelle in the rear-vision mirror. "Jan, the other night," he hesitated as he watched Tyler get out of his car, "Tyler asked whose baby was crying, I told him it was yours."

She shrugged. "I know. I should have told Ty about Teddy earlier that evening." Janelle sighed resignedly and went to meet Tyler.

Helen called out the window. "Shall we wait?"

"No thanks." Her friends drove away.

"Hello." Janelle said in a breathless voice. "Before you say anything, I have something I must tell you . . ."

"No, me first." Tyler moved to hold her tightly by the shoulders and looked down at her with soft blue eyes that expressed concern and something more. "I love you Jan. I want to marry you. I want to help you care for your baby."

She looked at him, eyes wide with shock. She felt his grip tighten. He gently shook her "Janelle! Do you understand? I want to marry you—to make a home for you and your child."

Janelle stood with silent tears rolling down her cheeks. Tyler pulled her into his arms and held her close "I don't care who the father is—I have no claim on you, and can only admire you for caring enough to bear this child alone. I want to marry you—share your life."

Swamped by her own churning emotions, she clung to him. Now she knew for certain why she'd never stopped thinking of this man. Even in the days when she'd thought he was gone forever she could not forget his gentle thoughtfulness despite all her doubts and objections. Her fears of rejection made no difference in her feelings for him. She loved the guy. Suddenly so calm, so sure, she wiped her eyes with the back of her hand and, with something close to a smile, she took his hand and led him into her house, through the living room, on to the sunroom, where Mrs. Rhodes sat in a rocking chair, holding Teddy. She took the baby herself, sat down, and sent Mrs. Rhodes away.

Sunshine streaming through the windows made a burnished red halo of the soft baby down on his head. Tyler slowly walked over to the two, and stopped at the side of the chair. The child looked up and studied the tall stranger. As Tyler observed the blue eyes, chin, forehead, the unruly fluff of reddish brown hair, he had to have seen that this child was the mirrored image of himself at that age.

He turned to Janelle with a puzzled expression on his face. She said quietly. "He's your son. His name is Teddy—the doctors were wrong, thank God."

He turned back and knelt down by the child and skimmed a fingertip over the baby's head. In a tight whisper he said, "Hello Teddy." Teddy gurgled his hello and smiled at Tyler who looked back with a tremulous smile.

Tyler stood and gingerly took the child from Janelle. Touching his cheek to the little boy's soft hair, he looked relaxed, comfortably natural. His eyes were moist when he looked over the child's head at Janelle. "I love you, Chamois." He whispered.

"I love you, Ty. I have ever since we bumped into each other."

Tyler broke the silence with a booming laugh. Teddy, suddenly frightened, burst into tears and leaned sideways with imploring arms extended to Janelle. The happy man's grin faded to a frown as he held the screaming baby out toward Janelle who made no attempt to take him. "What do I do now? He doesn't know me!"

"There's a remedy for that. It's called loving patience."

Teddy's cry was dissolved to a whimper as he again studied the man who held him. Reaching up, the little boy pulled on Tyler's string tie.

"That's it. Hold him cowboy." Janelle walked to them and wrapped her arms around Tyler and Teddy.

Thank you . . .

I wish to thank the following people for their help in my research: Scott McKinnis, James Wilson, George Tanner, G. L. Whitney, Pastor Daniel Berger, Doctor Michael Deery, my sister, Betty P. Luby, the many friends who encouraged me in my work, and a special thank you to my editor/publisher Nancy N. Baxter.

M.A.